Praise for

BETWEEN BEFORE & AFTER

"A beautifully layered story of secrets, hope, and change. This gem of a novel has all the hallmarks of a classic."

MEGAN CHANCE, bestselling, critically acclaimed, award-winning author of the Fianna Trilogy

"Maureen's flowing prose pulls the reader in closely to the harsh realities of life for children in 1918 New York City, but also conveys the strength of a sister's love for her brother when everything dear to them is ripped away. The duel narratives of Molly and Elaine grip the reader in a crescendo of suspense that pays off like a favorite fairy tale."

MARY CRONK FARRELL, award-winning author of *Pure Grit* and the upcoming *Standing Up Against Hate*

"This coming-of-age novel about a mother and daughter delves into the complex nature of relationships with an earnest voice and vivid details. Highly recommended!"

STEPHANIE MORRILL, author of *The Lost Girl of Astor Street* and *Within These Lines*

BETWEEN

BEFORE &

AFTER

MAUREEN DOYLE MCQUERRY

BLINK

BLINK®

Between Before and After
Copyright © 2019 by Maureen McQuerry

Requests for information should be addressed to:
Blink, *3900 Sparks Dr. SE, Grand Rapids, Michigan 49546*

Library of Congress Cataloging-in-Publication Data
Names: McQuerry, Maureen, 1955- author.
Title: Between before and after / Maureen Doyle McQuerry.
Description: Grand Rapids, Michigan : Blink, [2019] I Summary: In a dual
    narrative, Elaine struggles to protect herself and brother Stephen in 1918
    New York City, and Molly, her daughter, does the same for her brother,
    Angus, in 1955 San Jose, California.
Identifiers: LCCN 2018047870 (print) I LCCN 2018052918 (ebook) I ISBN
    9780310767299 (ebook) I ISBN 9780310767381 (hardback) I ISBN
    9780310767282 (softcover)
Subjects: I CYAC: Secrets—Fiction. I Brothers and sisters—Fiction. I
    Single-parent families—Fiction. I Family problems—Fiction. I San Jose
    (Calif.)—History—20th century—Fiction. I New York (N.Y.)—History—
    20th century—Fiction.
Classification: LCC PZ7.M24715 (ebook) I LCC PZ7.M24715 Bg 2019 (print) I
    DDC
[Fic]—dc23
LC record available at https://lccn.loc.gov/2018047870

Cover design: Brand Navigation
Interior design: Denise Froehlich

Printed in the United States of America

18 19 20 21 22 23 / LSC / 10 9 8 7 6 5 4 3 2 1

For my surprise brothers Richard and Roger.

We followed the breadcrumbs home.

And for Bill, who was lost in the woods.

~⊙~ PROLOGUE ~⊙~

*T*he year Uncle Stephen performed a miracle, all our lives changed. Of course, at first no one was sure it was a miracle; miracles aren't things you see every day, so how could you know? Even after the investigation, our lives kept changing. When a miracle invades, Uncle Stephen says, it sends out roots that reach backward and forward in time. It catches people by surprise when they discover that everything they've seen of nature so far is only one part of a system. They forget about the other part, the part running underground.

We were a family of believers. Oh, not in miracles, or God, or anything conventional—except for Uncle Stephen, who was on a first-name basis with God and taught at a Catholic boys' school. What we believed in was the power of stories—Angus, my mother, and me. My mother because they got her through, and Angus and me because we listened right from the start.

The best stories can be as unpredictable as miracles. They can surprise you, even when you think you know them by heart. So don't expect me to tell you everything right up front; you might not believe it. If there's one thing I've learned, it's that sometimes our minds prevent us from seeing the truth, even when it looks us square in the face.

Chapter One

PRUNING

SAN JOSE, CALIFORNIA—JUNE 1955

Molly

I found the envelope stuck at the bottom of my mother's lingerie drawer under some unmentionables. I was searching for a push-up bra to see if it could enhance my minor attributes when I made the discovery. The flap of the envelope was loose, no longer sealed by the yellowed piece of tape. Mom had taken my brother, Angus, to the dentist, and I was alone. I didn't hesitate to open it. The fragrance was faint but unmistakable. White Shoulders.

A few black-and-white snapshots of my mother with my father tumbled out. In one, they were seated at a white tablecloth restaurant, holding champagne glasses. Mom was wearing elbow-length gloves and a hat with a full rose. Her dress veed off her shoulders and nipped in tightly at the waist. The second showed them at a Chinese restaurant making funny faces. It must have been New Year's Eve because they were wearing shiny paper hats and party blowers littered the table. In the last one, they danced cheek to cheek. Mom wore a gardenia like a star in the red of her hair, her long neck the Milky Way. It made my throat tight to see them that way.

When I tried to stuff the photos back into the envelope, they stuck halfway in. Something more was inside. With one finger, I dragged out a tiny ring that just fit over my pinky. It was stiff and pale yellow. I ran my finger over it and held it up to the light. The ring was made of braided hair fine as corn silk! No one in our family had blond hair. I let it rest in the palm of my hand.

With the hair ring came a tiny clipping from a newspaper, nothing more than a headline: *Woodward Closes Its Doors.*

But let me back up and tell the story in order like Uncle Stephen says a beginning writer should. The trouble is knowing where to start. He says start close to the action. But life is made up of so many actions, big and small, that selecting the one that changes everything confuses me. You never know which will matter most in the end. I'll begin with this, a morning last month.

The morning of my decision.

The morning of the butchering.

The phone rang early. Angus was still in his pajamas watching *Howdy Doody.* I'd recently dragged myself out of bed after staying up late to work on the script my best friend Ari and I were writing for an end-of-the-year project. Mom, who was just settling down to work with a cup of coffee, answered it.

Dragging the phone into the laundry room, she closed the door on the cord, which always meant one thing: an adult situation we weren't supposed to know about. Recently, all adult situations involved my dad, who had been ordered out of the house right after Christmas when he said one too many times, "Bury your past before it buries you."

When Mom stalked out of the laundry room, white-lipped and silent, I made a point of staying out of her trajectory. I poured myself a glass of orange juice and watched as she streaked across the backyard and disappeared into the garden shed.

"What's Mom doing with the clippers?" Angus asked around a mouth of Trix as he watched from the sliding glass door.

"Pruning?" I said.

That had been Dad's job. He was the gardener; she was not. Now that he was gone, that job, like so many others, would probably fall to me.

I joined Angus at the window, juice in hand. Mom was striding across the yard, the long-bladed shears clenched in both hands. There was something about the way her hands gripped the black-handled blades that made me uneasy, like wind ruffling the surface of water.

"I don't feel so good." Angus moved closer.

The carnage began with the roses. She hacked at their ruffled blooms until they dropped into monstrous drifts of red on the parched yellow lawn.

Milk sloshed from Angus's bowl and trickled onto my foot. "She's chopping off their heads."

"Decapitation." It wasn't a word I had ever associated with flowers. I checked the clock. Ari would be here any minute. I couldn't let her see us like this.

Next, she attacked the geraniums, the ones in pots by the door, and then the pink-striped blooms that massed by the cement porch. Foreheads pressed against the cool glass, our breath made circles of fog on the window as we watched. Like a demented barber, she sheared the long hairlike fronds of the weeping cherry, leaving the tree twisted and bald. By this time, the yard was a red-and-pink wound, and Angus was pressed tight to my side. It was impossible to look away. A few hot tears dripped from my chin, but I scrubbed them away with the heel of my hand.

The doorbell rang. With all my might, I willed Mom to stop.

"Molly?" Angus's voice wavered.

"It's Ari. Don't say anything about Mom."

I opened the front door just as Mom, small petals caught in her hair like snowflakes, ricocheted through the kitchen and into the living room. The saliva dried in my mouth. Ari stared. Mom kept going. I held my breath until her bedroom door slammed shut.

"Okay, then," was all Ari said. She followed me into the kitchen, and I handed her the script we'd been working on.

"I made a few changes."

For Angus, toast and peanut butter solved most things. While I toasted the bread, Ari, dark eyes squinted in concentration, thumbed through the pages in silence.

I cut rounds of banana to make a smiling face on the toast and handed it to Angus. Even when I was done, I avoided glancing toward the window, hoping Ari wouldn't notice the damage.

"What happened to your yard?" She ran her tongue over her braces as she stared out the sliding glass door.

"Mom was pruning," Angus said. "At least she didn't pull up our vegetables."

Ari raised newly plucked eyebrows at me. I thought I knew her every expression. Aricelia Guetteriez Lopez and I had survived junior high together and, in a few weeks, we'd finish freshman year. She was everything I was not: caramel skinned, curvy, and quick to laugh. And if that wasn't enough, she had pierced ears. On her twelfth birthday, her abuela had given her tiny diamond studs to replace her gold hoops. This added instant glamor. She was striking, a word I quite liked but could never aspire to. The only thing in my favor was that I didn't have braces, while Ari did. I was the first one she told after Jimmy Schmidt stuck his tongue in her mouth in the backseat of her brother's car. She was there when my dad left. We shared secrets at sleepovers. But this time, what I saw in her eyes made me flinch.

I was someone to pity, set apart, as strange and vulnerable as an urchin without its shell.

I looked away, but she knew I'd seen it.

"I have to go. Mom's taking me shopping. Thanks for working on the script." Ari edged toward the door. "See you at school?"

"Sure," I said, knowing my disappointment flavored the word and hating that she probably heard it.

In the empty kitchen, my dad's ultimatum replayed in my thoughts like a scratched record. *Bury your past before it buries you.* I knew it was a metaphor. He was asking her to make peace with whatever haunted her and put it away for good. There was something in Mom's past that drove Dad away, something that was a threat to her and by extension, to all of us.

Chapter Two

HANSEL AND GRETEL

SAN JOSE, CALIFORNIA—JUNE 1955

Molly

Now I looked at the potential clues to my mother's past. The news clipping was brittle and yellowed around the edges. The ring was light as a whisper in my hand. But what that whisper said wasn't clear. I refolded the paper, then slipped both back into the envelope. It was time to call Uncle Stephen and discover what he knew.

I counted to ten, picturing each ring ricocheting off the walls of his studio apartment. Then I hung up. Maybe it was for the best. How objective could he be where his only sister was concerned? His loyalties would lie with her. Maybe it was better to leave him out of the equation. Her past would be mine to investigate and then bury, if burying was what it would take to hold our family together.

As far as I could tell, only two things kept my mother grounded to us: my uncle Stephen and stories. Most nights she still told Angus a bedtime story. He was only nine, the second-child surprise when she believed she'd spawned an only. My stories had been over a long time ago, but sometimes I still liked to listen. She'd sit at the foot of Angus's bed after tucking him in, hands folded in her lap. She was a different person then, more approachable, less like a skittish feral cat.

When I didn't feel like being alone or wasn't writing in my journal, I'd join them on my little brother's bed.

Her two favorite stories were "Hansel and Gretel" and the one she called "The Four Horsemen." *Hansel and Gretel* was the only book saved from her childhood. The cover was blue and most of the gold lettering had been worn off. Inside were strange and intricate pictures by Arthur Rackham. I kept it in the bookcase Uncle Stephen made, next to my writer's journal. "The Four Horsemen" had no book to hold it. It was my mother's story, and she knew it by heart.

"My father called my mother and her sisters the four horsemen. They were stair-step sisters, who boarded a boat in Ireland and sailed to New York. The oldest girl was twenty—"

"Tell us about your mother dying," Angus said. The dying part was always a favorite and he preferred to cut right to the action. His cold feet pressed against my thigh and I squirmed away.

"When the plague came, the Great Flu of 1918, coffins were stacked chest high in the streets. When they ran out of coffins, there were piles of bodies. I wasn't allowed out without a mask on my face. My mother, your grandmother, was the youngest sister. She was beautiful and good. Not like me."

"You're beautiful!" Angus was always ready to come to Mom's defense.

But I was more intrigued by why she claimed she wasn't good. I'd developed unconfirmed theories involving sneaking cigarettes and cutting school.

"Do you want me to continue with the story or not?"

We were quiet.

"Your grandma died. She was thirty-two, and had a new baby, my sister Claire. Claire died too."

"And you were an orphan," Angus added.

"I still had a father and a brother, your uncle Stephen. We had an Irish wake." She described the wailing, the aunts sweeping in, claiming the furniture and curtains, and then how they rolled up the one good rug that had come all the way from Ireland and took it away. "We were so poor, we had to steal food from the market so we could eat."

"Is that why you weren't good?"

I was skeptical. Stealing food because you were too poor to eat was in every sad story I'd read. Who would quibble over an apple or loaf of bread when survival was the issue? It was a writer's trick, a red herring she threw in to distract us from the truth. But no matter how I prodded and pleaded, she never elaborated.

"Will the flu come here?" Angus wanted to know. And every time he asked, she reassured him that it wouldn't. But how could anyone know about the things that might happen?

I grabbed a handful of covers and yanked them away from Angus, who had wrapped himself tight like a mummy. I was sure she was leaving the most interesting part out. My mother, Elaine Fitzgerald Donnelly, had been up to something more. But the story always ended here. No family jokes, no tales about school, no faded black-and-white photos of her childhood. Beyond that point, my mother's life was a blank.

"And then what happened? Who took care of you and Uncle Stephen?" I asked.

"We made do. When all is lost, Molly, things either die or get reinvented. There's no in-between."

She was obfuscating again, evading my question. I could play that game too.

"Uncle Stephen says that every story should leave room for miracles."

"Does he?" She arched one eyebrow. "Believe me, there were no miracles recorded."

She brushed her lips across Angus's forehead, and then reminded me it was a school night. As if I could forget.

I crossed the hall and shut my bedroom door. Slipping my hand under my pillow, I felt for the envelope.

There may not be miracles, but there were secrets. I let the envelope rest in my hand. The contents were almost weightless. I thought of her in the yard with the clippers.

What was my mother hiding? And what would it cost to bury it?

An excerpt from Elaine Fitzgerald Donnelly's "Hansel and Gretel"

In the dark of night, the woodcutter's new wife whispered her plans.

"Unless you desire to watch them grow thin with hunger and then expire, we must lead them into the forest." Her voice, when she wanted, could be honey. "It is the only reasonable choice. It offers a chance. They're strong; they've got their wits about them. Here, they'll have no chances at all."

So, bit by bit, against his good judgment, the woodcutter was persuaded, all his arguments chipped away like flint by his beautiful new wife. He was a man who had lost his convictions to loneliness. But at night, when he watched his two children restless with hunger in their sleep, he was filled with an inconsolable sadness. How would they make do? How would they ever understand that he was leaving them open for a miracle?

Chapter Three

THE NEW YEAR

BROOKLYN, NEW YORK—OCTOBER 1918

ELAINE

Bodies were stacked like cords of wood at the end of Flushing Avenue near the Navy Yard. The morgues were full that fall and there was a shortage of coffins. Elaine touched the mask crumpled in her pocket. Her mother didn't want her out of the house without it tied over her mouth and nose, but after wearing it for an hour, it began to smell funny. Besides, it was almost impossible to tell what another person was thinking when a mask covered both nose and mouth. The mailmen, the streetcar drivers, her teachers—everyone wore them. Elaine had never noticed before just how much a quirk of a mouth told you about someone.

All spring the newspapers had been full of accounts of a new influenza. In Spain, they called it La Grippe, but in the States, it was called the Spanish flu. No one knew exactly where it originated; some people said Germany, some said Spain, and some people blamed Aspirin tablets. Everyone was scared. This flu was fast and deadly, victims drowning in their own fluids in hours, and by August it had come for New Yorkers.

Elaine tucked the loaf of bread under her arm, crossed the street, and tried not to look at the flu's latest victims waiting to be collected by a death cart or a Red Cross ambulance. If she forced herself to count to one hundred by sevens, she could distract herself from that unthinkable pile. But her eyes, with a will of their own, persisted in searching out the empty faces. All their peopleness had vanished. What was left was the after-image: sprawled limbs, faces as empty as mannequins, and the strange formality of clothing. She grabbed the mask from her pocket and squashed it to her face, breathing fast.

Forgetting the sausages at the butcher's, she ran toward home, her heart outpacing her legs. She skidded around the corner onto Steuben Street and stopped short, almost colliding with four little girls jumping rope. Two were the younger sisters of girls in her class. They turned the ends of the long rope in lazy arcs while the two smallest girls jumped and sang.

> I had a little bird and its name was Enza,
> I opened up the window and in-flew-Enza.

Elaine smashed the mask more tightly against her nose and mouth. The faces of the corpses clung like cobwebs as she stumbled up the three flights of stairs that led into the safety of her family's flat.

Her mother, Anna Fitzgerald, looked up with swollen eyes from where she sat in the overstuffed reading chair soaking her feet in a tub of Epsom salts. The room was ripe with the smell of boiling cabbage. Elaine dropped the bread onto the table.

"What's wrong?"

"Your aunt Ellen died." Her mother's voice was flat as newspaper.

Auntie Ellen was her mother's oldest sister, who'd taught Elaine to sew. She'd watched her aunt's hands, big and red-knuckled after years of cleaning other people's houses, smooth fine cotton as tenderly as if it was silk. Each school year she made Elaine one new dress.

While Elaine had been out running errands, the influenza had quietly slipped under the door of their flat, changing the shape of her family.

"I saw her last night after work and she was fine." Her mother drew a shuddering breath. "Six hours, and Tom said she was blue." Then Anna Fitzgerald buried her head in her arms and sobbed.

She'd never heard her mother cry before, even when Anna gave birth to baby Claire six months ago. The sound found a hollow place inside Elaine and lodged there. She couldn't move. She had no idea what to do. Pop came in from the bedroom gripping a wailing baby Claire in his thick-muscled arms. The tattoo of an American flag, inked the day he became a citizen, glistened with baby drool. Stephen followed, biting his thumb, red eyebrows drawn into a frightened scowl. Pop wandered back and forth between his sobbing wife and son making comforting noises.

"Make your mother some tea."

Elaine opened the jar of chamomile, breathed in the grassy scent, and heated water on the stove. The faces of corpses haunted the shadowy corners of the room.

"Take your thumb out of your mouth. You're eight, not a baby," she snapped at her brother.

But even yelling at her brother didn't make her feel braver.

Late in the night, she woke to the sound of voices in the main room. She'd crawled into bed with Stephen to help him fall asleep. Next to her he stirred and whimpered. He smelled like pee. She wrinkled her nose and slid out of bed. The first frost had etched the windows, and her toes curled as they met the floor.

"We have to get the children out of the city now." Her mother's voice was tight and sharp.

Pop answered with a deeper rumble, saying the flu was everywhere, not just New York. It was a plague of God.

He was good at making pronouncements like that, and when he did, Elaine's heart believed him.

Somehow the flu missed them. By early Christmas, the death count had slowed. Her teacher had stopped wearing a mask to school and so had the policeman on the corner. Newspapers declared the epidemic was over. Pop read that in one year, 1918, life expectancy in New York had dropped by twelve years. All that mattered to Elaine was that her own family was one of the lucky ones. They'd escaped, all but Auntie Ellen. Her nightmares of corpses slowly vanished.

Then in January, when Elaine came home from school, she found Pop at the stove boiling water. He was working evening shifts that month and should have already been gone.

"Where's Mom?"

"Got a migraine. So keep the noise down. I sent Stephen across to the Malloys' so she could get some peace."

Elaine unwound her scarf. The sprinkling of snow was already melting into the dark blue wool, which just yesterday Patrick Newman had said matched her eyes. Elaine knew what to do for migraines; her mother had them often. Keep the room dark. Tea and cold washcloths.

"I can take care of her if you've got to leave."

Her father nodded, and Elaine poured the tea in her mother's favorite china cup with blue forget-me-nots. She balanced it in one hand as she opened the bedroom door.

"Mom, I'm home. I've brought you some tea."

The curtains were drawn, and the room was dim with a single light burning. Her mother moaned her thanks. As Elaine approached the bed she heard a strange whistle. Claire was lying next to her mother.

"You want a cold rag on your forehead?"

What's wrong with Claire? She set the tea on the bedside table and leaned closer. Her mother turned toward her and exhaled a sour cloud. White specks flecked her lips.

"Mom?"

Elaine touched her cheek. The skin was cold and clammy.

She reached for Claire, who was still making the same shrill whistle. The baby arched her back as Elaine lifted her. At the base of her throat, a hollow deepened with every breath. Bubbles burst on her lips.

"Pop!" With Claire in her arms, Elaine dashed from the room, knocking the teacup to the floor.

Later, what Elaine remembered were the sounds and the silences: the teacup smashing on the floor, steel-toe work boots pounding into the bedroom. The whistling stopped. Baby Claire never cried at all.

The new year, 1919, was one month old when the Fitzgeralds held a wake for two.

Chapter Four

AFTER

BROOKLYN, NEW YORK—JUNE 1919

ELAINE

After the funeral, Pop reverted. That's what her mother called it when he went on one of his drinking binges. He'd disappear for a day or two and then show up unexpectedly in the middle of the night once Elaine had finally gotten Stephen back to sleep after a nightmare. She'd stopped going to school weeks ago; someone had to take care of things. When the front door creaked open, she sat up in bed and smelled him enter, a mixture of whiskey and tobacco. The floorboards squeaked. He swayed in the doorway.

"Get up."

"Shh. I just got Stephen to sleep."

"Get up and make me some food." With one arm he steadied himself against the doorjamb.

Dragging herself out of her bed, she glanced toward her brother. If Stephen was awake, he was smart enough to lie perfectly still.

There was only one way out of the bedroom. Pop always bragged that he had fast hands. Darting through the doorway, she ducked her head as she passed him. But his hands were faster. Grabbing a hunk of hair with one fist, he pulled her head back. Fumes of whiskey and sweat rolled over her.

"You're growing up. You look just like your mother. Soon the boys will be swarming all over you." His hand splayed. Her neck snapped forward.

Keep walking. Don't stop. Don't acknowledge. She crossed to the stove.

"God did this to me. He killed her and left me with two kids."

She cut two potatoes into thin slices, then sizzled lard in the cast iron skillet. Grease spattered her arms as she dropped in the slices. Behind her a kitchen chair crashed to the floor. When she jumped, the skillet seared her forearm. This had been Mom's job, to come between Pop and the kids, to stand like a fence that couldn't be crossed. Now it was hers. She was the fence; she couldn't let him break her.

"Food's ready in a minute." And still she didn't turn.

"Where's my son? Stephen!" Pop bellowed. She heard him lurch back toward the bedroom. Elaine ran. But he'd already ripped the sheet off her brother, who lay curled tight as a sow bug.

"Get the hell up and show me what you're made of!"

"Your tea's ready!" Her voice came from a deep place. It was iron; it was steel.

Bloodshot eyes circled in her direction and then rounded back on Stephen. He was sitting up now, sheet reclaimed and pulled up to his chin. His milk-pale face soft and trembling.

Pop yanked him from bed by one arm. Stephen stumbled and slid to the floor.

"A man knows how to fight. Are you going to grow up to be a man?"

Pop feigned a punch at Stephen's chin. "Come on, fight me. Show me what you got."

"He's only eight!"

The smell of hot grease choked the air. The pan would catch on fire. She ran back to the stove. What was she thinking? She was no fence of protection.

Pop danced on the balls of his toes, making air jabs around Stephen's head. *Play him*, she willed. *Jab back at the air, laugh.* Instead, tears leaked from Stephen's eyes and dripped off his chin.

In a flash Pop backhanded him across the face. Stephen's head jerked, his mouth slid sideways.

"Toughen up or you'll never be a man." Then he pulled a small open bottle from his pocket. Reaching down, he grabbed Stephen's chin in one hand and forced the neck into Stephen's mouth. Stephen gagged and sputtered. Amber liquid spewed from his mouth and soaked the front of his undershirt.

Before she could think, she was across the room and circling Pop's bicep with both hands. He rocked, stumbled, slumped as loose as mud to the floor. Rank breath watered her eyes. Yellow snot ran in a stream from his nose into the dark stubble on his chin. "God's done this to me."

Still in his underwear, Stephen peeked out from behind the reading chair. He made a dash to her side and clung like a monkey to one leg. Together they made their way into the bedroom. Stephen's wet shirt pressed against her thigh.

Pop's snores were loud and guttural. Elaine checked for the hollow place that had opened inside when her mother died. It was still there, as small and cold as an abandoned bird's nest.

"Don't let him see you're scared. It just makes him meaner." She ran a hand through Stephen's hair. "Go wash your face." One of his eyes was already beginning to swell. Then she grabbed a pillow from her own bed and stuffed it under Pop's head.

Chapter Five

WALLABOUT MARKET

BROOKLYN, NEW YORK—MAY 1919

ELAINE

Pete the pigeon man rested one thick leg on an empty crate. Elaine watched him watch the market: the parade of horses and wagons delivering fresh produce; the wholesale stalls selling meat and fish; Elsie the flower vendor with one short leg, who'd take your bet on the ponies when the cops weren't around; the bald German baker offering fresh buns from his wagon and fake immigration papers on the side. Most of the time you stuck to your own neighborhood, but in the market you couldn't escape the foreign smells or languages: Yiddish and Polish, Italian and Chinese. Elaine liked to think of the market as a crazy quilt all stitched with people's hope for a better life.

Most grown-ups only glanced at the world; they didn't notice the details, but the pigeon man did. And she didn't want him noticing her today. Their plan was to steal apples. Only two—one for her and one for Stephen. It was a practice run,

26

giving them a chance to perfect their system. Elaine didn't normally approve of stealing things. Stealing was a backup plan to be used when all else failed. The problem was, all else was failing.

She would distract one of the vendors with an inquiry about a job. The earlier in the day, the more distracted everyone was: vendors set up stalls, produce arrived by truck and horse cart, workers unloaded crates. Tom Dougherty's produce stall was one of the largest at Wallabout Market. A few missing apples wouldn't hurt him. And he was fat, Stephen pointed out, meaning he probably couldn't run very fast if he tried to catch them.

"If we're caught, we won't just be in trouble. Do you know what will happen?" She needed to make sure her brother understood the risk.

"They'll take us to jail?"

"They'll start to poke around our business, and when the police find out Mom's dead and Pop's not home much, they'll figure we're half-orphans and send us to the Hebrew Orphan Asylum. Some kids never come out."

Her brother's face paled. That was good. She meant to scare him so that he'd do exactly what she said.

Stephen's task was to grab the apples, but Elaine explained that he must not run. Running was a dead giveaway. At her signal, he should tuck the apples into his coat and keep walking. She would assess the situation and decide which direction they would go. They'd talked it through at least ten times. Even so, her hands were cold with sweat and her heart couldn't keep a rhythm.

"I was wondering if you had any need for someone to stack and unload produce. Maybe to sell." As Elaine considered Tom's round face, his pug nose twitched.

"You don't have the strength to lift crates."

"I'm a hard worker and stronger than I look." She brushed the hair from her face. That was their sign.

Stephen grabbed the two largest Pippins from the bin, one

in each hand. But the apples were too big for a one-handed grip. As he fumbled at his coat, one dropped and rolled across the ground.

"Hey!" Tom called out.

Elaine's eyes flew to her brother and then back to Tom.

Stephen ran.

Head down, Elaine backed away, fast but not too fast. Not before Tom, his belly lunging over the dirty white apron tied around his waist, grabbed Elaine's arm in a meaty hand.

"What're you playing at?" His face was so close, she could smell the garlic on his breath. Her arm crushed in his grip.

"I don't—"

"Aaahh!" Tom dropped her arm and grabbed his shin. "Hooligans!"

"Come on, Lainey!" Stephen was at her side, pulling at her skirt.

They bolted. Dodging stacks of rye bread, carts of cabbages, and harried shoppers, they ran until Elaine's eyes swelled and her side stitched. She leaned forward, elbows on her knees, and drew a few shuddering breaths, expecting a policeman's whistle any second, but when she looked up no one was paying them any attention.

Stephen pulled the single apple of out his pocket, took a bite, and handed it to his sister.

"What did you do to him?" Her words puffed out with the last of her breath.

"Kicked him in the shin. I didn't want him to take you away!"

"Not so loud!" They were in a narrow aisle between a cheese monger and barrels of kosher pickles, near the permanent brick stalls. Only one person eyed them. The pigeon man. Elaine felt her face flame. He was looking right at them, and Elaine could swear she saw a smile twitching at the corner of his lips. Then he rubbed his hand across his mouth and bent down to check the water in the nearest crate.

When he stood back up, he was holding a fat pigeon with

feathers shiny as an oil slick. The bird didn't struggle. Its bright eyes blinked, then darted back and forth. With deft fingers, the pigeon man checked the band on the bird's leg and adjusted the tube. Then he cooed to her a bit and set her on his shoulder.

The apple gave a satisfying crunch when Elaine bit into it. Juice trickled onto her chin. The last apple she'd had was spongy because it was left in the barrel at the end of the day. She handed the next bite to Stephen.

Elaine spied one of the mounted police a few rows away and dragged Stephen in the opposite direction. Threading their way between the lace makers and barrels of curry powders and cardamom pods, Elaine led Stephen deeper into Wallabout. This was her favorite section of the market. On Saturdays, she used to come here with her mother. They'd run their fingers over silks and sniff the teas. The market was one of the easiest places to get lost in the city and stay lost, if you didn't want anyone to find you. And that was exactly what Elaine wanted now. The last six months had been the worst of her life.

Chapter Six

IN CASE ANYONE WAS WATCHING

SAN JOSE, CALIFORNIA—JUNE 1955

Molly

We moved to San Jose two years ago. Dad wanted a place in the country where a man could breathe. I wanted to stay at my school with my friends. Guess who lost?

We drove fifty miles south on the Bayshore Highway, past mudflats, past the white hills of the Leslie saltworks, and past Moffett Field air base with its aircraft hangar big enough to produce its own weather, away from the only home I'd ever known. Angus was young enough to think it was fun. I knew better. Moving to San Jose felt like being exiled to a foreign country. No city, no street cars, no friends, only track houses and miles of orchards. I even missed the fog.

I'd met Aricelia Lopez my first month here. Our houses had identical floor plans, but in reverse. We were the two new girls in seventh grade, the newest of the new. Now, sitting on the Lopez's front lawn, I was about to test that bond, but she preempted me.

"What's up with your mom?" Ari stood on her little brother's tire swing. As the swing slowly arced back and forth, webs of sun and shadow tangled across her face.

Her question was casual, almost careless, but I could read the subtext.

"She was upset." I shrugged. I plucked two stout blades of grass from the lawn, and focused on slitting one open with my fingernail and slipping the other one through to avoid the question in her brown eyes.

"I got that."

The sun glinted off the silver charm bracelet on her wrist as the tire swung a slow circle.

What was there to say? Ari had seen the underbelly of my family, the soft, vulnerable place I took pains to hide from everyone. There were other kids who had parents that were divorced, but I didn't know any whose mothers were crazy.

When I looked up she was watching me, but without the pity I feared.

"Your mom's a writer. They can be temperamental."

I was grateful for the pass. She wasn't going to press for more. And that made me feel even more guilty about having to drop a bomb.

"I didn't turn in the script."

"What? You know what that will do to our grade?"

"I know, I'm really sorry." I waited for an explosion. None came.

"It wasn't good enough to turn in." I didn't mention that after all the trouble in our yard, I'd just lost heart.

"So you took a C? Because it wasn't perfect?"

For some reason it felt worse to produce a less-than-perfect product than to turn nothing in at all. My regret was that it meant taking Ari down with me.

"I know. I'm an idiot. I should offer to do all your homework next year."

"Are you offering?"

"No. But I'm willing to grovel."

She shook her head as if I was hopeless. "Who needs English?"

It was an old joke. Her parents refused to let her speak Spanish at home unless she was talking to her abuela. They said it was important to "think and talk like an American."

"I don't want to be a secretary, and I'm not going to teach. I'll probably be an engineer like my dad or marry my cousin's rich friend and live in Mexico City. Maybe both. I was getting a C anyway."

"You're not mad? I would be."

She laughed and pushed off with one toe. Her dark hair whipped out behind her. "See what I mean about writers? They're temperamental. You worry too much."

I'd been planning on an A. And my mother had been expecting me to get one. Writers got As in English. I was a writer's daughter. I pictured the tight lines of disappointment in her face. It would be easier if she lectured. Instead, she'd turn away and retreat into herself. It might be days before I could coax her out.

"Jesse's got a job stocking at Woolworth's this summer, some counter work too. Feel like a milkshake?" Ari asked.

Jesse was Ari's sixteen-year-old, well-muscled, dimple-ridden, laughing-eyed brother. I was his kid sister's friend. Ari laughed as my cheeks grew hot.

"Can't. I have to beat the mailman home."

"Won't your mom notice if your report card doesn't come?"

I stood up and brushed off my shorts.

"She's a writer," I said.

As I turned to go, Ari called after me, "Hide the pruning shears, just in case."

When I got home, Angus was already on the front porch. The third Monday of every month, the mailman lugged a big box to our door and rang the bell, asking the same corny question each time.

"What you got there, a body or something?" Mr. Kaminski winked at me and then laughed a round belly kind of laugh. I always laughed back; partly to be polite, mostly because I liked to hear him snort.

He was the same mailman who delivered the *New York Times* every Saturday. My mother's one indulgence. He had a saying for that delivery too. "For my highfalutin family."

I rooted through the mailbox. A few bills, an ad for a new tire store, no report card. I let out my breath.

Angus had already tugged the box through the door, wrestling it into the middle of the living room where Mom was working. All day she sorted, muttered, clucked her tongue, and clicked the typewriter keys, her copper hair pulled back in a careless ponytail. I looked at her now. There was a rip in the shoulder of her blue sweater and a streak of something black along the ridge of her perfect nose, a nose I aspired to one day.

"I got here first." Angus said it matter-of-factly and wandered off toward his bedroom. It didn't really matter. The game was old. We both knew what was inside. It was nothing but papers and a few pictures; papers about people who were no longer living, my mother's box of alphabetical lives for the National Biography Project.

Outside, the sky puckered as if it was about to rain again. Mom hardly looked up. It was a *J* month, meaning the box was full of the lives of dead people whose last name began with *J*. At first, I'd shared her enthusiasm for this library of the dead. I read scraps of papers, old letters, yellow newspaper clippings, but the people never sprang to life for me. They were only ink people on paper, but they demanded more of her attention than we did.

33

I wandered off to Angus's room. The clutter made me nervous if I stayed there too long, and there was this little boy smell I didn't want to think too much about.

My brother had "the knack," or at least that's what I called it. He was born with it—the ability to take anything apart and put it together again, sometimes in ways that were even better than the original. No one taught him. He didn't inherit it. My mother couldn't even operate a can opener without swearing, and my father once added oil to the radiator in his car.

Angus was happiest when he was in his own room. It was his workshop, full of bits and pieces of things: springs and motors, miniature fans, and screwdrivers. He hummed, he chortled to himself as he worked, and in that way he's like Mom. I'm the only one who needs human companionship.

"Molly, pay attention. I want you to hold the throwing arm while I work on the catch." Angus furrowed his red brows at me.

"I'm listening to every word you say. It's just I don't care about making things." I grasped the ruler he called a throwing arm and held it still while he used two hands to do something with a rubber band and paper clips.

"You make things. You're always writing in that journal of yours."

"That's different." I sat back on my heels. I knew even as I said it that Angus had a point.

His tongue peeked between his lips. I could glimpse his crooked eyetooth that overlapped the tooth next to it. His magic tooth, as he called it, that gave him his special mechanical abilities.

"There, I've got it!' He scratched his nose with one end of a paper clip.

It had been raining on and off for most of the week; it was the beginning of summer vacation, and if we were like other families we might have plans to go somewhere, like camping or to visit a grandmother. But we weren't like other families. If I left Mom and Angus alone, they'd starve to death, dying in the same smelly clothes they'd been wearing for a week.

It was usually up to me to make dinner and run the laundry so that we looked like a normal family. In case anyone was watching.

Chapter Seven

BOXES OF THE DEAD

SAN JOSE, CALIFORNIA—JUNE 1955

Molly

My mother worked on a brand-new 1955 Smith Corona. It was her pride and joy, paid for with some of the advance money from the National Biography publisher after her old typewriter lost first the *s*, and then stuck every time you pushed the *i* or *p* keys. The last sound I heard most nights when I fell asleep was the tapping of keys, and sometimes in the middle of the night they tap danced through my dreams.

After giving up on Angus, I decided to offer Mom some help. I needed to be on her good side when the report card came. And more than that, I wanted to keep an eye on her.

She was chewing a lock of her hair as she read over her notes, a glass of iced coffee at her elbow, an uneaten grilled cheese I'd made that morning cold and dry on a paper plate.

"Who are you writing about?" I perched on the arm of the brown chenille sofa. Her gaze rose slowly like someone awaking from sleep.

"Oh, Molly. You startled me. Richard Nigel Jerome. You won't know anything about him. He was a clergyman who died a long time ago, nineteen twenty-three." She took a swallow of coffee, poked the cheese with her finger, frowned, and looked at me. "I forgot your sandwich."

"That's okay. I thought you might be hungry."

"Oh, Molly. I'm sorry." She nibbled a mouse bite and made a face. We both laughed. I felt a knot loosen in my chest.

"I thought maybe I could help you with the *J*s. You know, sort the papers or something."

"Well—" She looked at the half-emptied box, at the neat stacks of documents on the floor. I could tell she was afraid I might make more work for her, mess up her precious bits of paper. I swallowed the words that blistered on my tongue.

"How do you get to be in a box?" I began to sort through the files about someone named Robert Johnson.

"You have to do something remarkable, invent something, have a special talent. At least have a famous family." She took another swallow of iced coffee. "And you have to be dead, of course."

I dipped into the box, grabbed a folder, and spread Robert Johnson's life across the floor.

It said "Blues Legend Dies" in bold print under a picture of him playing a guitar.

"How dead? I mean, do you have to have been dead for a very long time?"

"Just dead, maybe two years before there's enough collected on the person to make a file."

"Then I guess Albert Einstein won't be in a box yet." He had just died a few months ago, but he was important enough to have an article about his theory of relativity in our science books at school.

She gave me a funny look and said probably not, but everyone knew who he was anyhow, and he'd probably been in the *New York Times* obituaries. If I was going to help her work, I couldn't ask so many distracting questions. And I thought, *This is how it always is—we are the distractions from the people in the boxes.*

I'd never looked at the obituary section of a newspaper. I opened last Sunday's *New York Times* and searched for the index. Obituaries were listed alongside marriages, lost and found, and missing persons. It seemed that there were many missing people in New York, which made me wonder what had happened to each of them. Someone was looking for a lady named MaryAnn Binder, who was a telephone operator and was last seen wearing a green coat. Another person was looking for his son, who disappeared New Year's Eve. An insurance company wanted anyone who'd witnessed an accident on June 1 to call them.

It was then, while I was still looking at the classifieds, that I had my grand idea.

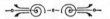

*T*he idea came to him when he eavesdropped. The woodcutter's house was small and full of secrets. Hansel was good at listening in. He never fell asleep as quickly as his sister, and their small sleeping alcove was separated from the main room by the thinnest of partitions. From his bed, he heard the rumors in the wind that clawed against their windows. He heard the voice of his stepmother, as persuasive as honey. He heard all kinds of things that Gretel missed. And what he heard this time made his heart beat faster, his palms grow cold. If they were careful, if he could fill his pockets with chips of stone, they would survive. He looked at his sleeping sister. His plan would see them through.

Chapter Eight

THE CIGAR BOX

SAN JOSE, CALIFORNIA—JUNE 1955

Molly

The investigation into my mother's past needed a starting point. I had the clues from her dresser; now I'd write a classified ad. I wasn't sure what it would say yet or how to go about getting it published, but the thought made me feel lighter. If hope was a bird, like my teacher and Emily Dickinson liked to say, I'd throw a net over it.

It's funny how one good idea seems to coax others out of the shadows. Not only would I write a classified ad, I'd begin a biography box for her like the ones she excavated for the National Biography Project.

From the lineup of items on my bookcase I selected a favorite Uncle Stephen had given me a few years ago. It was a square wooden cigar box with a picture of a white owl perched on a cigar under the words *White Owl Brand*. The cigars had been a gift from a grateful parent and Uncle Stephen had smoked every one of them. Every time I opened it, I could still inhale the sweet scent of tobacco.

Small and ornate, the cigar box closed with a tiny brass lock. A perfect container for my mother's biography.

I got my journal and a pencil and began writing the ad, but it wasn't as easy as I'd thought it would be. Mom wasn't a missing person. But there were parts of her that were. What I really wanted was information about who she'd been. I read the ads over and over, picked out key words, and finally settled for:

Seeking information about Elaine Fitzgerald Donnelly born in Brooklyn, NY October 26, 1904. Contact Molly Donnelly 3308 Kirk St. San Jose, CA.

An address was safer than a phone number. I knew when the mail came, and I could be certain that I was the one who retrieved it.

Beginning the biography box required an accomplice. I knew I had to return the envelope with the ring and newspaper headline to her dresser in case she ever went looking for it. But I thought it might be wise to document my sources.

Angus was young and unreliable. I'd already decided enlisting Uncle Stephen would only complicate matters. I considered Ari. Not only was she my best friend, we were brain doubles. We shared each other's thoughts. At least until recently. In the last year, boys had begun to take up significant brain space that used to belong to me. But she was still my go-to person when adventure called, and she'd already witnessed my mother's dark side. She also had access to the very thing I needed, a Polaroid Land camera.

In a matter of minutes, I was back at her front door. Her family was getting ready for their yearly summer trek to visit cousins in Mexico City. After explaining the basic concept of the biography box and enlisting Ari to help me with my research, I made my case for the Polaroid.

"We can take pictures of the clues and put the pictures in

the cigar box. We need to borrow the camera from your dad for the greater good."

Resting her hands on her hips, she said, "He'd kill me. Boil me in burning oil. Hang me by both thumbs. That camera is new. You know what he's like."

I knew exactly what Mr. Lopez was like. He doled out bad puns like candy. He bought the newest gadgets, and several weeks later they collected dust on his shelves. Ari's mother came from a wealthy family in Mexico City. Her father was east LA, and Ari's mother never let him forget it. I liked the way her parents were with each other, the way they teased, the way Mr. Lopez circled her waist from behind and nuzzled her neck. Even when she swatted him away, she laughed.

"Your dad will never know. We'll borrow it and return it before he gets home. I'll let you take the pictures." The last concession was very hard for me. I would dearly love to take an instant photo with a real Polaroid Land camera.

Ari adjusted the sunglasses on top of her head.

"I don't know."

I sighed. "I'll write your next two essays for English."

"Done."

We shook hands.

A car pulled into the driveway. Jesse and two friends emerged. They'd been playing basketball and were in sweat-soaked T-shirts and shorts.

Laughing and talking, they pushed past Ari and me into the house. Jesse bumped my shoulder. I caught a whiff of sweat. It wasn't at all like the smell in Angus's room. It was warm and musky and made my stomach tighten in an unexpected way.

Ari was talking, and I missed most of it.

"Are you sure you want to do this?" she asked.

"What do you mean?"

She crossed her arms and dropped her voice.

"I mean, what if you discover something you don't want to know? Then what? Not all secrets are good, Molly."

My mouth said, "Don't worry so much." But in my head, I knew that was what I feared the most.

"If you're sure, go distract my mom while I get the camera." She slid the sunglasses over her eyes.

I gave a quick nod. Did I want to know? Maybe some things in life should remain a mystery; examining the details could only lead to disappointment.

Twenty minutes later, two photos lay in the bottom of the cigar box. While Ari was home packing her new two-piece for her cousin's pool, I was on my way to the corner mailbox with an envelope holding two dollars and twenty-two words addressed to the *New York Times*.

Chapter Nine

PIGEONS

BROOKLYN, NEW YORK—MAY 1919

ELAINE

Masks had disappeared for good in the spring. Faces again had noses and mouths. And there were other changes. Soldiers returned and prowled the streets. Some of the men were missing arms or legs. Others had afflictions Elaine couldn't identify and didn't like to think about. In March, Pop had taken the train into Manhattan to see the welcome home parade for the 27th Division. He said people threw cigarettes and candy while the troops marched in full army gear with a French goat parading beside them as a mascot. Some of the wounded rode in cars, but many of them watched from the street corners.

Elaine tried not to stare at the injured who haunted the market. Wallabout was her escape from their flat, where her mother's ghost still moaned in the corners, where Pop raged, and where her school books collected dust.

For one entire week, Elaine and Stephen shelled peas for a wall-eyed woman. They made twenty-five cents apiece each day. But Stephen was slow and kept getting distracted by the crates of pigeons in the next stall over. At the end of the week the lady said she didn't have any work for them, and shouldn't they be in school anyway?

"Lainey, couldn't we visit the pigeons for a minute?"

She was tired and cross, but without another plan she couldn't think of a reason to refuse. "Why not? We don't have anything else to do."

"Look at their feathers; they've got rainbows in them."

"Pigeons are nasty, disgusting birds, shatting all over everything." She made sure she was quiet enough that the pigeon man didn't hear her comments. "Besides, you might get the flu from them."

"But these ones are messenger birds. You write a secret message on a little piece of paper, roll it up, stick it in the little tube, and the bird delivers it. Then he comes back home again." Stephen was bent almost double peering into a crate of shuffling birds.

"How's he know where to go and how to get back?" Elaine found herself more interested than she pretended to be.

"Ah, that's the mystery, i'n' it?"

Elaine jumped when the voice boomed right in her ear. She looked up into the watery eyes of the pigeon man. Her first thought was to hurry Stephen away, but his voice was kind. A big gray bird rode his shoulder. A smear of white pigeon dropping ran the arm of his jacket like trim. He probably didn't even care.

"Homing pigeons got a sense about 'em. Used 'em in the war, they're that smart. Why, one even got a medal of some kind. A kind of magnetism tells 'em which way to go." He was talking faster now, and he reached up to scratch the top of the bird's head. The pigeon cocked its head toward his thick finger and closed its eyes as if having its head scratched was the best thing in the world. "You can't send messages just anywheres. You can only send 'em to the pigeon's home. This pigeon is Lucky." He continued to scratch the gray-and-green giant on his shoulder. "One of the smartest birds there is. She'll always come back to my coop. That's her home. Say my friend Dom want to send me a message. He takes Lucky somewhere, writes me a note, and she'll bring it to me. She'll always find her way home."

"Can I hold her?" Stephen was looking so eagerly at the big man that Elaine didn't have the heart to drag him away.

Pete pushed his finger under the bird's chest and it stepped right up as if it was climbing on a perch. He carefully placed her on Stephen's narrow shoulder. Her yellow feet grabbed on and she ruffled her feathers. The bird was almost as large as Stephen's head.

"There's a good lady, Lucky. Nice little feller here wants to hold you." Pete looked over at Elaine. She looked away quickly, not wanting to find pity in his eyes or have him start asking questions. When he cleared his throat, all that came out was a deeper version of Lucky's coo.

But Elaine didn't notice; she was watching a lady.

The lady was wearing a hat with a mist of black veil. Her dark, thick hair was caught up in a roll above her slender neck, and her shoulders were covered by a fine lace shawl. On her arm was a basket filled with onions and lettuce. Her gloves neatly met the lace-edged wrists of a green silk suit short enough to show off her black-stockinged ankles. She was beautiful. Elaine sighed, and for a moment she was reminded of her mother. The pain was so sharp and unexpected that it strangled her breath. Not that her mother had ever owned anything so fine, but something about the way the lady carried herself, about the way she joked with the old woman selling bread, brought back Anna Fitzgerald so intensely that Elaine wanted to throw her arms around the woman.

"What's the matter with you?" Stephen asked, poking her in the side with his finger.

She pushed his hand away, still unable to speak.

"Lainey, I'm hungry." He grabbed at her sleeve.

Elaine pulled her eyes away and looked at her little brother. His hair needed washing and stuck to his head in ragged clumps. She had been too tired to heat up water for baths this week and his face looked like it hadn't been washed in a few days. The pigeon preened on his shoulder. Stephen's ankles stuck out of his pants. Thank goodness his shoes still fit, because it looked like he was growing.

She didn't want the woman to notice how dirty and poor she and her brother looked. When she looked down at her own skirt, she could feel blood rush to her face. Not only had there not been time for baths, but there hadn't been time for laundry either, and she noticed there was a coffee stain on the front, vaguely in the shape of Africa.

"Give the man back his bird. I've got four pennies. Enough for one sugar bun for each of us, but that's all you'll get 'til we get home. So don't whine for more." There really wasn't anything more at home, but it made her feel better to say it. "If we get them now, just eat half and save the other half for later, okay?"

"Fine, but let's hurry. My stomach's burning." Stephen pushed his finger under Lucky's chest as he'd seen Pete do and the bird obligingly climbed on. Pete was busy selling onions to an old man, so Stephen helped the bird back into its crate. "That's a good girl, Lucky."

Elaine followed him over to the bakery stall, darting glances at the fine lady in the lace shawl.

Stephen was already handing the bread seller, an old lady not much taller than he was, his pennies for a day-old sugar bun. The day-old buns were kept in a bag in the back and all the children knew about them. They weren't as soft as fresh buns, and sometimes Lainey suspected they were much more than a day old, but they still had the same sugar crust on the top and that was worth a little extra chewing. Stephen opened his mouth for the first bite when a man balancing a load of boxes clipped his arm. The bun spun from his hand onto the damp ground. It landed half in a puddle of muddy water. When the man's boot stomped on top of it, Stephen began to wail. Elaine hurried over as fast as she could, grabbing for Stephen and the bun at the same time. But the squashed bun bore the muddy imprint of a boot.

"Shush now. I'll give you half of mine if you stop crying." People began to turn and stare, and one of them was the lady in the green dress. Stephen wailed louder.

"Here now, it can't be that bad." The woman pulled a handkerchief out of a small pocketbook that was tied to her waist and brushed at Stephen's face. It was a pure white cloth with edges of lace. It startled him into silence. And that was the moment their luck changed.

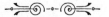

*A*nd so the children set out in the gray dawn with their father and stepmother, who lead them deeper into the forest. All that long day, Hansel held his hope close. After all, he had a pocketful of white stones, gathered by moonlight the night before. Every few steps he looked back at the way they had come and dropped one white, shining stone to mark their path. Those stones would change their fortune. The woods were dark and unpredictable, but this way they could always find their way home no matter what happened in the forest.

Chapter Ten

MAY GOSSLEY

BROOKLYN, NEW YORK—MAY 1919

ELAINE

"It's okay, I can buy him another sugar bun." Elaine rummaged in her pocket as if there really was enough money. She didn't want this lady to think Stephen was there by himself with no one to look after him, and she wouldn't be seen as a charity case. When the lady turned toward Elaine and smiled, faint lines laced the edges of her eyes. She was older than her mother had been when she died, thirty-five at least, Elaine guessed.

"I'm sure you can, but why don't you let me?" The woman didn't wait for an answer and asked for two fresh buns. Lainey could see them resting in her gloved hand, white and soft, light brown tops crusted with sugar. Saliva pooled in her mouth.

"We don't take things from strangers."

Stephen's lip began to tremble again.

The lady pursed her own painted lips. "Then I won't be one. My name is May Gossley." She took Stephen's dirty hand

48

in her gloved one. And then handed him the fresh bun. Half of it disappeared in the first bite.

"I'm Elaine Margaret Fitzgerald, and this is my brother, Stephen." The fragrance of lavender water pinched her heart. It was a fragrance she could still smell on her mother's slip. She'd hidden it in the bottom drawer of the dresser she shared with Stephen so Pop wouldn't find it. When life got to be too much, she'd bury her face in its silky folds and inhale.

"I'm very pleased to meet you, Elaine Margaret Fitzgerald. Consider this a gift." May handed the other bun to Elaine. Elaine ran her tongue over the rough, sugary crystals. Her stomach growled so loudly that her face flushed.

"Are you shopping by yourselves?"

"No, ma'am, my sister is looking for work." Stephen spoke with bulging cheeks and Elaine looked away.

May's eyebrows rose in two brown arches. "What kind of work do you do?"

"I can clean and cook, mend and sew a little."

"You're a talented girl." She looked closely at Elaine, right through her skin and into her bones. Elaine stiffened her spine.

"Can you read?"

"Of course. I'm fourteen. I've almost finished the eighth grade." She stared back into the keen gray eyes and longed to take another bite of her bun, but she didn't want to be caught with her mouth full like Stephen.

"You're looking for a summer job then. There are still a few more weeks of school this year."

"She don't go now cuz our mother is dead."

Elaine glared at her brother. How could he have said it right out loud? That pain was private. She might as well be naked in front of the world. And there was always the threat of the orphanage hovering like a great cold shadow.

"I'm sorry to hear that. What about your brother?" Her eyes stayed fastened on Elaine.

"He'll be going back to school in the fall." She reached for

Stephen's hand. This spring he'd missed more days than he had attended; she couldn't always make him go.

"I see." May narrowed her eyes the slightest bit. "I have a son a few years older than you, Elaine. He's in the eleventh grade. Schooling is very important. Have you ever read to anyone before?"

"Only to my brother, and he likes it when I do."

"Well, Elaine Fitzgerald, I have a proposition for you. My father is very old, and he can no longer see well enough to read. In fact, he's almost blind. He still likes to hear the news every morning. I have commitments that often take me away from home in the mornings. I would be willing to pay someone to come and read newspapers and books to him every weekday for an hour or two."

A tremor ran through Elaine like a small earthquake. "I could do that."

"Then I could pay you two dollars a week if you could begin as soon as school's out. You would need to be at my house by eight."

Two dollars! And newspapers and books to read. The numbers sang in her head. Elaine bit her lip so she wouldn't grin. The end of school was only a week away.

"Where do you live, ma'am?"

"I'll write down my address. It's not too far from the market." May reached back into her pocketbook and took out a tiny silver pencil and piece of smooth, creamy paper. In a neat hand, she wrote down the house number and street. "See that you're not late."

She had a real job. Money they could count on. What would Pop say? She shrugged off her tiredness like last winter's coat. It was spring, and with every step she felt lighter.

Elaine decided they should detour past Sacred Heart on the way home. She'd never seen this particular church before, even though it was only a few blocks beyond the market. They had gone to their parish church, Holy Family, every weekend of their lives to say confession, but all that had changed since Mama died.

Sacred Heart filled an entire block between Claremont and Adelphi. Elaine looked up at the rose window set high in a brick wall. Mama had promised Stephen that, once he was old enough, he could be an altar boy and wear vestments and walk ahead of the priest at Mass. Seeing that it was Friday, and that they hadn't been to confession since Mama died, Elaine decided they should stop. She still had her pennies deep in her pocket. It would be enough money to light a candle and say a prayer. She had watched people do this before and knew that the prayers kept your soul from purgatory, which was a place that was neither here nor there, like waiting at a bus stop for a ride that never came. Even though she was sure her mother had gone straight to heaven, Elaine didn't want to take any chances.

"Stephen, we're going in to say prayers for Mama."

"Okay, but I'm still awfully hungry."

Elaine dragged him up the steps before he could start whining. Inside, the darkness swallowed the day, silencing the noise of the outside world. Candles flickered in red glass, casting moving shadows on the painted walls. The echo of their footsteps was no more than the sound of a rock breaking the surface of the East River, a small splash soon absorbed. The air smelled holy.

She gripped Stephen's hand. The last time they had been in church, Stephen had been frightened of the statues, especially the one of Christ, blood dripping from his head and hands. In the flickering light, the blood appeared to trickle from real wounds that hadn't healed. Mama had reassured him that wasn't the case. But sometimes, she had told them, the statues did bleed for the sins of people and for the sadness in the world. Then it was a miracle. Now Elaine walked cautiously, hoping a miracle for them was lurking in the shadows. Maybe they had already found one, and it was named May Gossley.

"Don't forget to bless yourself." Elaine dipped her hand into the holy water font and made the sign of the cross, touching forehead, chest, left shoulder and then right. Solemnly, Stephen copied whatever she did. The church was mostly deserted except for two old ladies with lace scarves on their heads and a man kneeling in the front pews. Elaine pulled Stephen toward the rows of candles under the Virgin Mary.

"We're going to light a candle under the Virgin."

"Was that Mama's favorite saint?"

"I don't know, but she's mine."

The mother statue. She would understand how much Elaine missed her own mother. She'd understand about Pop and the way she hated and loved him at the same time until everything inside her was all tied up in knots. She'd even understand how much Elaine wanted to finish school and get away from Brooklyn. Looking up, she whispered, "Thank you for the job, and please make sure Mama makes it to heaven." She didn't add what she really thought. That maybe God should have worked a little harder to keep her mother alive. But she knew the Virgin saw the bitter seed rooting in her heart. Elaine clinked her last pennies into the metal box and selected one of the small white votives.

"Let me light it!"

"Okay, but don't shout. You light it from one of the other candles and then you say a prayer. If you don't say a prayer, you can't light it."

"What prayer do I say?

"You can say the Hail Mary. I'll help you."

A priest walked silently across the stone floor. Elaine watched him from the corner of one eye. He paused to look at them and then disappeared into the dark closet of the confessionals.

On the way out, Elaine pointed to the statue of Saint Stephen. A long robe fell to his ankles and in on one palm he held a pile of rocks. He looked too young to be a saint.

"That's who Mama named you after." No sense in telling Stephen his namesake had been stoned to death.

Stephen considered the statue. "Lainey, I'd rather he wasn't wearing a dress."

Chapter Eleven

MCDONALD'S

SAN JOSE, CALIFORNIA—JUNE 1955

Molly

I heard Uncle Stephen as he came up the walk. His whistle could imitate a bird; it could slide up and down the scale like a piccolo. It always made me feel better. I pushed my face out into the rain, letting the fine mist bead on my eyelashes. Today he was whistling "Yankee Doodle" something fierce. He wore a long tan raincoat, but his head was bare, and rain had plastered his wild gray-and-red hair to his scalp, making his ears stick out even farther than usual. There was something about his long, angular frame that always reminded me of a crane—not that I had ever seen a crane in person.

"Molly, he has no bags!" Angus complained.

And he was right. Every Tuesday and Sunday, Uncle Stephen carried bags of groceries into our kitchen and then set them ceremoniously on the kitchen counter. Today his arms were empty, hands stuck in his pockets.

Angus beat me to the front door, where Mom already waited.

"And how's my favorite nephew?" He scooped Angus up into the air. "And the two prettiest girls in the Santa Clara Valley?" Then he shook his head like a wet dog, and Angus giggled as the drops splashed on our faces.

"Look what I have here!" He pulled a slightly damp newspaper from his raincoat pocket. I could hear Mom come into the room behind me, almost feel her smile. "In two weeks, *The Lady and the Tramp* opens."

Angus let out a whoop.

"Ah, but that's not all. This"—and still in his wet raincoat, he spread the paper across the coffee table—"this is the piece de resistance! Disneyland!"

Spread across two pages was an artist's rendition and photographs of the Magic Kingdom. We had been hearing about it on the television for months now. It had been built in our state, near Los Angeles. Maybe one day— I didn't want to let my thoughts wander any farther than that. I didn't do too well with disappointment. I looked at the picture of Sleeping Beauty's Castle and tried to imagine walking in through the gates.

"Are we going?" Angus's eyes were round with hope.

"Now see what you've started, Stephen!" But I could tell Mom wasn't angry. Uncle Stephen was the only person who could draw her out. "Take off your coat and dry your hair." She handed him one of the pink towels from the bathroom.

"Why should I, when we're going out for dinner?"

That was why there weren't any grocery bags. "Where are we going?" I asked.

"McDonald's!" He bowed with a flourish while Angus whooped and hollered.

I wanted to go. Everyone at school had been talking about it, but I hadn't planned on going with my family. I'd already imagined being at a table with Ari and a crowd of kids from high school. Jesse would walk in. He'd notice us across the room and saunter over to the table. It was really me he was coming to see. He'd lift a french fry from my plate and stick it between his lips like a cigarette. We'd both laugh. Then he'd ask me if I wanted a ride home. Ari would catch my eye and smile. Before Jesse and I drove off into the night, we'd turn the music up loud and roll all the windows down.

Mom's voice cut in. "Are you sure we can afford this? You're spoiling them."

"Elaine, it is my treat. After all, San Jose's first McDonald's is nothing to sneeze at. Milkshakes and burgers for everyone! Besides"—and here his eyes twinkled—"burgers are only fifteen cents!"

I ran to get my raincoat. The cigar box and my journal were on the floor by my bed. I'd have to be more careful now that I had a real secret to hide. I grabbed them both and stuffed them in the back of my closet.

The first thing I noticed about McDonald's was the two thin golden arches spanning the building. The second was the long line winding out the door and a few yards down Meridian Avenue. Angus kept jumping up to see over the heads of the people in front of him and asking annoying questions, like if we would see famous people because it was the grand opening, or trying to make us guess what flavor milkshake he was thinking of. I spotted a few kids from school in letterman jackets ahead of us in line. I kept my eyes on the red-striped tiles, hoping no one would notice me.

As soon as we were inside the front doors, Uncle Stephen slipped off his raincoat and sniffed the air like a cocker spaniel. "Boy, do I smell french fries! When is the last time you kids had fries?"

Angus screwed up his face to think, but I knew right away. "At the boardwalk in Santa Cruz. You wouldn't remember, Angus, because you were still in a stroller." The smell of the ocean and french fries, the image of us as a family of four, Dad pushing the stroller, came rolling back so strongly, my eyes stung.

"I'd forgotten all about that time, Molly. I'm surprised you even remember it; you were only five or six." Mom scooted us forward in line, but her eyes were on their own journey, somewhere far from here.

"Can't have french fries without a milkshake, Lainey. What flavor are you going to have? I'm partial to chocolate." Uncle Stephen's voice called her back, refused to let her brood.

For a minute I was afraid she was going to refuse or, worse yet, say that milkshakes weren't healthy. Instead, she smiled even though her navy blue eyes still hadn't reached us. "I think I'll have a strawberry one."

McDonald's was mostly a take-out place, and I would have preferred that. But Uncle Stephen found a table with four seats, and declared it was his lucky day. I scrunched into the orange plastic chair.

It was the shade of orange that reminded me of a headache, the kind that throbs in the front of your head above your eye.

There were no plates, so we spread our hamburgers on napkins like it was a picnic. Angus and I shared a packet of fries. I had a chocolate shake like Uncle Stephen and Angus had a vanilla one. Immediately, he peeled the paper half down his straw and blew. The paper shot off his straw and landed on the lap of a women at the next table over.

Mom glared. She leaned over to the family. "I'm so sorry. You know how children are."

But I was sure I saw Uncle Stephen's lips twitch.

"I read *Beowulf* to my students last week. Not all of it, but we made a good start. You know, not a single one of them had even heard of it before," Uncle Stephen said.

"There're only high school boys, Stephen, not scholars." Mom swirled her straw around in the thick pink. "I don't think I read that until I was twenty-five."

"Kids are smarter now. They learn things earlier." He took a big bite of his double cheeseburger.

"What's *Beowulf*?" Angus asked.

I could see the pickle all mixed up with catsup and a little meat in Angus's mouth when he talked, and my stomach did a flip-flop.

"It's a romance."

Angus pretended to gag.

"Not that kind. Romance means high adventure. It's the story of a hero from Sweden named Beowulf who travels to Denmark to kill a monster named Grendel. It's full of battles, honor, and courage. In the end, he must defeat Grendel's mother as well, and when he's an old man he slays a dragon."

"And what are they supposed to learn from that?" Mom raised her dark-penciled eyebrows a fraction of an inch. I could tell she was teasing Stephen, but he answered seriously, talking to her but looking at me.

"Well, we all have monsters in our lives, but good stories aren't written to teach lessons. I tell the boys they're incarnations. They give life to characters and send them to walk around in our hearts and minds. If we learn anything from a story at all, it's through identification. That's why politicians and priests tell stories. Even Jesus told stories. There's something in the human heart that needs a story. *Beowulf*'s a good one."

Mom sniffed and took a very tiny bite of a french fry. "Perhaps Jesus should have done more miracles and less storytelling." There was danger in her voice. My stomach drew in tight like the cinch on a horse. I looked around to see if anyone had noticed.

I knew it was time to change the subject. *Nothing* gets Mom more riled up than religious talk. I don't think she has ever forgiven Uncle Stephen for teaching at a Catholic school. She says that she and God parted company a long time ago.

Mom directed her glare at me. I'd been caught in those headlights before. "Stories are entertainment. Don't let your uncle confuse you."

This time a few heads swiveled in our direction, so I kept

my mouth shut and stared into my empty milkshake cup. I really wasn't sure what Uncle Stephen meant when he said stories were incarnations, but I liked the sound of it. It made me feel like a story could be more than words on paper, a living thing that might change in unpredictable ways.

The tension ebbed as Mom finished her milkshake and Angus told a stupid knock-knock joke. An older woman began wiping down the table next to us. She shot a few "this is supposed to be fast food" glances in our direction, but we took our time. A few of the people working the counter were teenagers. I wondered exactly how old they were. All spring, I'd lobbied Mom for a job. She told me I'd have the rest of my life to work and that fourteen was way too young to start. But I pictured the summer stretching ahead of me like an unbroken expanse of concrete—hot, barren, and deadening in its sameness.

"Maybe I'll get a job here when I grow up." Angus sucked the last of his shake from inside his straw. Sometimes he can read my mind like that.

Thinking about jobs reminded me of the one plan I did have, to search for clues for Mom's biography box.

"What was your first job, Mom?"

She was curiously still, as if she hadn't heard me, and I noticed a faint flush to her cheeks.

"Go ahead and tell them, Lainey," Uncle Stephen said.

Still she said nothing.

"It was at Wallabout Market. She supported the whole family," Uncle Stephen supplied when she still failed to talk.

"How old were you?" I tried to picture her somewhere in New York, selling apples at a market, but I couldn't picture her anywhere without her desk and typewriter. As soon as we got home, I'd add the name Wallabout Market to the cigar box.

Angus leaned forward and poked her with his straw. "Go on, tell about it."

"It was a long time ago." And then she stopped. "It wasn't a real job at the market."

"How old were you?" I asked again.

Uncle Stephen stretched out his long crane's legs. "She was fourteen."

And she told me I was too young to get a job this summer! How did this new piece of information fit into the jigsaw of her life? Uncle Stephen had to be joking about a fourteen-year-old supporting the whole family.

"Okay, then when was your first real job?" I asked.

"It was later that same summer," she said, "reading to an old man."

But before I could pursue this line of inquiry any further, she began to gather up our hamburger wrappers and cups as if she was ready to leave.

Uncle Stephen cleared his throat. "Before we go, I have some news to share. I'm going to New York."

"What?" As a fledgling writer I dreamed of going to New York. It was where famous writers got their first break. No one famous got their start in San Jose.

"I want to go with you."

"Not this time, Molly."

Angus frowned. "Why are you going?"

"I've become involved in a miracle."

Chapter Twelve

INVESTIGATION

SAN JOSE, CALIFORNIA—JUNE 1955

Molly

"Involved how?" Mom asked

At the same time Angus said, "Did you do a miracle?" in a voice loud enough to stop the conversations around us.

Heads turned.

The family with the toddler leaned in. A girl from my school whispered behind her hand to her friend. I sank down. Any hopes I had of going unnoticed or at least pretending to be a normal family vanished.

"I don't know, Angus. I certainly wasn't planning to. That's what this investigation is all about."

"Enough!" Mom shot up from her chair like a jack-in-the-box. She leaned forward, pressing her fingertips on the table so hard they turned white. "We'll talk about this at home."

Her word was final. As she jerked her arms into her yellow raincoat, we stood as one and followed her stiff back out of

McDonald's. I stared straight ahead, consumed by my dread of being a spectacle.

Before we got to the car, Uncle Stephen began whistling "You are My Sunshine," and Angus joined in. My mind whirred like a hamster on its wheel. I kept sneaking glances at Uncle Stephen's face, looking for hints of the miraculous. You couldn't do something big like a miracle without it leaving a mark. But his face was still familiar in the way a true miracle worker's could never be.

In the back seat, Angus and I sat in silence. Outside, the rain had washed the sky clean of clouds. Hundreds of stars blinked back at me. Just beyond our neighborhood, cherry and walnut orchards bloomed. Beyond the orchards, the forested hills of the Santa Cruz Mountains sloped down to cliffs, cliffs that stood with their toes in the great Pacific Ocean.

As we pulled onto our street, I noticed the dark sedan parked in front of our house. A man waited on the steps, his silver hair haloed by the porch light.

"Who is—" Mom began.

But Uncle Stephen cut her off. "Monsignor Martin." He was out of the car and up the walk before my foot hit the curb. We followed them in.

Monsignor Martin was tall and gray, his bushy hair the color of rain clouds. Even his eyes, under curling brows, were the color of steel. I thought of the Tin Man in *The Wizard of Oz*. A snicker escaped.

Uncle Stephen sent me a sharp glance. I could feel it on the back of my neck.

"Monsignor Martin, this is my nephew, Angus, and niece, Molly. My sister, Elaine."

Next to the gray man my mom looked like a sunset, her red hair glowing above the yellow rain slicker. She held out one hand, and in a voice she reserved for door-to-door salesmen and missionaries, said, "Pleased to meet you."

When the monsignor smiled, his face opened. I don't know

any other way to describe it. It reminded me of a tightly closed bud that fast forwarded into a flower. Suddenly the grayness was beautified.

The Tin Man and my uncle disappeared into a bedroom and closed the door. I snuck into mine and pressed one ear against the wall. But all I heard was the rise and fall of male voices. I'd often thought my own life didn't have much of interest to write about. Now it appeared that might be changing.

I opened my journal and was finishing a note about Wallabout Market and the fact my mother's brother might be a miracle worker when I heard the front door close. Mom was already in the living room, and Angus was curled up on the couch. He'd fallen asleep watching *Walt Disney's Disneyland*. I paused in the dark end of the hallway, where no one could see me, journal still in my hand. In the living room, Mom and Uncle Stephen were illuminated like actors on a stage. Uncle Stephen walked over and turned off the sound on the TV. He massaged his forehead.

"It appears there will indeed be an investigation."

"What does that mean?"

"The church has to verify that an actual miracle occurred. I don't even know the answer to that question."

"This is crazy, Stephen. Miracles are wishful thinking. Something happens that seems too good to be true, and people call it a miracle. Remember when Angela Fabrino almost died of cancer? One day the cancer was gone, and people said it was a miracle. It was her cells fighting off the disease. Why can't we leave it at that?"

Mom spoke in that hissing kind of whisper that meant she was trying not to yell. When he didn't respond, she continued. "Is this about wanting to be famous, Stephen?"

My uncle flinched and turned away. Her words hovered in the silence between them. I knew the question was a dig about my uncle's ex-roommate, who had moved to LA two years ago to pursue his dream of being in the movies. Mom had never liked him or his close friendship with Uncle Stephen.

Ignoring her dig, he continued. "The Fabrinos were different people after his wife was healed. Joey Fabrino paid back all that money he owed folks." He walked into the kitchen. "I'm going to make tea."

Mom followed. I could still see her, one hip against the kitchen counter, taut as a bowstring. If you touched her, she might shatter. "It's superstition, Stephen, like rubbing a rabbit's foot. He thought if he didn't do all those things, God might make the cancer come back."

Uncle Stephen was out of view, but I could hear him filling the kettle. "We can't know what's in a person's heart, Lainey. Miracles are about transformation and people always change one way or another."

"This is my fault. If I hadn't left, you never would have been brainwashed by the priests. And what about us, Stephen? Where was God when we needed a miracle? Why didn't he save me?" Her voice was as bitter as the white layer of flesh in a lemon.

Uncle Stephen's reply was so quiet I almost missed it. "Don't you think I ask myself that question every day?"

My mother had left her brother, and they had needed saving. From what?

Her voice ran on. "I'll tell you what I think. If there is a God, he winds the universe up and then stands back and lets it run itself out."

Chapter Thirteen

HOT DOGS

BROOKLYN, NEW YORK—MAY 1919

ELAINE

Elaine opened the door. Brilliantine, cigarettes, and beer. Pop was home. But he wasn't in the main room or in one of the two bedrooms that ran shotgun, one opening into the other.

"Pop's on the fire escape!" Stephen called. The fire escape cantilevered over the alley off Steuben Street, where even on the hottest days a breeze funneled down the narrow channel between apartments.

Elaine hesitated. Should she tell him about her job right away? Her aunt always said approaching Pop was like walking on eggs; you had to be careful where to put your foot. But no one really walked on eggs. Elaine thought of him like a tomcat. Sometimes he'd hiss and spit, and other times he'd rub against your legs and purr. The problem was, you never knew which cat to expect.

Pop leaned an elbow on the railing as if he was on a ship's deck staring out to sea. That faint breeze ruffled the thick, dark hair he arranged so carefully in the mirror every morning.

The tip of the black comb he always kept at hand peeked out above his back pants pocket. His sleeves were rolled up to the elbows and one sinewy arm rested on Stephen's narrow shoulders. Like a painting of father and son, Elaine thought, and she waited a few seconds before interrupting the scene.

"Pop, I've got a job, a real job for two dollars a week!"

When he swiveled his head in her direction, she noticed new lines rumpled his face. She wanted to reach up and smooth them like sheets on an unmade bed.

"That so?" His voice was flat, measured, and his gaze drifted away again out over the alley.

Elaine held her breath.

"Never expected a daughter of mine to be working so soon. But I guess we could use some good news about now." A tic vibrated his cheek. "An extra paycheck would be good news."

She expelled her breath.

Then Pop swung around. "What the hell are you thinking? No daughter of mine's going to quit school!" His eyes sparked blue fire.

Stephen wiggled out from under his arm and scooted back into the apartment.

"I could do it for a little while, just the rest of this summer. Then I'd go back in the fall, promise."

Pop began to whistle under his breath, jingling the loose change in his pocket. "She wants a job and she's even talking back to her old man."

"I'm not talking back. I said I could be back at school in the fall." Her chest was tight and her eyes stung.

A thick hand flew up to cut her off. Air moved against her face. She blinked, but she didn't flinch. Those hands had a life of their own. Boxer's hands, he told people.

"I'm not saying it's a bad idea. Just takes some getting used to." He whistled through his teeth. "I've a bit of news myself. I'll be helping Harry Ames out with his horses regularly. It isn't much, but it should put something on the table."

"That's great." She could hear the tremble in her own voice.

"Won't pay enough to keep us in this place though." He pulled at his lower lip. "You'd only work through the summer and then be back at school in the fall?"

"Promise."

He spit on his hand and extended it to her. "Man's handshake's his word, Princess."

Elaine spit on her own hand and grabbed on to Pop's big warm one. Then he dragged her into his chest. At first, she stiffened. But his familiar scent surrounded her. She buried her face against him and breathed in. Maybe he was coming back to them after all. He'd always been good with animals. Horses were his special love, and Harry Ames supplied them to most of the delivery services in town.

Pop took a step back and pushed her out to arm's length. His eyes traveled her face as if it was a territory he hadn't visited in a long time. "Tell me about this job of yours."

Elaine told him all she knew while he listened, his eyes parsing every word. Then he pulled the comb from his back pocket and ran it through his hair.

"Let's see this fine house where my daughter will be working. A little foray into the neighborhood."

It was less than a mile from their flat on Steuben Street, between Myrtle and Flushing, to Clinton Avenue. Even in that short distance, the landscape changed. As they walked west, away from the riverfront, factories and light industry dropped away. Flats changed to houses. The houses stood farther apart, leaving space for small gardens and trees. And right in the middle of the block was a new women's college, St Joseph's. Elaine eyed the wide college yard and solid brick buildings. Maybe one day she would go there and be the first in her family to be educated. With a job, anything seemed possible.

The Gossley house was white clapboard with tall windows fringed by black shutters. And in the very center of the house was a glossy black door with a brass knocker. There was a handkerchief front yard with a tree and a row of lipstick-red tulips lined up like soldiers. A boxwood hedge separated the yard from the street. It was the type of house Elaine liked to imagine she lived in.

"If I lived here, that would be my bedroom." Stephen pointed to an upstairs window where a chestnut tree brushed the glass. "I could climb right out and down that tree."

"I wonder how many rooms are in that house." Elaine counted the windows.

Pop nodded. "Looks like a place for a princess to me. You stumbled into a piece of luck. What about your brother?"

"I talked to Mrs. Malloy. She'll watch him with her grandson this summer. Then he'll be in school in the fall like me."

"In school," Pop repeated. "My boy's going to grow up better educated than his old man." And he bent down so that his face was level with Stephen's. "Don't let me hear that you've been skipping school or church, or you'll end up like me." With one fist he chucked Stephen under the chin. "How about I treat you both to lunch? Hot dogs on me."

Elaine took one of his big square hands and Stephen the other, and they walked back through the weak spring sunshine. For the first time since her mother died, she felt hope stirring, faint as the breeze in their alley.

The lunchtime crowd was swarming the hot dog cart, and the warm, savory smell made Elaine woozy. Stephen squirmed by her side. Had they even eaten today?

"Wait here." But as Pop pushed forward between a man in a bowler hat and a stout woman in black, a hand landed on his shoulder.

"Mr. Fitzgerald?"

Pop spun around. Elaine watched as his eyes widened and then narrowed to blue slits. A cop had materialized from nowhere, and he stood so close to Elaine that she could smell the garlic on his breath as he spoke.

"You'll be needing to come with me."

Pop shot a glance at Stephen, but his eyes settled on Elaine, landing no longer than a bird on their balcony and then flitting away.

"I can walk myself." He shrugged off the policeman's hand and tossed the coins to Elaine. "Buy yourselves a dog."

The coins spun and clattered to the ground. Stephen scrambled to one knee.

"Pop?"

Why didn't he say there was some mistake? He didn't look at them again as he walked away.

—◦═◉═◦─◦─◦═◉═◦—

*B*ut Gretel's legs were short, and she had to run to keep up. Every time Hansel paused to wait for her, he'd catch a glimpse of glittering eyes watching from between the trees. Their father and stepmother never broke stride or looked back as the woods closed around them.

Chapter Fourteen

THE MIRACLE BOY

SAN JOSE, CALIFORNIA—JUNE 1955

Molly

I crept a little closer to the kitchen, so close that if Mom or Uncle Stephen weren't completely distracted, they might see me in the dim light of the hallway. I considered it worth the risk. What did Mom mean about leaving Uncle Stephen, and where did she go? Why did she need saving? I wrote both of her comments in my journal, bracketed by big question marks. So far, I couldn't tell who was winning this discussion, Mom or Uncle Stephen. I could see Uncle Stephen sitting hunched at the table; Mom was just out of view.

"Listen, I don't want you filling *my* children's head with nonsense. They need to be prepared to live in the real world, not in the church like you do!"

I heard a chair drag across the linoleum floor. I pictured Mom sitting down next to my uncle at the Formica table.

"You go on believing what you want, but Molly's already too much of a dreamer, and Angus, well, I don't know what he's thinking half the time." Her hands moved into my line of sight. One gripped the other as they rested on the tabletop.

Uncle Stephen reached out a bony hand and covered up Mom's elegant ones. Even with bitten fingernails they were long and slender.

"Molly's a fighter like you, and she's a thinker. She's going to be a tremendous writer one day."

My heart swelled, and at that moment I loved Uncle Stephen more than anyone.

"And Angus, he might be a genius."

Just as quickly, my heart deflated to its normal size.

"Geniuses can't always pay the bills." She pulled her hands away. And I knew she was thinking of my father, who was some kind of mathematical wizard but never held any one job for too long. Mom had said he was always too busy thinking great thoughts.

"Don't worry, Lainey. They're good kids, exceptional kids, and you're a good mother." That's when the crying started. The cry of a wounded animal, the same noise Ari's dog made after it was hit by a car. It was the sound of bone rubbing bone, the sound of tearing flesh.

My hands couldn't stop shaking. I dropped my journal, but I didn't look away. Uncle Stephen disappeared and reappeared with a tissue in his hand. Then he sat down, again crossing his forearms on the shiny tabletop. He didn't say anything. That was one of the many things I liked about my Uncle Stephen; he knew when not to talk. When the cries subsided to jagged sobs, Mom loudly blew her nose. She scooted her chair to the same side of the table as my uncle, and for the first time I saw her face. It was blotchy. My heart skipped a beat. Her voice was thick. "You haven't been sleeping again, have you?"

He shrugged. "It's difficult. Always has been since you went away."

Away. That word again. I concentrated so hard on listening that my head hurt.

"So, tell me about this miracle of yours."

This was what I'd been waiting for: the miracle details. As quietly as possible, I scooped up my journal from the floor.

"It's not my miracle, Lainey. I don't even know if it is one. Some days I don't even believe miracles exist. I just happened to be there when something extraordinary happened. Remember Robbie Crater, the boy who came to class with a helmet every day?"

Mom nodded. "He'd had a brain tumor and didn't have any balance."

"That's the one. Well, he hated wearing it. The other boys teased him; you know how kids can be. They chew up anyone who is different. They called him a Martian, stuck gum on his chair, drew ugly pictures and left them on his desk. I never could catch them at it, but I had a good idea who it was."

He got up and brought the teapot over to the table, pouring a mug for Mom and another one for himself. "The doctors hadn't gotten all the tumor and he had these horrible headaches. It was only a matter of time for him, although I don't know if he knew it. He'd stay in at recess and I'd give him little jobs to do. Things got so bad, he'd make up reasons not to come to school. I didn't know what to do. So last month, when he was eating lunch in my room, I asked him if I could pray for him, and—"

"I'm sure his parents had been praying for him all along," Mom cut in.

"I'm sure they had. Anyway, I prayed, and for some reason I took the helmet off his poor head and put my hands on his bony scalp. It seemed the thing to do."

"And what happened?"

"Nothing. Nothing that I could see. We went back to eating our lunch, and he didn't come to school the next day or the rest of that week, and I didn't think too much about it. I told you he'd been making up reasons not to come to school. And I got busy—" He turned up his palms in a helpless gesture. "I may not even have prayed for him again that week. After the second week, I got a call from his parents asking if they could come in and see me. Of course, I agreed. I had all the homework he'd missed laid out for them, but that's not what they were interested in. I must confess I was a bit nervous too. What if his folks thought I'd overstepped myself? His father's a big man, used to be a football player. He leaned right in to my face and asked what I'd done to their son."

I tried to breathe as quietly as I could so that I wouldn't miss a single word.

"The tumor was gone, not only reduced in size but gone—the whole thing. That was when Robert spoke up. He told them he knew it was gone because the headaches and the dizziness were gone. They asked him when that happened, and he told them about my laying my hands on his head and praying. He said he felt different right away." And Uncle Stephen let his hands fall limp on the table. He looked down and shook his head.

"It probably would have cleared up on its own like Angela Fabrino and hundreds of other children who are healed," Mom said.

I was writing as fast as I could. Mom's reactions interested me as much as my uncle's actions.

Mom wasn't about to give in. "We don't know everything about the human body."

"You're probably right, Lainey. Whatever happened didn't have much to do with me at all. Maybe it was coincidence or maybe God used my hands when he had some work to be done. How can I know?"

Mom slapped the table hard enough for the teacups to rattle. "I'm glad for the little boy. Who wouldn't be? But I think you're taking this too far—going to New York to prove you worked a miracle when you're not even sure they exist. You've always been soft, Stephen, too willing to believe."

Why was she so mad about a miracle? Weren't miracles

good things? As soon as she said New York, my heart started summersaulting again. I needed to finagle a way to go with Uncle Stephen. Not only was New York a real city, but the secret to Mom's story was there. I could almost smell it. And if it was her story, it was my story and Angus's story too.

Uncle Stephen was quiet for a long time. When he finally spoke, his voice was the hardest rock in the world. He said each word slowly, like he was dropping them into a pond. I had never heard him speak that way before.

"I'm going, Lainey, because I'm being sent. I don't know if it was a miracle. If it was, it wasn't about me at all, maybe not even about Robert. Belief isn't a soft thing. It's hard, more work than rolling over and being bitter like you."

"I'm a realist, Stephen. Call it what you like."

"No, you're bitter. It's like a sliver that you refuse to pull out. Even when it's poisoning you."

Mom was silent for a long time, at least a hundred heart-beats. When she spoke again she was calm. "Believe what you want." Her voice held that note of finality that could end any conversation. "You were in the right place at the right time, and God had nothing to with it."

There wasn't much interesting after that. They both went back into the living room separately, and Mom turned the TV's sound back on. I crept back into my room intent on making sense of my notes and adding them to the cigar box. I didn't know what to think about Uncle Stephen being a miracle worker. I had trouble separating miracles from magic. I knew that most of the things I considered magic as a kid involved tricks and had logical explanations. But it was hard to give up the idea that the world was peppered with magic, that the unexplainable might happen any time. Where miracles fit in, I wasn't sure. Were they a different kind of unexplainable? And by this age, shouldn't I know the difference?

I had theories about why Mom said she needed to be saved. My favorite one was that she had done something really dangerous, the kind of something she was always warning Angus and me not to do. Right in the nick of time Uncle Stephen, or maybe Dad, had saved her from certain death. But I didn't have any facts. Other clues, I was sure, were in New York. A tapping on my door made me stash my journal under my pillow. Uncle Stephen poked his head into the room.

"You still up, Molly?"

I nodded but didn't meet his eyes. "I've been writing."

"If you keep writing, I'll probably be teaching one of your books someday. I wanted to say good night."

"Wait. Will you take me with you to New York?"

He leaned against the doorjamb. "Not this time, but I'll take you next time."

"But—"

"What's so special about New York?"

"Lots of writers get their start there—Walt Whitman, F. Scott Fitzgerald." I paused. "I can name more."

"I'm sure you can."

"Besides, it's the largest city in the country. Things happen there." How could I put the longing I felt into words? "It's full of opportunities. San Jose is . . . small."

"In my experience, big things can happen in even the smallest places."

I wondered if he was thinking about his miracle.

"But I understand what you mean. Sometimes a person has to stretch her wings. Next time, you'll go with me."

"Promise?"

He drew an *X* across his heart with one finger and quietly shut the door.

While he talked, another fear had crept in. What if this miracle business did make Uncle Stephen famous and he left us for good?

I crossed to the window and looked out, letting my mind play with this new thought. I rested my chin on my hands. New York and all its glittering possibilities felt a million miles away. The night cooled my cheeks. I inhaled the scent of night blooming jasmine and the smell of rain on asphalt, which had a perfume all its own. Under the streetlight right across from our house, a blue car idled. I could see the silhouette of a person sitting in it.

Minutes later, when Uncle Stephen stepped out onto our porch to leave, the car sped away. I was sure I'd seen that same car on our street earlier in the day. It caught my attention because it was my favorite color, robin's egg blue, and because I'd never seen a car parked with a grown man sitting in it in the middle of the day as if he had nowhere to be.

⁻ₒᵌ═◉⁾⁻ₒ⁻⁽◎═ᵌₒ⁻

So Hansel and Gretel made their way into the woods and obediently gathered firewood all the long afternoon. As the shadows drew close, their stepmother told them to eat their piece of bread and rest by the fire while their father finished cutting wood. The warm fire and good bread lulled them to drowsiness and they soon fell asleep to the sound of the axe. When Gretel awoke, it was dark and the two children were alone. She began to whimper. Hansel woke with a start and begged his sister not to cry. "Wait until moonrise. The stones are our clues. They will lead us home." And sure enough, when the moon rode high in the sky, the chips of stone glowed like fallen stars and led the children back to the woodcutter's house where they lived.

Their stepmother met them at the door and rebuked them for staying so long in the forest. But their father met them with joy, for his conscience had not given him a moment's peace since he left the children alone in the woods.

Chapter Fifteen

WOODWARD SCHOOL

SAN JOSE, CALIFORNIA—JUNE 1955

Molly

The first thing I did the next morning was look out my bedroom window. No blue car. I sat crossed-legged on the floor in my pajamas and read over my notes from the night before, then added a few more questions for Mom's biography box. I pictured myself telling Angus and Ari all about Uncle Stephen's miracle. Then a peculiar kind of shyness came over me. Maybe this was not the kind of thing you bragged about. Maybe God wouldn't like it. I wasn't too sure what I thought about God either, having heard both sides of the story my entire life from Mom and Uncle Stephen. Worrying about God was complicating my life.

When the mail came, I could take care of another complication. An envelope from Lincoln High School was mixed in with the bills and advertisements. I tucked it away and then riffled through my few dresses, piles of shorts, and a Halloween costume I'd outgrown, until I reached the back shelf of my bedroom closet where I hid my journal. Without opening the envelope, I set it on the shelf. Looking at the C in the space next to English would only depress me. With any luck, Mom would never ask.

There was no response from my ad in *The New York Times*.

At the end of every school year, it was our tradition to help Uncle Stephen pack up his classroom. It was also a way to earn a little summer spending money. He paid Angus and me a dollar each to spend half a day boxing books, making an inventory, wiping down shelves, and cleaning windows.

The high school smelled of old chalk and dusty books and a tinge of mold, an aroma I preferred over the familiar pong of old school lunches and overheated locker rooms at my high school.

Today, Angus had brought his book on Leonardo da Vinci with him. "Molly, did you know da Vinci made a flying machine?"

I could tell by the gleam in his eye he was winding up for one of his long explanations. So could Uncle Stephen.

"Angus, I want you to pack up the bookshelf. Molly, I've made an inventory list, and you need to check off every-thing that is here." Uncle Stephen seemed more at home in a classroom than in any other place. His stature grew in front of orderly rows of desks like an actor commanding the stage. He handed me a four-page list written in his small, cramped script. I had my own agenda: find out more about Mom's life in Brooklyn.

"Why don't I get to do the inventory?" Angus furrowed his brow, and when his chin jutted forward I noticed how much he looked like Mom.

"Because whoever packs the books has to lift the boxes, and they're heavy," Uncle Stephen explained and then added,

"Besides, Molly is more meticulous than you when it comes to keeping track of things."

Angus scowled, but didn't complain again. "Are we going to listen to the baseball game?" The San Francisco Seals were playing the Los Angeles Angels, and it was all everyone seemed to be able to talk about.

"Later. The game doesn't start until one," Uncle Stephen said. He handed Angus a large packing box.

I began checking off the books in Angus's bookcase first, and then moved to the shelves in the back of the room.

Uncle Stephen whistled as he began to file the tower of papers looming on his desk. Now, while he was half distracted, was the time to start asking questions.

"Uncle Stephen, where did you go to high school?"

"Holy Cross in Brooklyn, and I can tell you it was a tougher place than this school. We had nuns who rapped our knuckles if we didn't study hard enough."

"Didn't they get in trouble for it?" Angus asked with a kind of fascination.

"Not in those days. Teachers had more authority then. Of course, not all of them used it well."

"Did you ever get your knuckles rapped?" Angus was sitting cross-legged on the floor, piling books from the bottom shelf into the box.

Uncle Stephen laughed, a great, booming sound. "More than a few times. And I've still got a few scars to prove it." He looked at his knuckles. "I wasn't like your mother. She always did her homework."

I saw my chance and dove in. "Where did she go to high school?"

I noticed a brief hesitation in his response. "Lainey didn't go to my school. She went to an all-girls' school."

"What was it called?" I persisted.

"I think it was called Woodward. Now don't be missing anything on the list, Molly."

Aha! The name in the newspaper headline. The school that closed. I was relentless. "But I bet she helped you with your homework like I help Angus."

"I help you with your math," Angus said matter-of-factly.

Again, that beat of hesitation. "It was a boarding school, so I didn't get the benefit of her good habits." And he began whistling again, burying his head in the file cabinet.

A boarding school! I hugged this new tidbit of information close. "But I thought you were poor! Who paid for her to go there?"

"Oh, her employer saw to it, a lady named May Gossley. We lived with the family for a few years. They were always good to me. She gave your mother her first real job. The one she told you about."

"Wow, that was nice of her." I rested the clipboard on his desk, thinking I'd hit the mother lode of information. May Gossley was the next clue for the biography box.

He snorted then from the depths of his files. "I'm not sure kindness came into it. She probably did what she thought was best."

"Was she very rich?"

"Yes, Molly, very rich. But she didn't know everything."

"What do you mean?"

"Well, we knew nothing was not enough, but she didn't know that everything was not enough either. It never could be."

Sometimes Uncle Stephen talked like that, in riddles. Before I could fire off the next question, he continued. "I don't think she was a happy person."

"Who, Mom?"

"I was speaking of Mrs. Gossley, but maybe your mother too."

The door to the classroom swung open. The priest who had come to our house, Monsignor Martin, walked in.

"I see you have helpers. Hello, Angus and Molly."

I smiled in response.

"Stephen, can I speak with you in my office?"

Uncle Stephen nodded. "Keep up the good work, you two. Lunch break soon." And Uncle Stephen followed him out of the room.

"Molly, why do you always ask so many questions?" Angus was looking at me, his face in a knot of puzzlement, or maybe it was annoyance.

"That's what writers do. It's how they gather information."

"You're not a writer. You're fourteen." Angus could be so literal.

"Almost fifteen." My birthday was only a month away. "And why do you have to be so annoying?" I threw an eraser that hit him square in the chest, sending up a puff of chalky powder. I should have known better. Angus had a continual supply of rubber bands in every pocket. For the next ten minutes, there was a truly satisfying war.

When the door opened again, Angus and I stopped mid-attack. We were covered with the white marks of our battle. I felt an explanation rise in my throat, but before I could say anything, Uncle Stephen cut me off. His face was paler than usual and his left eye was twitching.

"Some things have developed that I think you should hear first from me."

This was not the way he usually talked to us. He stood with his hands clasped behind his back as if he was delivering a lecture.

"I mentioned that I'm testifying about a miracle, but it looks like I'll be investigated as well."

"Are you going to be arrested?" Angus's eyes sparked like exclamation marks.

"For doing a miracle? Don't be stupid!" I said.

"Both of you, stop!" He held up his hands. I could see wet marks peeking out like dark eyes from underneath his shirt-sleeves. A vein throbbed in his temple.

I worried that everything in our lives was about to change.

Chapter Sixteen

RAYMOND STREET

BROOKLYN, NEW YORK—JUNE 1919

ELAINE

While Stephen scooped the coins from the ground, Elaine watched Pop's back recede. He walked with his shoulders thrown back, arms swinging as if he was out for a stroll, not being led away by a policeman.

"Come on." Elaine tugged Stephen's arm. "We've got to follow them."

"Where's he taking Pop?"

"Stop sniveling. It won't help anything."

Stephen blinked up at her through wet eyes.

She regretted her words as soon as she'd said them, but she couldn't find any kindness inside. She was too busy wondering what Pop had done.

They followed Pop for six long blocks, dodging pedestrians and street carts down the length of Dekalb, past Fort Greene Park to Raymond Street past the Brooklyn City Hospital. Pop never looked back. They passed the police station and unfamiliar brownstones until stopping at the corner of Raymond and Willoughby Streets, where Pop climbed the steps to a bleak gray-stone building that quashed any hope just by looking at it. The sign over the entrance read Raymond Street Jail. All this time, Stephen had remained quiet, but when the door closed behind Pop, his sniffles turned to shrieks. Elaine grabbed his arm.

"Stop it. People are staring. It's probably a mistake." Pop had a job, he'd been home most nights . . . If she couldn't convince herself, how would she convince Stephen? What did someone have to do to be taken to jail? She looked down at her brother, and realized it did no good to stand in the street and wonder while Stephen cried.

"We're going home. Pop will be back before bedtime. You'll see." She wouldn't let Stephen see her fear. Gossip spread fast as the plague in Brooklyn. It wouldn't take long to ferret out the truth.

By the time they reached their flat, Stephen had stopped crying. Elaine sent him outside to join a group of neighborhood kids playing stoop ball.

"Don't say anything about Pop. I'll see what I can find out from Mrs. Malloy, then I'll make us some supper."

Instead of going to the Malloys, however, she dropped into the reading chair and stared into space. How do you help someone in jail? She didn't have any money to bail Pop out. He'd almost been arrested once before for fighting, but had gotten off with a warning. She rested her head on the back of the chair and closed her eyes. What would happen if the Gossleys found out?

Elaine was stirring a pot of potato soup when the door banged open.

"Go wash your hands!"

"Since when does my daughter tell me what to do?"

She spun around. Pop dumped a half pound of salt pork and half a loaf of bread on the table.

"Get rid of that long face. It was only a case of mistaken identity." He sat at the table, tipping the chair back.

"That's it?" She put her hand on the table to steady herself.

Stephen crashed through the door, saw Pop, and hurled himself into his lap. Why was it always so easy for her brother to show what he felt?

During supper, Pop told stories about what he saw at the jail. But Elaine saw shadows moving in his face, a tremor in his hands, and noticed he drank only water. In the morning he'd already left to help with Harry's horses by the time she was up.

On Monday morning at eight a.m., Elaine stood at the Gossleys' front door in a dress with the sleeves rolled because they no longer met her wrists and a hem that was too short to do much about. She'd woven her hair into two braids that slapped against her shoulder blades as she ran the last few blocks. Despite her best persuasion techniques and the promise of two stories at bedtime, it was still almost impossible to get Stephen over to the Malloys for the day. The fear of being late for her first job had also made it impossible to eat, and her eyes felt hollowed with sleeplessness.

As she waited for someone to answer the door, she smoothed her skirt, trying to smooth her worries with the same small gesture. What if she misunderstood and they really didn't want her after all? Or worse yet, what if she couldn't read well enough for the old man and was sent away?

The black door swung inward. A maid in striped apron and dust cap blocked the entrance to the foyer.

"There you are. Better come in, then. Punctual, that's good."

As she moved aside, Elaine hoped for a smile, but the woman's face was as still and placid as the river in summer. Black-and-white tiles checkered the floor, and a large mirror edged with gilt framed Elaine's tight face and shadowed eyes.

"Mrs. Gossley will be down in a minute. I'm Pat Theilen. Missus Theilen to you. Don't fidget."

Elaine stilled her hand, which she realized had been twisting the folds of her skirt, and let her eyes roam. A dark wood banister ran up the stairs, and two doors opened off the entry hall. A thick Oriental carpet sat like a prize in the middle of it all. When May, dressed in a dove gray suit, descended the stairs, Mrs. Theilen disappeared behind one of the doors.

"Elaine Marie Fitzgerald," she beamed, "and right on time."

"Margaret," Elaine said. "Elaine Margaret."

May continued as if she hadn't heard. "Father's in the morning room drinking his coffee." She pushed open the second door and motioned Elaine to follow. "Don't stare at his eyes. He'll know."

Chapter Seventeen

A REAL JOB

BROOKLYN, NEW YORK—JUNE/JULY 1919

ELAINE

The walls were buttercream. Blue curtains with patterns of flowers and birds were tied back to let the morning sun flood the room. At a long cherry table, a very old man sat holding a cup of coffee. His bald head topped the folds of a thick red shawl like a white marble statue, and it startled Elaine when he moved. As they entered the room, he turned his head toward them. Pale blue eyes latched on to Elaine's face. Could they be mistaken about his blindness?

"Dad, Elaine has come to read to you, like I promised."

She stood quite still, pinned by those cloudless eyes, unsure what to do next.

"Go over to him and introduce yourself," May whispered.

Not knowing where to look, Elaine inched forward. She tried not to stare at his eyes. It was impossible. She extended her hand as a test, and when he didn't move, drew it back again. "I'm Elaine Margaret Fitzgerald."

The old man cleared his throat. "Can you read?"

"Yes, sir."

"Well, get busy then. I'm a day behind because my daughter is always gallivanting about after some cause or another. And don't leave anything out. I'll know if you do."

"When you're done, Elaine, let Mrs. Theilen know. She'll see to your lunch. I've got to leave now." She pecked her father on the cheek, tossed Elaine a smile, and sped out the door as if she couldn't exit fast enough.

Elaine considered the stack of newspapers on the table. Unsure where to begin, she rifled through the pile. "Which one do you want to hear first?"

"Start with the *Tribune* first, Sunday edition. It has the real news, not sensationalism like the others. Don't stutter, do you?" And he leaned forward and widened his sightless eyes.

"N-n-no, sir." But the *n*s tripped from her lips in a nervous staccato as his blank eyes searched her. A thin trickle of perspiration crawled down her spine. Settling into a high-backed chair, she searched through *The New York Sun, The New York Herald* and *The New York Daily* for the Sunday copy of *The Tribune*.

She hadn't known that New York had more than one newspaper. The only one her father ever read was *The Herald,* and only when someone else had discarded it. She decided to begin with the headlines and willed her voice to hold steady.

"Congress Passes the Nineteenth Amendment." Elaine had heard of the Nineteenth Amendment. It would give women the right to vote. Pop had said nothing'd make him prouder then seeing his daughter voting like a good Democrat one day.

"Does that mean women can vote now?"

"It has to go to the states for ratification." May Gossley's father snorted. "Cursed Russians! They're behind this suffrage business!" His pale face infused with red. "Women don't have the mind for politics."

"I'd like to vote one day." She swallowed. Maybe this wasn't the way to start, contradicting her new employer. She gripped the paper tighter.

"So you speak your mind. Same as my daughter."

She wasn't sure if she was supposed to respond or not.

"And how old do you think I am, young lady?"

Elaine regarded the freckles on his pale head, his wrinkled hands that curved in like pigeon feet. Ancient, but she couldn't say that. She couldn't lie, either.

"I'd say seventy, sir."

"Seventy-eight. At least you didn't try to flatter me. A man my age has experience. I know how the world works."

"Yes, sir."

He nodded as if they'd agreed upon something, but Elaine wasn't sure what it was. "Keep reading."

Elaine read about profiteering landlords and the rise in milk prices, and most interesting to Mr. Seward, the upcoming fight between Jess Willard and Jack Dempsey.

"Can't believe people with a lick of sense would pay good money and sit in the hot sun to watch two criminals fight! Ever seen a boxing match?"

Elaine shook her head, then realized he couldn't see it and said, "No, but my father has. He tried for the Golden Gloves once."

"Did he now? Your father's a fighter, is he? I used to enjoy a good clean fight. They're all engineered now."

She discovered Mr. Seward had an opinion about nearly everything she read.

"The Bolshevists will be running New York and we'll all be taken over by Russia. Do you know what a Bolshevist is?"

She'd heard the word, but no clear definition came to mind. "No, sir."

"I thought you were educated. A Bolshevist is someone who wants something for nothing. They want everyone to be the same; they want revolution. They're out to destroy us. Take my daughter, for example. She's great for causes, always giving my money away. She's being manipulated by the Bolshi and she's too pigheaded to see it!"

Elaine wondered if she should defend May, but decided it might be better to say nothing.

"They're infiltrating our government even as we speak. Government run by short-haired women and long-haired men. How'd you like that?" He wheezed. "You don't have short hair, do you?"

"No, sir."

"Come over here and let me feel it."

Elaine stiffened when she looked at his curled hands and long fingernails and imagined them touching her hair. But she inched her chair closer.

"Well?"

"It's braided today." When she held out a braid, her hand trembled.

He grasped it in both hands and ran it between his fingers. Then he yanked.

"Ouch!" She pulled back, but he hung on.

"Had to see if it was real or not," he said as he passed one hand up the braid until he reached her scalp. Satisfied, he patted her head. "See that you keep it long while you're employed in my household."

Angry words boiled on the tip of her tongue, but she pressed her lips together. Without this money, they'd be dependent on Pop showing up for Harry Ames's horses every day. And she knew how likely that was.

"What color is it?"

"What?"

"A simple question, young lady. What color is your hair?"

"Red."

And then he laughed, a deeper, fuller laugh than a dried-up old man should be able to produce. "Red? I've always been partial to red-haired women." When his laugh sputtered to a cough, Elaine poured him a glass of water from the pitcher on the table.

"A redhead, my Bolshevik daughter brings me a redhead!" A bit of the water dribbled down his chin. "Do you have breasts yet? Anything for a man to look at?"

Elaine folded her arms across her chest. Then remembered again that Mr. Seward couldn't see. It didn't matter; her face still burned. She stood up and shoved the chair back. In seconds she could cross the floor and be out the door.

"Sit down. I'm trying to determine how much of a distraction you'll be for my grandson. He has no morals."

On the outside she stood completely still, but inside her heart jackknifed and her brain chattered. Walk out now or stay and finish today's job? Without the job, she'd live her life taking care of Pop and Stephen, never go back to school, never make it to college.

"I can see I've offended you. All women grow them eventually."

When she still didn't speak or move, his voice gentled. "Well, get back to reading. What are we paying you for?"

She hated him. After righting the chair and making sure it was well out of Mr. Seward's reach, she picked up the paper and prepared to read. But different words sprang from her mouth than were on the page, the words that had piled on her tongue. "It doesn't matter how rich you are, you can't treat people that way. I don't belong to you." She took a shuddering breath. "I'm here for a job. To read. You've no right to make comments about my person."

"I've offended your sensibilities. Said more than I should have." He coughed into a handkerchief. "I speak my mind plainly. I can see you do too. I like that. In the future I will be more circumspect, Elaine Margaret."

It wasn't an apology, not quite, but he'd heard what she said. And she wasn't fired, yet. Elaine began again.

This time she read about the bombings that had happened earlier that week in eight US cities.

"Anarchists! They're trying to destroy our country."

Elaine stopped mid-sentence.

"Did I tell you to stop reading?" He swiped the air with one hand, knocking over the glass of water. She grabbed a cloth napkin and began wiping the table and floor.

"Damn it! Can't even see a glass of water!"

If he wanted her to feel sorry for him, it wasn't working. The sooner she could get out of this house, the better. But as she read, her anger wandered into the stories and got lost. She forgot about everything beyond what was on the page. There was so much in the world she didn't know about, so much she wanted to know.

It was some time later when Mr. Seward began to make a funny whistling sound. His head slumped forward on his chest, his mouth opened, and a thin trail of drool connected his chin to the front of his white shirt. He snorted, readjusted himself, and began to snore.

Elaine looked at the mantel clock above the tall fireplace. It was eleven o'clock. She'd been reading for almost three hours, and her throat was sore. She poured herself some water. Despite Mr. Seward, she couldn't deny the pure pleasure of reading the paper.

A bathroom was what she needed now, but she didn't know where to find it. Where was Mrs. Theilen? After shifting uncomfortably in her chair for several more minutes, she stood and crossed to the window.

The door behind her swung open. She heard the soft *swish* as it grazed the carpet. Turning, she was face to face with a tall, brown-haired boy. A strawberry birthmark stood out like an island on his left cheek.

"Oh, hello there. Thought I'd see who was reading to the old man." When he smiled a dimple appeared in each cheek. "My name's Howard, Howard Gossley. I expect you've heard about me."

Chapter Eighteen

THE "T"

BROOKLYN, NEW YORK—JUNE TO AUGUST 1919

ELAINE

Dinner that night was more of a celebration than anything Elaine had experienced since her mother's death. Pop purchased a shank of lamb. They ate it boiled over potatoes with cake for dessert sent home compliments of May Gossley. Stephen told about his day with Mrs. Malloy and her grandson. They'd met a new kid on the block who'd moved to Brooklyn from somewhere in the south. When Stephen imitated his accent, Elaine laughed so hard milk squirted from her nose.

Pop told about Harry Ames's horses, how the big chestnut, Danny Boy, tried to trick him.

"Every time I'd draw the cinch up tight around his great belly, the beast'd hold his breath 'til his stomach swelled up like the fattest balloon you ever saw. Then when he'd let his breath out, the saddle could roll right off."

"What did you do?" Stephen asked.

"I punched him in the stomach. It's the only way to treat a

horse of his nature. All the air came out in a blast. He farted so bad I could hardly stand the stink!"

Now it was Stephen's turn to roar with laughter. Pop described each horse by name. This is good for him, Elaine thought. Maybe we'll be a real family now. And he drank only one beer with the entire meal.

Elaine thought carefully about what to share about the big house. She didn't want to make Pop feel bad or say anything that might make Stephen feel like he was missing out. So, she told about Mr. Seward. He was an old, dried man who yanked her hair to make sure she wasn't a Bolshi woman. She told about the preparations for the Dempsey and Willard fight, about the smell of warm bread in the Gossleys' kitchen. But she didn't mention Mr. Seward's other question, the one that almost sent her home, or Howard with the strawberry birthmark.

That night as she cleaned the kitchen, she sang one of her mother's favorite songs, and the words felt good in her mouth. How long had it been since she sang? As she lay in bed listening to Stephen's regular breaths beside her, she thought about her day and the things she didn't share. There was no reason to keep secrets, but she liked to have something that was hers alone. In their small flat, the only secrets anyone had were those locked inside themselves.

Howard was seventeen, three years older than she was. That was intriguing enough, but there was also his grandfather's warning: *Howard has no morals.* Those words made her nervous, but there was a thrill buried there too, and his stories made her laugh.

As the weeks wore on, they ended up eating lunch together at least twice a week. Nothing was ever formally arranged; it just worked out that way. They ate in the kitchen where Kay Baggot cooked, feasting on warm bread right from the oven, and roast chicken or beef sandwiches.

He told her he'd been sent home for pranks. Twice. The twenty mice loose in the Latin classroom had made old Hayes scream like a girl. Glue in the drawer lock where his math teacher kept his flask made the man cuss in front of the nuns. Each time, May made him promise he'd never do it again. He always agreed. Doing the same prank more than once would spoil the pleasure of it.

After his stories, Elaine knew his world. Sally Ann, who always wore her skirt tantalizingly higher than midcalf, had the best legs in school. His buddy, Teddy Schwartzman, got caught kissing Agnes in the cloakroom with one hand under her shirt. Agnes's father had threatened to shoot Teddy if he ever talked to his daughter again. Howie impersonated every teacher. Elaine was his audience. He never tired of performing; she never tired of listening.

"Elaine, my newspaper princess, I've got something to show you in the side yard." Howard leered at her.

Elaine felt blood rush to her face.

"Ah, I see what you're thinking, and can't believe you'd consider me so debased. What I have to show you is a simple matter of mechanical ability."

"That makes it sound worse."

"My intent exactly."

Howie grabbed her hand and pulled her to the gravel drive where his father's new 1919 Model T gleamed in the sun. The T was totally enclosed, unlike most of the rare cars on the roads. She knew Mr. Gossley worked in banking and had something to do with the stock market. He left for work early and came home late. But occasionally he came home at lunchtime and napped in the middle of the day. Then the T sat in the driveway, ostentatious as an oversized diamond in a ring. According to Howie, he washed the car every Sunday and then buffed it with a special cloth. No one else could clean it.

"Care for a spin in the T?" Howie's eyes challenged her.

"And who's going to drive us?" Elaine crossed her arms and tried to look stern. Her brain voice whispered this was not a smart thing to do. But her heart spun like a Ferris wheel.

"I am, of course." Howie climbed in the left door to set the spark and throttle.

The Ferris wheel spun faster. "What if we get caught?"

"Worried? Then we won't get caught." He climbed back out and with two hands circled the crank. The engine sputtered, then roared.

She could lose her job over this. Gravel crunched under her feet as she took a few steps back toward the house. "He'll hear you and wake up."

Howie was instantly at her side. He took her hand.

"A carriage for the newspaper princess." His brown eyes locked with hers. They were his best feature: almost girlish eyes, with long, curling lashes. She didn't want to pull her hand away, and wasn't sure she even could as it was now melting into his. Her brain shouted to walk away but she let him lead her to the car.

"Do you know how to drive?" Her voice was a whisper.

The seats smelled like new leather, felt like the shoes she touched in stores when no one was looking. Howie released the hand brake and the car slowly began to roll. Every muscle in her body clenched. Howie's thigh was inches from her own. His long hands slid across the steering wheel. As he pressed his left foot on the slow speed pedal, they glided from the drive to the street.

"Isn't this far enough?" She imagined she could feel Mr. Gossley's eyes drilling into them from the bedroom window. She was afraid to turn her head to check.

"Once around the block and no one will be the wiser. What's the matter—don't you trust me?" A grin split his face.

"Give me one reason I should." Then, "It's not that, but if we get caught."

Just as quickly, his grin disappeared. "That's what's wrong with you, you know. You don't know how to have fun."

Fun. The small word bristled with barbs. What did he know about her life? She blinked back startled tears and turned her head away so he wouldn't see. Howie was right; she didn't know how to have fun. She could barely remember peace.

The car was pointed south, toward Myrtle Avenue. The afternoon sun was warm on her face. She allowed her shoulders to relax. As Howie accelerated, Elaine let herself feel an exhilarating rush. It must be the same thing Pete's pigeons felt when they launched into the sky.

The next moment a car rounded the corner from Myrtle and shot straight toward them, blowing its horn. Howie pulled his foot off the pedal and swerved. The car lurched toward the hedge. He slammed his foot on the reverse pedal. The car shot back and smacked into the brick post at the edge of the drive.

Elaine snapped back and forth in her seat. Biting down hard, she tasted blood on her tongue.

"Of all the blasted bad luck!" Howie pounded the steering wheel. He looked at Elaine. His face was white, but a flicker in his eyes made her think he was enjoying it.

Pieces of hedge poked in through the open window. Howie leaned his head back on the seat and laughed.

Elaine closed her eyes and imagined telling Pop how she'd lost her job.

"It's the best fun I've had all week!"

"Fun? We've crashed your father's car." She swallowed. "I need this job."

"What are you talking about? It's only a scratch."

By then Kay was puffing down the driveway. Mr. Gossley followed, still in his shirtsleeves.

"Are ya all right?" Kay peered in the window, her face as red as a tomato from her garden.

Mr. Gossley had yanked open the door. His nostrils flared, and he made a strange clicking sound with his teeth.

"Get out."

Elaine couldn't catch her breath. She stepped down to the street, followed by Howie.

"Father, a thousand apologies. It was all my fault. I persuaded the young lady to be my accomplice."

"What in tarnation do you think you're up to?" Mr. Gossley's voice shook. "I should get out my belt and beat you black and blue."

Her head throbbed where she'd knocked it on the window. The tang of blood was still sharp in her mouth.

"You're the young lady who reads to my father-in-law. I trust my son hasn't brought you to any harm." Mr. Gossley didn't look at her or even wait for an answer. Instead his nod was like a period to a conversation.

Elaine knew what that nod meant. She was dismissed. Her job was over. Howie caught her eye and winked. Should she leave? What would happen to Howie? He'd been showing off and she could have stopped him. But neither Howie nor his father looked at her again. Instead, they examined every inch of the car.

The brilliance of the September afternoon faded. Head down, eyes locked on the pavement, Elaine walked away. How had she managed to destroy the one good thing that was handed to her? She should have stopped Howie. Instead, she would be banished, never allowed to see him again. At home, they wouldn't make the rent on Pop's salary alone. Which fate was worse? She wasn't sure. Either way, her new life was ended.

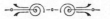

*B*ut the difficult times were not yet over for Hansel and Gretel and their family. The famine continued to plague the land. Once again, their stepmother spoke vehemently about returning the children to the woods, so that they might not all starve. And their father, having been persuaded once before, now toppled quite quickly under the force of her words.

Hansel was not caught unawares. His vigilance never relaxed; he had been waiting for the second shoe to drop, and when it did, he was prepared. Their safety hinged on a loaf of bread he had hidden in advance. When his stepmother again urged them to return to the heart of the forest, he brought the loaf concealed under his jacket.

As they trudged the narrow path into the woods, he worried pieces of bread from the loaf and dropped them on the forest floor. Hansel was certain the crumbs would lead them home again, as surely as the white stones had done before. The rest of the loaf would sustain them on their journey. For just as he predicted, this time they would be led deeper into the woods.

Chapter Nineteen

PROOF

SAN JOSE, CALIFORNIA—JUNE 1955

Molly

Everything looked the same, but everything felt different, as if we had walked into a classroom on the other side of the looking glass. Without being told to, Angus and I each sat at a desk as if we were Uncle Stephen's students. Angus busily picked at a scab on his knee, a leftover from the last time he went roller skating.

"Some things have developed that I think you should hear first from me," Uncle Stephen said again. "I think Molly may already know what I'm going to say."

He shot me a look that pierced me like an arrow. I sat up straight and wondered how much he knew about my eavesdropping.

"As I mentioned when we were at dinner, it seems I've fallen into what might be one of God's miracles."

I could no longer restrain myself. "So, are you a miracle

worker?" I half expected him to levitate right then and there to prove his point.

"It's God's business," Uncle Stephen said. "It doesn't really have very much to do with me, except that I may need to answer a few questions about what occurred."

"What did you do?" I asked for Angus's benefit, but I hoped the question might deflect the issue of my eavesdropping.

"All I did, Molly, was pray. I didn't even give it much thought. Then God did something big. He made one of my student's tumors go away." He was quiet for a minute. "Completely away." And he shook his head. "What it means is that the church is going to investigate to see if this is a real miracle. You might hear things that are confusing, things about me."

"What kind of things?" I asked.

But Uncle Stephen kept on talking as if I hadn't said a word. "The important part to remember is that Robert is healed." Then he deflated as if he was a helium balloon that had run out of air, and sat down abruptly on his teaching stool.

"But will you be doing more miracles?" I dearly wanted to see him do something miraculous right in front of us.

"We don't choose when or how miracles happen. God does. Period." I felt rebuked enough to keep my mouth shut for the next few seconds.

"How do they prove it?" Angus looked up for the first time. His red eyebrows were furrowed in the way that told me he was working something out in his head and had been listening all along.

Uncle Stephen cleared his throat again. His long, bony hands hung over the edge of his knees. "The verification of miracles includes some pretty specific rules. There are investigators who certify that something inexplicable took place, and then the case goes on to a panel of bishops and cardinals, the Roman Congregation." He checked to make sure we were following along. I nodded my head like any good student would.

"Here's the part you're interested in, Angus—it must be

scientifically inexplicable. A healing miracle requires that the person couldn't have survived otherwise. The prognosis prior to the event has to be fatal."

Angus looked as if he understood exactly what Uncle Stephen meant. But despite my nods, all that I could think about was Uncle Stephen telling me that good stories, the ones that really mattered most, leave room for miracles. Did he know that a miracle would change the story of his life? This miracle was also changing Robert Crater's life. It seemed to me that a miracle changed the trajectory of any story it touched. And then I thought again about levitation and invisibility cloaks. Surely those were miracles too, changing what was possible? The more I thought, the more tangled up I got.

"Does it include breaking natural laws like gravity?" Angus had that gleam he got when he was on to something.

Outside the window I could see a lemonade stand across the street with a cardboard sign and two little kids. For those kids, it was an ordinary summer day. But we had left ordinary territory far behind.

"Well, remember that a miracle has to be something totally outside our ability to produce or contrary to the way nature usually acts. It breaks the natural laws because God has interfered."

Angus persisted with his gravity questions. "Like a man flying, without an airplane."

Uncle Stephen stared at him for a minute, like he didn't know what to say.

"I guess if a person flew without any kind of aircraft, it might be miraculous. Not all miracles have to do with healing people. Remember Saint Paul on the road to Tarsus?"

I did, because Uncle Stephen had told me the story at least a dozen times.

"Molly, Angus, the reason I'm telling you all this is because I may have people asking me questions, and it's possible they could ask you questions too." He shook his head again.

"What kind of questions?" He hadn't answered the last time I asked. This time I wasn't going to let it go.

"Things about our family, about me or your mother. You're not required to give anyone information. In fact, it would be better if you didn't."

"I don't see what that has to do with whether or not it was a real miracle." I knew my uncle Stephen never lied. If he claimed the boy was healed, we didn't need any investigators to prove it.

"I'm not sure I understand it all myself."

I thought about the blue car that watched our house. Maybe it was one of the miracle investigators Uncle Stephen talked about. I was ready to ask, but there was another question that needed answering first.

"And you'll be making more trips to New York?" I tried to keep my voice as neutral as I could, but I was thinking about my unanswered ad in the *Times* and about his promise to take me with him next time.

Uncle Stephen looked at me strangely.

"Now, it's funny you should mention that. I thought I would have to go back to the diocese where I was confirmed, but I was told a few minutes ago that all the investigations can happen right here, for now."

I couldn't believe what I was hearing. "But what do people in a place like San Jose know about miracles? There aren't any miracle investigators in San Jose!" I realized my voice had gotten louder, but somehow I couldn't stop.

My trip to New York—the one place where Mom's secrets were hidden, where my own future as a writer might begin—was slipping away before it even got started. I knew I was acting younger than Angus, but the wave of disappointment was so strong it towed me right under.

"Molly, that's enough." Uncle Stephen's hand was on my shoulder and even Angus was staring at me with an incredulous expression.

I couldn't help it; tears leaked from my eyes.

"Molly, you're spoiling everything!" Angus's voice shook.

I watched through gummy eyes as he turned to Uncle Stephen and asked, "Do you think performing miracles might run in families?"

Chapter Twenty

A LIBRARY JOB

SAN JOSE, CALIFORNIA—JULY 1955

Molly

The investigation started the first week in July. It was the same week Uncle Stephen was politely told to move out of his apartment by his landlord. *Just 'til this blows over,* the landlord said, not quite meeting my uncle's eyes. *Can't have the other tenants disturbed. Miracles make people uncomfortable.*

How he discovered news of the investigation, we never knew. My uncle took up residence on our couch. I could tell by the set of Mom's face that she was worried, but he was her brother; she would never say no to him.

Two miracle investigators—Fathers Rickard and Pasquali— arrived by car after flying into San Francisco. Uncle Stephen greeted them at our front door. They wore dark suits and white shirts with clerical collars. Rickard was very tall and had a long neck like a giraffe. Pasquali was wide and dark like a penguin. That's how I'd think of them, Giraffe and Penguin.

We collected in a curious knot right inside the front door:

Mom, Angus—in his bathing suit because it was Wednesday and on Wednesday he had swimming lessons—me, and Uncle Stephen.

"It's an honor to meet Stephen's family." Penguin extended a short, thick arm. I tried not to think of flippers.

Mom took his hand and nodded.

"Are you going to question my uncle now?" Angus, as I have mentioned, had no discretion.

Giraffe tipped forward so that his face bobbed over Angus. "We'll spend the day with your uncle discussing certain events. Tomorrow we will meet with the family of the boy."

Mom thrust her sunglasses on her face. I was sure I heard a snort. "We have to be going." She opened the door.

"If you're going to do any more miracles, can you wait until I get back?" Angus threw Uncle Stephen a pleading look as Mom dragged him out the door.

Penguin turned to me. "Molly, we especially look forward to chatting with you."

An alarm pinged inside me, and I cast Uncle Stephen a look that was supposed to say, "Help me out here," but he merely nodded and followed the investigators to the shiny rental in the driveway. Two things bothered me: When Penguin smiled, he wasn't very penguin-like at all. He was more like a she lion stalking her prey. And Uncle Stephen hadn't smiled once all morning. That was something that had never happened before.

It was almost nine o'clock, and I had the house to myself for a good hour. I'd taken swimming lessons too when I was Angus's age, but Mom had given up on me pretty fast. No matter how hard I tried, I could never get comfortable putting my face in the water and turning my head side to side to breathe. Angus took to the water much better than I did. Today, I was glad to be left behind. I went to my bedroom, collected the cigar box from under my bed, and opened it. The notes I'd written were right on top. To the paltry list of clues about my mom's life I'd added two significant pieces of information: her brother is a miracle worker (because he healed a boy dying of a tumor) and Wallabout Market.

It wasn't enough to have random clues. They had to add up to useful information. Or better yet, a story that would explain how everything was connected. There was still no response from my classified ad, so I picked up the photo of the newspaper headline for Woodward School. If I couldn't go to New York myself, I would start from this. But the research was a library job. Not the pink San Jose Public Library bookmobile that showed up on the corner of our street once a month, but the main library downtown that used to be the San Jose post office.

The phone jangled me from my thoughts. I dashed to the kitchen. It was Ari, back from her trip.

"Come over?" she asked. That was all it took; I was on my way.

I opened her screen door a crack and knocked on the front door, not too loudly because her father was working nights that week and sleeping during the day. She must have been waiting for me right on the other side, because the door swung open as soon as I was done knocking. Ari sashayed out on to the porch. I gaped. Her straight black hair had been cut to her shoulders and was a mass of curls. And then she flashed a smile. Her teeth were white, naked, and perfectly straight. For once, I was speechless.

"Well, what do you think, chica?" She laughed. "Got my braces off yesterday, and when we were in Mexico, my auntie Irena gave me a perm."

I wasn't sure what I thought. Her legs were deeply tanned beneath rolled jeans that were cinched in tight at the waist, and I suspected there might be extra padding in that bra of hers. My best friend looked at least sixteen.

"You look great," I said, even though her new image made me feel kind of lonely inside.

We wandered to the front lawn and sat in the grass under the shade of the cherry tree. She told me all about her vacation, and a cute boy, Paulo, she'd met at Chapultepec Park, then unfolded a scrap of paper where he'd written his phone number. "He's sixteen, almost seventeen. He might come visit next summer." She blew a large bubble and it popped, sticking in a pink ring from her nose to her chin.

This was more like the Ari knew.

"What did your mom say when she saw your report card?" Ari said.

"She hasn't yet. It's in my closet."

"She's gonna ask for it sometime, and it won't be pretty when she does."

The funny thing was, I almost wished she would ask, no matter what the consequences, because it would mean she was paying attention.

Next, Ari asked the exact question I was hoping for.

"What else have you found for the box?"

I told her about clues three and five: Wallabout Market and Uncle Stephen claiming my mom had left him alone. But I was careful not to mention number four: my uncle might be a miracle worker.

"So, how do you think we find out about Woodward School in New York?" I included the "we" because I wanted to remind her that she was part of the investigation. Besides, I needed another resource she could provide.

Ari stretched out on her back in the grass. "That's a library job."

I was glad our thoughts were still in sync. "That's what I thought, but we have to figure out a way to get over there." I pulled up a few blades of grass and twisted them around my fingers.

"We can ask Jesse. He wants any excuse to drive and the library's a good one."

Exactly the response I'd hoped for. The hardest part would be persuading Mom to let me go with him in the car. This reminded me of the blue car I'd seen loitering in the neighborhood.

"Maybe it's a boy who has a crush on you." She squinted over at me, and looked me up and down with a critical eye. "Well, maybe an old pervert or something."

I could always count on her to boost my ego.

Jesse agreed to drive us after work. It was one of those perfect San Jose summer evenings when the air is like a gentle breath on the back of your neck. We rode with all the windows down, Ari shotgun and me behind Jesse, admiring the way his hair was just a little too long and curled over the edge of his collar.

"What's up with you two, going to the library in summer?"

"Research project," Ari said.

"Who does research when it's not homework? Sure you're not meeting some guys?"

"And if we were?" she shot back.

"Don't get all frosted on me. Two good-looking girls like you."

His eyes met mine in the rearview mirror. My face flamed. He laughed. Then like I had imagined, he cranked up the Platters singing "Only You," and the three of us let our arms trail out the open windows as we sailed through the warm California dusk.

The main library had a sandstone clock tower, a turret, and arches over the entry. Whenever I came here I felt like I was entering a castle. This time I entered with a faint fluttering in my ribcage. I was about to connect one of the pieces of my mother's past. Jesse let us go in first, whether that was because he didn't want to be seen with us or because he wanted to let "Rock Around the Clock" play out, I wasn't sure.

During the drive I mentally rehearsed what I'd ask the reference librarian.

The librarian would say: "Why don't you ask your mother where she went to school?" I would reply: "I'm planning a surprise, a kind of *This Is Your Life* surprise," which was a very popular TV show she was sure to have heard about.

The librarian would smile, give me a wink, and retrieve all the information I wanted.

Still, I approached the desk with trepidation. But Ari began the conversation before I said a word. "My friend, Molly, needs some information."

The librarian looked up, smiling. "How can I help you?" She was a pretty woman, with a freckled nose and thick black hair.

I took a deep breath. "I want to find out about Woodward School in New York, in the 1920s. My mother went to school there and I'm making a surprise for her birthday."

"I see." Her eyebrows were thickly penciled arches and a mechanical pencil was stuck behind one ear. "Well, let's see what we can find. Follow me." She crossed to a set of large volumes with gold letters on the spine that read *History of New York State*. She reached for the volume that read *1800–1940* and flipped to the back. "First, I check the index." She talked us all the way through the process as if she were teaching a class. "Do you know what city she lived in?"

"Brooklyn."

The first volume didn't seem to have anything that was helpful. "Let's look under education, private." The librarian's voice was full of never-ending good cheer as she muttered and flipped through the pages. Then she stopped, a slight crease appearing between those arched brows. Finally, she turned to us. "I'm sorry, but there doesn't seem to be anything in the public or private school system listed as Woodward School. The closest thing I can find is a reference to a Woodward Home." And here she paused and looked away. That strange fluttering began below my ribs again. "A place for girls in need of guidance," she concluded.

She spread the book out on the top shelf. I stood next to her shoulder as she tapped on the entry with her pencil. *Woodward House was established as a Residence in 1845 to help delinquent girls in New York City rebuild their lives.*

There was obviously some mistake. I looked at Ari. Her eyes narrowed. My voice was stuck somewhere deep inside. Finally, it squeaked out.

"That must not be the right Woodward. She went to a boarding school." I had pictured girls in uniforms all in a line like the *Madeline* book I read when I babysat the neighbor's twins.

I remembered to add thank you before we walked away.

"What if your mother was a delinquent?" Ari bumped my shoulder. "That would explain why she never talks about her past. What if she did something really awful?"

For one moment I looked at my best friend and imagined strangling her on the library floor. "She had a job and a rich lady paid for her to go to a private school." Inside me the fluttering had grown to a flapping, as if a large bird had roosted in my rib cage and was beating its wings.

Jesse was checking out the latest detective novels, so I had a few extra minutes. While Ari flipped through a movie star magazine, I looked up the word *delinquent* to see if there was any definition I wasn't familiar with. But the dictionary confirmed my worst fears: *a tendency to commit crime, particularly minor crime.* I thought about the hair ring.

What had my mother done?

Chapter Twenty-One

DOPE

SAN JOSE, CALIFORNIA—JULY 1955

Molly

Angus's bedroom door was closed when I got home, but even from the outside there was a curious odor. I pushed open the door. Even at the best of times, Angus's room was a laboratory of his latest experiments, a collision of smells to assault the senses. This was not the best of times. Angus was painting a clear substance across a piece of beige canvas cloth. I recognized the fabric as something from the scrap bag Mom kept in the laundry room. I pinched my nose.

"Angus, that stinks! What are you doing?"

"Dope."

"Don't call me a dope when you're the one about to asphyxiate us!"

He looked up. An infuriating smile twitched his lips. "I'm spreading airplane dope on this to make it stiff."

I came closer. Crude sketches of wings, wings of all shapes and sizes, littered the floor. The da Vinci book lay face down, pages spread wide like a fallen bird. I picked it up and crossed the room to open the window. As fresh air poured in, I noticed Angus had left the book open at an illustration of wings.

"*Ornithopter,*" I read. "*Man bird.* Angus, what are you doing?"

Now his look was all impatience. "I told you. I'm spreading dope—"

"No, I mean why. What are you making wings for?"

"I plan to fly."

The next morning, Mom sat at her desk like she always did, but the typewriter keys were mostly silent. The Smith Corona was a barometer of her moods, one I trusted completely. As far as my state of mind, the thought of Woodward House was like a third presence in the room I couldn't ignore. I found myself searching for a delinquent girl under the surface of my mother's efficient demeanor in the same way I searched my uncle's face for the miraculous.

There'd been no word from Uncle Stephen since yesterday morning when he left with the investigators. I tried hanging out near Mom's desk, hoping she might talk to me about all this miracle stuff, but she didn't.

Angus was still in his room, absorbed with his idea for wings. Ari had a follow-up orthodontist appointment; I was at loose ends. Fourteen was a powerless age, I decided. Too young for work, still dependent on others to get most places, and too old not to mind. I wasn't sure fifteen would be much better. I tried reading, but found my brain had other ideas. Every thought led it back to the home for delinquent girls. By lunchtime we still hadn't heard from Uncle Stephen, and Mom had given up pretending to work.

"It's an awfully nice day outside. I was wondering if you and Angus might want to walk down to Thrifty Drug with me and get an ice cream cone. I'm out of stamps and envelopes," she added as an explanation.

It was better than my aimless wandering, so I retrieved Angus while she went to put on some lipstick and brush her hair. Thrifty Drug was only a fifteen-minute walk from our house, in one of the new shopping centers that seemed to sprout overnight.

I tried to imagine what Uncle Stephen might be doing at that very moment. I'd envisioned a tableau of the Penguin and the Giraffe kneeling in front of my uncle when I noticed the Bel Air again. The car was idling just down the street from us.

Apparently, Angus noticed it too, because he said in an unconcerned voice, "There's Arthur."

Mom gave him one of her sharp looks. "Arthur?"

"In the blue car that's always around our house?"

Now her look was more than sharp; she was a hawk descending toward its prey. "What do you mean, always around our house, and how do you know his name?"

"He told me when I asked him if he wanted a lemonade."

I could tell by the catch in his voice that he realized he'd wandered into dangerous territory, and he shot me a desperate glance, hoping for a way out.

It was too late now. I shook my head.

"Molly, read that license plate to me." She rummaged through her purse for a pencil and paper.

The car was already moving away from us. I squinted. The sun glared off the metal bumper as the blue Bel Air turned the corner.

"I couldn't get it!"

Then, as Mom's frown deepened, and deepened again until it seemed her face would crack, I explained how the car had been in the neighborhood for weeks, often parked near our house. With a short, stabbing stroke, she recorded everything.

"I'm surprised at both of you. You know that there are people out there who want to harm children. Molly, you're

113

almost fifteen years old—what were you thinking?" She wiped a small trickle of sweat from her forehead.

I looked down. How could I answer that I thought the car was interesting, that it might be a mystery?

She shook her head in disbelief. "Come on, let's get out of this sun."

As we pushed open the door of Thrifty, Mrs. Bolger, on a smoke break, pushed out. She stopped, a pack of Camels in her hand, a cigarette dangling between her lips. She stared. Her mouth opened and closed like a fish, and the cigarette, rimmed with pink lipstick, fell to the sidewalk. She ground it out with the toe of her pump. I could tell Mom wanted to hurry past her, but Mrs. Bolger blocked our entrance to the store.

"Elaine Donnelly," she said, "I hear your brother's a miracle worker. He healed that little Crater boy, the one with a tumor in his brain, just by laying his hands on him."

I could sense Mom gathering herself as she took a deep breath. "We're all pleased the boy is well. But don't believe everything you hear, Beverly." And with that, she swept into the store, Angus and I trailing at her heels.

We ordered our ice creams fast. I kept my head down and scuffed at the brown linoleum with the toe of my sandal. I'd already felt self-conscious walking to get ice cream with my mom and little brother, but this was worse. The curious stares of strangers peeled away what little poise I had. Once again, our family would be labeled as different and I would never fit in.

We passed Beverly Bolger without a word. She looked at me and exhaled a circle of smoke, then crossed herself as we passed as if it made us holy being related to Uncle Stephen.

We walked home in silence, acutely aware that our lives were now open to public commentary. As the sun beat on my shoulder, my Dutch Chocolate turned into a gooey mess that trickled down my hand and onto my wrist. I'd lost my appetite even for ice cream. Angus was the first one to our porch, the first one to see the lit candles and the photo of the little girl in leg braces.

Chapter Twenty-Two

CROSSING THE LINE

BROOKLYN, NEW YORK—AUGUST 1919

ELAINE

Elaine didn't mention the car incident at home. She never had the opportunity. For the second night in a row, Pop didn't show up for dinner. He didn't arrive before nine when she put Stephen to bed, or by ten when she finished laying out the laundry to dry. She propped open the window to the alley. The air was still and heavy, smelling of waste left too long in the sun.

When she sat on her bed, the springs squeaked.

"It's too hot to sleep." Stephen sat up in bed. "Lainey, where do you think Pop is?"

"I don't know. Maybe he had to stay late to help with the horses."

"I don't think horses are out at night. Maybe all that work made him thirsty."

She paused a beat, not knowing what to say, glad for the dark that hid her face. "Maybe he stopped off to see some friends."

"Well, when do you think he'll get home?" The whine in his voice frayed her nerves like a paring knife.

"Doesn't matter. He can stay away for all I care."

"You don't mean that." Stephen curled on his side away from her. "You're just mad."

Of course she was mad. Mad enough to kill. It wasn't only the stifling heat that set her nerves on edge.

She stood and ruffled his hair. It was damp with sweat.

"Don't keep hoping things will be the way they were."

Then she crept over to her own bed and lay on top of the covers. Before she fell asleep she liked to think about going back to school, having books to read, learning things she didn't know. But she couldn't find that location in her mind anymore. With money from the Gossleys they could still manage the rent, barely. If she lost her job because she was with Howie when he crashed the car . . .

The bittersweet smell of tobacco filtered into Elaine's sleep. Then a scraping noise in the front room. A chair being dragged across the floor. She struggled to wakefulness. Pop was home.

She pulled on her robe and, careful not to wake Stephen, walked into the front room. In the darkness a red pinprick of ash punctuated Pop's silhouette. He'd dragged a chair to the open window and, elbows resting on the sill, stared into the dark. No faint breeze offered relief.

Pop didn't turn toward her. For a moment she believed he didn't know she was there. He flicked the cigarette. A shiver of sparks dropped into the night and disappeared.

He spoke without turning his head.

"I've never really cared for horses. Did you know that, darling?"

"I thought you liked working with the horses." Sweat dampened her temples. A wild thudding began in her chest as she crossed to his side.

"They're feckless beasts. I'm meant for better things than

shoveling muck and brushing their sorry hides. Do you know what it's like being a man who's meant for bigger things?"

The thudding in her chest expanded to her head. Did she know what it was like? Every day she cleaned, cooked, read to an old man, while her dreams of going back to school, maybe college, were like a receding shore. No matter how hard she paddled, she'd never reach land.

His head slowly swiveled in her direction, eyes glittering in the streetlight. "I've gone and lost my job again. What do you think of that?" He exhaled a cloud of smoke. "Your old man's a disappointment to you."

This couldn't be happening, not when she'd probably lost her own job. It wasn't the horses who were feckless. Instead of answering she turned her back as if she hadn't heard, walked into the bedroom, and shut the door.

Stephen stirred and mumbled.

"Go back to sleep."

"Pop's home." He must have heard his voice.

"You can see him in the morning."

She bent over him and straightened the sheet. No point in telling him the unhappy news now. Despair could always wait 'til morning.

Pop was gone when Elaine got up, and maybe that was her fault, but it spared her having to tell Stephen the news. She was determined to show up for work and beg for her job if she needed to. Would she at least have the chance to say goodbye to Howard? He'd be worried about what happened to her. All the way to the Gossley house, her brain churned.

As she rounded the corner to Clinton Avenue, morning sun fired the leaves of the small maple. The gravel drive was empty, so she wouldn't have to face Mr. Gossley, only May, and she would be bad enough. No matter how many deep breaths she took, they didn't steady her heart.

But when she knocked on the kitchen door, Kay let her in as usual, and said Mr. Seward was waiting in the morning room. She hurried through the hall expecting May's voice sharp with reproach, but the hall was empty and silent. Mr. Seward swiveled toward her as she entered. His skin shone like wax as the east light played across his face.

"I hear you and Howard got into a bit of a scrape Friday."

And here everything ended.

She should have known he'd get right to the point.

"Well? What were you thinking, allowing that boy to persuade you into such foolishness?" He beetled his eyebrows over his sightless eyes. "Didn't consider you could lose your job for a prank like that?"

She was ready. Stopping halfway across the room, she began the speech she'd prepared. "I'm sorry. I should have been more responsible. It's my fault; I should have stopped him. But if you—"

Mr. Seward leaned forward. "Responsible for that boy? It's not your job to protect Howard from himself. You could no more prevent his pigheadedness than stop the wind. But you can keep yourself from being carried away with it."

Why didn't he fire her and be done with it? She dug the toe of her shoe into the soft carpet.

"My grandson is the one who should have thought of the position he was putting you in, but he never will. Can't see beyond his own nose. His vision is worse than my own."

"That's not true. Howard's been very kind to me."

"There are some lines that shouldn't be crossed."

"Howard was just showing off."

"That isn't the line I'm talking about."

Something was squeezing her chest. "I don't take his kindness for granted."

"I'm not worried about you doing the taking." His voice was softer now. "If anything, you're miles above him."

"You're wrong. He's—"

He held up his hand to silence her. "It's time you started reading. The news will be old before I hear it."

Tears pricked her eyes. She wasn't fired? Silently, she crossed to her chair and the pile of newspapers waiting on the table. Unfolding the *Tribune*, she began with the headlines. While she read about race riots in Knoxville, her mind traveled in its own direction. How could Mr. Seward think she was better than his own grandson? Howie deserved better. He'd tried to protect her when his father discovered them in the car. His grandfather didn't know him at all, not like she did. Hopefully his punishment hadn't been too bad. She'd never had a boy defend her before and she found she liked to think about it.

By lunchtime, Mr. Seward was dozing as usual. Elaine looked at the clock. Five past twelve. She hurried into the kitchen. Howard usually was there, waiting for her with stories about his day. Today, Kay whipped potatoes for a shepherd's pie.

"I saved you some of last night's stew." She dipped a ladle into one of the cast iron pots on the stove.

"Thanks, but I'll wait 'til Howard gets here." Elaine pulled out a chair at the wood table. The savory smell of rosemary and roasting meat warmed the room. It made her dizzy with hunger.

"Then you'll be waiting all day. He told me not to expect him for lunch this week."

⚬≥◉⚬⚬◉≤⚬

*A*gain, the woodcutter and his wife left the children sleeping in the dark of the woods. When the cry of an owl woke Hansel from his restless dreams, he could no longer hear the singing of the ax. They were abandoned in the woods just as he expected they would be. But Hansel didn't worry, for he had left a trail of breadcrumbs to see them safely home.

Full of hope, he shook his sister to wakefulness. In the moon's light, the breadcrumbs would shine like white pebbles and lead them home. But once they began walking, there were no breadcrumbs to be found. They tried walking in every direction, but still the forest floor was bare.

The children heard a rustling in the branches above them. All manner of birds craned their feathered necks to look down on the two ragged travelers and blinked eyes that glowed like jewels in the moonlight. Hansel knew that ordinary birds were bedded safe in their nests at night. But these strange birds had eaten every crumb. Hansel shook his fist at the conniving birds and tried to comfort his sister, who had begun to weep.

"There, there, Gretel, the moon is bright, and with any luck we can still find our way." So huddled close, the two set off to retrace their steps. The night was clear and cold. The twisted trees took on terrifying shapes in the darkness and blocked their path at every turn. Soon Hansel knew they were hopelessly lost.

Chapter Twenty-Three

HANSEL AND GRETEL

BROOKLYN, NEW YORK—AUGUST/SEPTEMBER 1919

ELAINE

That summer, August trapped the city under its hot, damp hand. Everyone who could escaped to the shore or to lakeside cabins. Those who remained slept with their windows open or set mattresses on fire escapes in hopes of the slightest breeze. Nerves frayed, tempers flared, and drunks were left to sleep it off on the streets because the jails were full.

May and Howard spent three weeks at the family's lake cabin in Connecticut, but Elaine was still expected to read every day. Mr. Seward refused to let the weather dictate his actions.

For Elaine, the days were a long, lonely slog. Not even the news could draw her in. Without lunch with Howard to look forward to, it was hard to muster the will to face Mr. Seward. His disposition was worse than usual, and at least once a week she considered leaving, but they were still dependent on her income. Mrs. Malloy continued to watch Stephen and let him run wild with her two grandsons in exchange for Elaine helping her sew altar cloths on the weekends. Pop showed up sporadically, sometimes with a little money, more often without.

September was a welcome relief. The air cooled, school started, and Elaine looked forward to life in the Gossley household returning to normal.

"You can't come with me whenever you feel like it. You've got to be in school." Elaine eyed her little brother; he did look pale.

"My stomach hurts, and I'm hot." Whenever he complained of feeling unwell, Elaine had a moment of panic and thought of her mother and Claire, how quickly they'd died and how helpless she'd felt. She wondered if her mother could see her trying to do her best with Stephen.

"All right, then. Come with me, but bring your books. You'll have to read and keep yourself busy while I work."

"You don't work. All you do is read."

"Then I'll let you pay the rent next month."

It was a day for walking in parks. Fall was offering them a few weeks of Indian summer, a last grand gesture before she disappeared into winter. Perhaps today Howard would again be waiting in the kitchen to share lunch with her. But what would she do with her brother?

May met them at the door. It had been several weeks since Elaine had seen more than a glimpse of her employer. Today she was in her dressing gown, hair pulled back in a loose bun, a cup of coffee in her hand.

"I see we have a visitor this morning."

"Yes, ma'am. Stephen wasn't feeling well, and I thought that maybe he could sit with me. He brought his school books along and he won't be any trouble, I promise." Elaine's stomach tightened like the cinch on one of Pa's horses. If only Stephen would keep quiet.

May measured Stephen with pursed lips and squinted eyes. "Yes, I believe you're right— he won't be any trouble at all. But first, a little breakfast might cure what ails him."

Elaine's shoulders dropped a notch, her muscles loosened.

"Patricia, please take this young gentleman to the kitchen and feed him something." And Stephen, smiling and humming to himself, grinned over his shoulder at Elaine, then stuck out his tongue.

She might kill him one day.

"I'm sorry I've been gone so often when you come, but Prohibition needs an army. And it looks like they're making me its general." May repinned a loop of hair to her bun. "You know what Prohibition is, don't you? Eliminating alcohol is a small price to pay for strengthening society. This is a war, Elaine. There are those who already want the law repealed. But we'll make sure that never happens."

Elaine nodded, thinking of her father. She wondered what May knew about him.

"I'm home today because my father is not feeling well. You may still read to him, but I want the reading to be kept short. Then I will have some work for you to do, folding pamphlets." She paused, cup to her lips. "My father is very fond of you. We all are, and I think that at some point very soon we should discuss your future. You're obviously very bright. We should have a little heart-to-heart."

Elaine flushed and looked down as May brushed a stray hair from Elaine's face.

"Now go see if you can cheer up my father. Nobody else seems capable of it."

They cared about her. No one held the car incident against her even though it was still fresh in her mind. May wanted to talk about her future. Elaine had no idea what that might be, but maybe St. Joseph's College wasn't completely a dream.

When she opened the door to the morning room, it made the familiar *shush* across the deep carpet.

"Don't expect me to wait all day for you, young lady." Mr. Seward's voice was sharper than usual and punctuated with a raspy cough.

Elaine smiled. "Sorry I'm late. I had to bring my little brother Stephen with me today."

"Where is he? I don't hear anyone else."

"Mrs. Gossley sent him to the kitchen, sir. For breakfast."

"Just what we need, another mouth to feed. Do you all think I'm made of money?"

"No, sir. I can get him if you like. He probably hasn't eaten much yet." That was most likely a lie. He was always hungry.

"What's done is done. I'm waiting for my papers."

Elaine began to read. Mr. Seward's head dropped to his chest and then jerked upright like a marionette every few pages. Reading was easy now and it left one part of her mind free to wonder about Howie Gossley.

She didn't hear the door open or Stephen steal in on quiet feet to stand by her side, but Mr. Seward did.

"Well, where are your manners? Aren't you going to introduce us?" He was fully awake now, leaning forward in his chair. His milky eyes fastened on them as if he could see.

Elaine saw Stephen's face grow white. She gave him a little shove in the direction of Mr. Seward. "Mr. Seward, may I present my brother, Stephen." She mimicked the way May introduced guests and hoped that it was right.

Mr. Seward stretched out one freckled hand and placed it on Stephen's head. "How old are you?"

"Nine." Stephen's voice was barely more than a whisper.

"Speak up. Why aren't you in school?"

Elaine clenched her hands.

"I didn't feel well. I wanted to come with Lainey." This time his voice was louder.

"You sound well enough now." Mr. Seward coughed a wet, fleshy cough and then felt for a glass on the table. He brought it up to his mouth and spat. "What can you do?"

Stephen was quiet for a minute. "I can play the penny whistle. I can read, though not as well as Lainey, but I can draw better than she does."

Mr. Seward's hoot of laughter made Elaine jump.

"There's honesty for you. More than I get from most people. Well, Stephen, I can't see your drawings, but I expect to hear the penny whistle next time you come. Now I have something that I think might interest you both, writer and artist. Bring me that book on the end of the table."

Elaine looked across to the far end of the table, where a slim blue book lay.

"Well, bring it to me!"

Gold lettering embossed the spine: *Hansel and Gretel.* She knew that story. But what was Mr. Seward doing with a book of fairy tales?

She set the book in his outstretched hands. He ran his knobbed fingers over the cover. "In nineteen thirteen, before I lost my eyesight all together, I came across a book full of the most wondrous illustrations I'd ever seen. The artist is a fellow named Arthur Rackham. He's won a few awards."

Here he paused, coughed, and spit into the glass again. Elaine tried not to look at the thick foam of spittle running down its side.

"I'd heard that he had a new work come out—this *Hansel and Gretel.* It's a great disappointment to me that I can't see it with my own eyes, but an artist of his caliber needs to be supported." He paused a long time.

Stephen's breath was hot on her neck as he peered over her shoulder.

"Go ahead, open it up."

Stephen released a great sigh behind her. The illustrations sucked her into the page. It was like falling down Alice's rabbit hole. In the drawing, two children—brother and sister—looked up into the face of an old woman with an enormous nose. Her eyes glittered. Elaine could feel the woman's dangerous smile in her ribcage. The old lady leaned on a stick, on the steps of a house surrounded by a forest. The trees had faces.

"You know the story, of course?"

"We know it! Our mother used to tell us fairy tales." Stephen traced the picture. "That's the witch."

Elaine grabbed his hand to make sure his fingers were clean.

"I thought you might it enjoy it, Elaine."

"I love it. Thank you for showing it to me." She turned to the next page.

"Showing it you! I'm giving it to you!"

She tried to speak, cleared her throat and tried again. She had no books. Stephen had his few school texts on loan. "For me? It's too beautiful."

Stephen kicked her shin.

"I want to support this fellow, and no one in my house would care a thing about it. It should be valuable one day. See that you take care of it."

"Thank you." Her voice was someone else's voice. It was the voice of a girl who owned a book, a beautiful book full of magic. Someday she would own hundreds of books like this. She hugged it to herself. "We'll take good care of it, sir."

"I expect it. Son, make yourself unobtrusive while your sister finishes reading me the papers."

Stephen opened the book and sat crossed-legged on the rug in a puddle of sunlight. Elaine read about the rise in living wages.

Within thirty minutes, both Mr. Seward and Stephen were fast asleep. Elaine looked at her little brother, one hand rested across the open book. His bony wrists protruded like pale, peeled sticks from his cuffs. His face was thin and pale too, but so like her mother's. How long had it been since she had really looked at Stephen? There was a difference between looking and seeing, she thought. She hadn't really seen him these last months, being so busy with work and worrying about Pop. Stephen wouldn't be little much longer. No wonder he was always hungry. Gently, she eased the book from under his hand. He sighed and shifted in his sleep. For the next hour, Elaine was lost in the pages.

When the clock chimed noon, Elaine looked up. She heard a familiar whistle in the hallway, heard the kitchen door slam, and then nothing more. She waited for the door to open. It didn't. May didn't arrive to invite them to lunch. Her stomach rumbled. Finally, the morning room door pushed inward. Elaine smoothed her hair.

"I thought you and your brother might want to have lunch with me in the kitchen today. Howie's been home and gone. I wouldn't mind the company." May had changed from her dressing gown to a gray silk dress that whispered like wind in grass when she walked.

The fluttering in Elaine's stomach stilled. A heavy weight dropped in to take its place.

May glowed with good will. "Every September, we celebrate my father's birthday with a picnic. I'm not sure why he likes picnics so much, but he does. In my mind, summer's the time for picnics, but he won't hear of anything else." May paused. "I was hoping you and your brother might be able to join us. I know it would please my father immensely. And now wake up your brother. I'd like to talk to both of you about school."

Chapter Twenty-Four

HOPE

SAN JOSE, CALIFORNIA—JULY 1955

Molly

With a sharp yelp, Mom had jerked the picture of the girl in leg braces off the front porch and marched it into the house. Then, without speaking, she'd blown the candles out and dropped them one by one into the trash. "Who'd put that picture there?" Angus had asked. "Should you do that?" I'd worried at her. "Maybe God wouldn't like you throwing those candles out." She'd sent us both to our rooms.

It was growing dark when Uncle Stephen came striding up the path. He'd been with the investigators so long, I'd about given up on seeing him today. I met Uncle Stephen at the door with Mom and Angus right behind.

"What happened with the investigators?" Mom blocked the entrance.

He pushed past her without speaking.

"How soon will this be over?" Her questions fell like blows.

Uncle Stephen held up his hand to ward them off. "I'd appreciate a drink and a bite to eat."

We followed him into the kitchen and sat around the table. Mom soon clattered a plate of Chef Boyardee in front of each of us.

"*This* was our welcome." Mom pulled the photo out of the kitchen drawer. The glass was cracked.

"And some candles," Angus added.

Uncle Stephen picked up the small frame in one hand and held the photo close to his face, then set it back on the table. After a long pull from a bottle of beer and a mouthful of spaghetti, he said, "More expectation than welcome. If I hadn't moved in with you, you'd be spared this."

"How did they know you're here?" I asked.

"I must have been followed—me or the investigators. I don't know."

I looked at him sprawled in our vinyl chair, his long crane body, protruding ears, bruised eyes, and red hair fading to gray. There couldn't be anybody who looked less like a miracle worker than my uncle Stephen.

"The doctors agreed—Robert's completely healed. Bishop Gurly was there along with the investigators. That poor kid—what they put him through! It's been called an 'instantaneous and complete cure.'" Uncle Stephen held up his hands and looked at them. Then he let them fall to the table, long fingers splayed. "Cause and effect."

I had no idea what he was talking about.

"Seems to me that's what a miracle's all about, effects we can't predict."

Angus picked at the last worms of spaghetti on his plate. Mom poured herself a beer, and I thought I noticed her hand shake. "Mrs. Bolger said something about it when we went to the Thrifty today."

"What did she say?"

"She said, 'I hear your brother's a miracle worker.'"

"Unfortunately, Lainey, I think things will only get worse. Mr. Crater's been telling people even though the bishop asked him not to. I can't blame him. It's hard to hold good news in, and I can't imagine better news than having your kid saved."

The last bits of color drained from her face. "What happens next?"

"If it was as it should be, nothing. We'd all go back to our normal lives and Robert would go on with life."

"Did you suggest to them that it might be a coincidence?"

Uncle Stephen sighed. "Maybe miracles happen more often than we think. Perhaps we aren't looking in the right places."

"You don't really believe you worked a miracle, do you?" Her voice skittered up an octave. "I thought you had doubts too."

Angus sucked in the last long strand of spaghetti, letting it slide from his chin up over his lips and into his mouth, like we were never allowed to do at the table. My heart raced a little faster.

"I have no idea. Whatever happened, I had very little to do with it, Lainey. But denying something happened? Well, that wouldn't be honest."

Uncle Stephen set up for another night on our couch. He said he didn't want to hear another word about miracles. As a result, we watched some boring nature show about bats that Angus wanted to see until my eyes were gritty. But even when I could no longer hold them open, I couldn't sleep. The last I looked at the clock, it said three a.m. So it was no surprise to me it was almost nine when I woke up. The surprise came when I walked into the living room still rubbing away the sleep.

The curtains were drawn and the room was dark. Mom and Uncle Stephen talked in whispers. Angus was still in the spaceship pajamas he favored.

"There are people in the yard, Molly. *Lots* of people."

"What do you mean?" I slipped behind the drapes at the picture window. An audience hovered on our patchy lawn, all eyes expectantly pointed on our front door. Most were people I had never seen before, but a few I recognized—men, women, and kids. Cars choked the street. A pyramid of candles burned in the bright summer sunlight. And there were flowers: single long-stemmed roses, grocery store bouquets of frothy pink blooms wrapped in paper, hot reds and oranges all lining our walkway.

"Get away from the window." Mom dragged me back. "I called the police. Those people have been here since the sun was up." She turned on Uncle Stephen. "You've got to tell them there's been a mistake. We can't live like this."

"They just want some hope."

"Hope is made, not given." Mom's voice was dangerous, and she looked right at Angus and me as she spoke to make sure we understood her position.

"Are you going to do more miracles?" Angus looked hopeful.

"Not that I'm planning," Uncle Stephen said. "Look, Molly and Angus, there are some people out there who have heard about this boy being healed. They probably think I can do this for them too. They don't understand it has nothing to do with me. But I want you to know that. Whatever God is up to is his business."

"Maybe you should talk to them," Angus said.

"Angus!" Mom shot him one of those looks.

And for once I was grateful. This wasn't the kind of celebrity I ever aspired to. This was a spectacle that would completely destroy any pretense of normality in my life. It would mark me as freakish, and once marked, it was all anyone would see when they looked at me.

Uncle Stephen took Angus seriously. "Maybe I should."

And he opened the front door.

"Get back here!" Mom rushed to the door.

Too late.

I hid behind the partially open door, watching my uncle and wishing for the first time I could disown him.

He raised a hand. The crowd cheered. Then everyone fell silent except for a baby who continued to wail.

"All you good people have come here because God did

something miraculous. That's right, he did. I didn't. I have no more idea what God is up than you do, but I do know this. God has a habit of interfering in the world for his own purposes. It has nothing to do with me, and as far I know nothing like this will ever happen to me again." Here he paused. I held my breath and blinked back tears. I thought I recognized Jesse's face in the middle of the crowd.

"If nothing else, God has reminded us he's still working. I know I tend to forget that sometimes."

The crowd murmured in response. Then a woman with a black lace veil on her head crept forward on her knees. She grabbed Uncle Stephen's pants leg. He looked down at her as she uttered one word. "Please."

The word was like a collective sigh. It swelled with hope. It floated like dandelion down on the morning air.

"I don't have any special power." He sounded embarrassed. His face was red, but he helped her to her feet. "You should pray to God."

I didn't think that was what the lady wanted to hear.

"*You* pray for me."

My hands went cold with sweat. He put his hand on the lady's head, and I could almost feel her tremble.

Two things happened at once before he spoke: a police car screamed in from one direction and a TV crew drove in from another. So the whole thing—Uncle Stephen on the porch with his hand on the woman's head, the crowd, the few policemen breaking everything up—was filmed for the news. Mom slammed the door shut before Uncle Stephen came back inside, and made us go to our rooms to get dressed.

The phone rang while I was pulling my clothes on. Mom appeared in my doorway. "It's your dad. He wants to talk to you. I want you and your brother in the house today. It's a volatile situation out there."

I hurried into the kitchen. We talked every Saturday, but this was a Friday. Mom hovered right behind me.

Dad's voice was sharp with concern. "Molly, are you and Angus okay?"

"We're fine, but there are people all over the yard, and we might be on the news."

"I heard your Uncle Stephen has been acting crazy."

"He's doing miracles."

"Exactly what I mean."

There was a short pause, and then, "I have to be out of town with work for a few days. But I want you to promise that you'll call me if things get out of hand. I'll find a way to come get you."

I wanted to say that things had been out of hand for a while, but he kept talking.

"Promise me."

"Okay. Dad, are you coming back soon?"

He sighed. "It's complicated, Molly. But I mean what I say about getting you and Angus. Now let me talk to your mother."

I handed the phone to Mom and went to the window.

The police were leading people off our front lawn. At the edge of the crowd, I saw Ari. I wanted to catch her attention, to tell her that Uncle Stephen hadn't meant this all to happen. Right behind her was the blue car with the man Angus called Arthur leaning out the window.

Chapter Twenty-Five

VULNERABLE

SAN JOSE, CALIFORNIA—JULY 1955

Molly

When I came back into the living room fully dressed, my hair gathered into a bushy ponytail, Mom was wearing that look that said this is grown-up business and don't you dare interrupt. I thought this might be a good time to practice those observation skills Uncle Stephen told me all writers need. I sat down by the coffee table and opened my journal. No one paid any attention.

The first thing I made note of was that Uncle Stephen looked pale, his skin almost transparent under his eyes, and a vein throbbed through the thinning hair at his temple. He was pacing back and forth; every now and then he'd grab his earlobe and give it a tug, then his hand would fall limply to his side.

"Did you see all those people? I don't have any idea what I'm supposed to do. Do miracles need a response?" he asked.

I couldn't tell if he was talking to Mom or to himself.

Mom sat in her desk chair, which was spun to face him. I noticed spider webs in the pale skin around her eyes. Even though it was summer, she was wearing a baggy sweatshirt that came down to the tips of her fingers. In it she looked very small.

"How dare you give them hope? What about the ones who aren't saved? What about the kids who die every day even after people pray? Where are those miracles?"

"I don't know, Lainey. I don't know!"

"This is going too far! If you go on like this, I can't protect you anymore."

Now Uncle Stephen stopped dead. His head snapped up, and he looked at Mom for a beat before he said, "Protect me?"

"I've spent my entire life protecting people. First Pop, then you, now the children." The tips of her fingers disappeared inside the sweatshirt sleeves. Her voice was low and throaty, like she might cry. "God abandoned me just like the Gossleys did."

"You took good care of me when I was younger. But you didn't protect me, Lainey. That was God."

"Was it God who got you to school every day? Who worked so we weren't living on the streets? Who stood between you and Pop when he was raving drunk and then cleaned his vomit off the floor? Who lied so that you'd stay with the Gossleys, where you had a chance?"

Then her small white hand shot out of the sleeve and closed around the mug. She hurled it, coffee and all, at the wall. Brown liquid sprayed up across the white paint. Blue shards rained into the carpet, across the surface of her desk.

"Lainey—" Uncle Stephen looked at me. There was a warning in his voice.

"How dare you! Everything I did was for you!"

She was on her feet, running the few steps it took to reach him. He stood, the only thing moving the blue vein throbbing on his temple.

"And now you're taking *his* side." She pummeled his chest with both fists. "Choosing a God who watched our mother and sister die. You're choosing him over me all because you think you've done a miracle! There are no miracles!" Crying now, Mom let her hands drop.

Uncle Stephen set both of his long hands on her shoulders, but she shrugged them off, her glance rounding on me. Our eyes locked. And in those seconds, what I saw was similar to the look of a trapped animal—pain, fear, and threat. My gut twisted. When she bolted down the hall, the slam of her bedroom door shook the wall and clattered my school picture to the floor.

Uncle Stephen stood rigid, staring after her, the blue vein still pulsing.

The starburst of coffee dripped down the wall. The whole room smelled of it. My brain was frozen, caught in a repeating frame of the mug flying from her hand. Why *did* God let people die? I made a gurgling sound. Uncle Stephen turned in my direction. In two strides, he was next to me.

"I'm sorry you had to witness that, Molly. Your mother has had some awfully hard things in her life. She didn't mean to hurt me. This miracle business has been more than we all bargained for."

I couldn't swallow, much less talk.

Uncle Stephen gave a light tug on my ponytail. "Miracles aren't comfortable things. But we'll get through this, you'll see."

I was crying now too, and buried my head on his shoulder. Mom's words were clashing cymbals in my brain. What about the ones who never got the miracles?

Mom stayed in her room the rest of the morning. Uncle Stephen said to let her be, and he busied himself cleaning up the kitchen. I picked the shards out of the carpet and scrubbed at the wall, but the coffee had left a dark, weeping trail on the light wall. A small crack had allowed the stain to soak below the surface of the paint. I rubbed hard, and while the stain lightened, it wouldn't disappear completely.

When Uncle Stephen got out the vacuum cleaner, I decided to make myself scarce, in case he had any idea of co-opting me into service. I wandered toward my room, but found I couldn't keep from staring at Mom's closed door.

Angus had been in his room through the entire debacle. I cracked open the door.

"Angus, what are you doing?" Angus stood on his bed with his arms outstretched. Attached to his arms was an enormous pair of wings. I don't mean feathery wings. These were as wide as his body, draped with the stiff cream fabric he had attached to wooden ribs with dope. From where I stood, they looked as though they had sprouted from his shoulder blades, and he was smiling, his crooked incisor shyly lapping its neighbor. In his own strange way, my brother was beautiful.

"Don't tell anyone." Angus carefully unstrapped the wings and slid his arms out.

"You can't fly with those." I poked at the stiff fabric and wondered at the design. But the truth was, I wasn't quite sure.

"Leonardo thought you could, and mine are like his. Only better."

"He was a grown man and you're a little kid." I hated it when I found myself copying Mom's tone of voice.

"So? It means I have less weight to carry. Besides, I understand how these things work. And I'll let you watch my first trial, only if you promise not to tell."

"Trial?"

"Didn't you hear what I said?" He looked at me like I was complete idiot. "I'm going to need to make certain adjustments, so I'll have to make trial flights, and then write up any changes I make. That's how inventors do it."

"Don't you need wind?"

"It would help, but the thing that would help most is flapping wings. My design is a glider. I'm going to jump off the backyard fence as a test." He paused to make sure I was paying attention. "It may not be high enough. I have to get myself horizontal." Then he looked down. His voice shook just the tiniest bit. "What's wrong with Mom?"

"She thinks Uncle Stephen likes God more than her."

Angus met my eyes. He shrugged. "He probably does. He's God. We're supposed to like him more."

It was snowing in the living room. At least that was how it looked. The couch was buried beneath mounds of white sheets. Socks and underwear were stacked like snowmen while white shirts billowed over the backs of chairs. I tried not to look at the dull stain patch on the wall, but I couldn't ignore the faint bitter smell of coffee.

Uncle Stephen smiled sheepishly. "I thought I might do a little wash." He stood like an awkward crane in drifts of white, sorting, piling, folding.

I carefully stepped over a pile of undershirts. He must have included his own laundry with ours. I lifted a corner of the drapes and peered out. People had returned to the yard with armloads of flowers and candles. Like before, some waited, staring at the door, as if something magical might happen at any moment. I quickly let the drapes fall closed.

"They're the faithful, Molly. But what occurred is not what they think."

I began sorting Angus's socks from mine. "What do you mean?" I glanced again down the hallway toward Mom's closed door.

"What most people don't understand is that miracles aren't always benign."

"What does benign mean?" I felt that certain flutter, right behind my ribs, that a new word always caused.

"Benign . . . harmless." He dipped his chin to pin one end of a trailing sheet while he folded the two sides inward with albatross arms. "When people ask for a miracle, they think they are sending in an order to be fulfilled. But miracles are terrible things."

"Getting healed isn't so terrible." I rooted about for a missing sock.

"Terrible meaning awesome, full of fearsomeness and wonder. You can never know the consequences once your life has been invaded."

Invaded made me think of our duck-and-cover drills at school. The teacher would shout "Duck!" and we'd dive under our desks, heads buried beneath our arms, waiting for the bomb to come. Invasion was a terrible thing.

Uncle Stephen piled the folded sheet on top of an already towering mound of white. "In the Bible, people were raised from the dead. A dead man coming back to life must be a fearsome sight."

I wouldn't want to see something that had been dead for a while appear in my room. My uncle had a way of showing everything from a different angle.

"Are you going to talk to them again?"

I didn't like the feeling of all those eyes watching our house. I didn't like being trapped inside on a sunny day in the middle of July. But it was more than that. Suddenly Uncle Stephen was a stranger to me. There was a part of him, a secret life, that had nothing to do with me. It was the same way I felt about Mom when I heard the words *Woodward House*, as if the people I had known my entire life had suddenly grown a tail. They had a life that was apart from me, and knowing that, I couldn't look at them the same way anymore.

"I think your mother's right. It's best to let the whole thing blow over, if it can."

"Is Mom going to be okay?" My question was so quiet, and he waited so long to respond, that I wasn't sure he heard.

"Sometimes it's hard to understand why bad things happen, why it feels like God has left us on our own." A pair of white boxer shorts dangled from one hand. "Existential angst. Your mother feels like God left her all alone. She wonders if her life has meaning. Maybe it's my fault. I haven't done a good enough job of telling her it does."

The phone shrilled.

We both froze. White towels draped from Uncle Stephen's arms.

It shrilled again, and I hurried to answer it.

"Hello?"

"Stephen Fitzgerald, please. This is the *San Jose Mercury* calling."

I put a hand over the mouthpiece. "It's the newspaper. They want to talk to you."

"Tell them I'm busy."

I thought he'd at least want to speak to them, to explain his story. "He's busy right now."

"Who are you, his niece?"

"My name's Mo—"

Uncle Stephen grabbed the phone from my hand. Towels and washcloths drifted to the floor. "Please don't question my family. I have nothing to say." He set the phone down quietly and stood there not moving.

"Uncle Stephen?" I asked.

Then I heard it too, faint voices singing. A flight of song was rising from the yard, a strange melody I did not know.

By mid-afternoon, Mom came out as if nothing in the world was different. She'd changed from her sweatshirt into a new blouse and even added a touch of lipstick. Piles of neatly folded laundry punctuated the room, which now looked as tidy as she did. She sat down at her typewriter and began to work, but not before I caught her glance at the wall.

Angus and I, clearing a pile of towels off the couch, tried to watch TV, but every few minutes the phone rang, until Uncle Stephen took it off the hook.

"We are besieged in our own home," Mom said without looking up.

"I'm truly sorry that it's come to this. I'll get a hotel. I'll leave right after dinner and make sure they see me go." Uncle Stephen picked up the book he'd been reading between interruptions.

"That won't be necessary."

"It's unfair to put you and the kids through this," Uncle Stephen spoke to her back.

Mom turned to look over her shoulder. "You're my brother. Fairness has nothing to do with it."

The doorbell rang. Like the phone, it had been ringing on and off most of the afternoon. This time the bell was followed by several sharp raps. Angus peeked under the corner of the drapes.

"It's the Penguin and the Giraffe."

Uncle Stephen sprang to his feet and hurried to the door. When he opened it, Pasquali waddled in. He was a hot, sweating penguin today. The Giraffe loped after him. He was so tall, he had to duck his head to come in our door. It looked like his clothes had been stretched to fit him.

"Quite a group of pilgrims outside." The Penguin spoke quickly. "Hope doesn't wait for official verification. We strongly suggest you do nothing to encourage them." The Giraffe nodded.

Mom went to the kitchen and returned with glasses of lemonade on a tray.

"Tell me, do you really believe my brother has performed a miracle?" Mom leaned forward as if eager for their wisdom. She was using her researcher voice; maybe no one else recognized this, but I did. Penguin looked at Giraffe and Giraffe's Adam's apple did a two-step. Then Penguin folded his hands— white hands thick with black hair.

"There are different degrees of miracles. It appears that your brother has performed a modal miracle. A boy's body underwent an extraordinary or miraculous cure."

"So how would you define a miracle?" Mom looked up from under her thick eyelashes. It was a deceptively sweet look. She was waiting to attack.

"They're wondrous, divine deeds with spiritual purposes." Penguin folded and refolded his hands.

"And how do you know that what happened was miraculous?"

I caught Angus's eye. How could we know? Proof was a complicated word.

"That is an issue for the Roman Congregation to consider. We've sent off all the information we have on this case. Doctors concur the boy is healed from his tumor."

I could tell that the two investigators wanted to talk to Uncle Stephen. But Mom was relentless.

"How do we even know that miracles exist?"

This time the Giraffe spoke first. His voice was deep, like the rumble of thunder. "If you believe in an omnipotent God, you've opened the possibility that we don't live in a closed system. The world becomes vulnerable to miracles."

A shiver went down my spine. There was something about the word *vulnerable* that made me want to run away and hide.

Chapter Twenty-Six

GIRLS WHO ARE DIFFERENT

SAN JOSE, CALIFORNIA—JULY 1955

Molly

The house was hot. Every window was closed. Every drape was drawn. The afternoon sun beat against the glass. Sweat dampened my temples. After three days of forced confinement, it felt as if the walls were closing in, as if I might suffocate in my own house. I needed to see Ari, to remind myself that there was a real world apart from the drama surrounding our house. I wanted privacy to talk and to explain that things weren't what she probably thought they were.

No one would notice if I left. Uncle Stephen was building a model airplane with Angus in his bedroom. Mom was working at her desk. I slipped out the kitchen door and into the backyard. Here, you would never know our front lawn was under siege. Without the news presence, Uncle Stephen predicted that interest would fade by the end of the week. I wasn't so sure. Besides, I couldn't wait for the interest to fade. I thought about my possible escape routes. If I ducked out the side yard gate I might be able to skirt the crowd. Besides, they were focused on the front door. It wasn't me they were interested in.

I clicked open the gate latch and peered out. The noonday sun was merciless. The crowd on the lawn was also larger this morning. People loved a spectacle, and word of mouth spread fast. The one news clip of Uncle Stephen on the porch with raised hands hadn't helped. I eased out the gate and paused for a minute, my back against the warm wood, watching. Cars choked our once quiet suburban street. I recognized one or two neighbors, but most of the crowd were strangers. All were expectant, all were waiting, but for what? For my uncle to perform another miracle? To be healed? What hopes drove them to our door?

I edged forward along the fence line, keeping my eyes on the sidewalk only yards away. Once there I could blend in and keep walking like any neighbor hurrying home to escape the sun. I'd almost reached my goal when a little boy sitting next to his very pregnant mother shouted and pointed at me. A murmur started, then built like a wave, a terrifying wave that might suck me under. I ran.

No one followed me as I rounded the corner to Ari's house. Once I was completely out of view, I felt safe enough to slow to a trot and then a walk. My breath came in gasps, my shirt stuck to my back. I untucked it and let it hang loose over my pedal pushers. My legs trembled. I watched the windows I passed for the flick of a curtain. It felt as though there were eyes everywhere.

By the time I approached Ari's house I was sticky with sweat, my tongue was gummy and stuck to the roof of my mouth. From her side yard, I heard the *swish-click* of lawnmower blades and inhaled the unmistakable scent of hot new-mown grass. Jesse rounded the corner of the house, brown muscled arms pushing the mower. A line of sweat plastered his T-shirt to his chest. My heart did a summersault.

He stopped when he saw me on the walk, and with a forearm wiped the sweat from his face.

"Ari's not here. She's at the movies with some friends."

Friends that didn't include me. My heart contracted.

He squinted at me as if he could read the confusion in my eyes. "Look. What's going on at your house has made people nervous."

"But it doesn't have anything to do with me."

He walked to the hose bib, turned on the faucet, and took a long drink from the end of the hose. I watched him swallow, feeling my own saliva dry in my mouth. Water splashed his neck.

"Maybe not, but you're involved by extension. That's how people think." He sprayed his head and shook the water off like a dog. "Do you believe he did it?"

"A miracle? I don't know. I don't know what I think."

"Want a drink?" He held out the hose.

I nodded and crossed the lawn to take it from him. The water tasted like warm rubber, but it bubbled into my mouth and soothed my throat. I wanted to douse my head like he had. Instead I handed it back, and he dropped the hose on the ground.

"You've heard of Darwin, right?" he asked.

"Sure." Although I was a bit fuzzy on the details.

"My science teacher says science may do away with religion entirely. But people aren't ready to hear that yet. They only hear what they're ready to hear. Anything beyond that makes them nervous. What your uncle did makes them nervous."

Drops of water sparkled in the dark curls of his hair. The sun beat on my head.

"You're a nice, cute kid, and it's too bad you had to get caught up in all this."

I winced at the word *kid*. "Don't you think it's important to figure out what to believe?"

He leaned a long, tanned arm on the mower handle. "Sure I do. But let me give you some advice. Let all of this go. Guys don't like girls who are different, girls who overthink things."

"Then I guess that saves me from worrying about what to wear to prom." My pulse pounded in my ears. "I'm not going to stop thinking because it makes some guy uncomfortable. I'll ask whatever questions I want!"

He threw his head back and laughed. "Suit yourself, but you'll end up like the rest of your family."

The water still poured onto the grass from the discarded hose. I grabbed it, and as I tilted my head back I let water sluice over my hair, stream down my neck, and run under my shirt. Nothing had ever felt so good. Then I dropped it at Jesse's feet. His tennis shoes flooded as he watched me with a half-open mouth.

There was nothing more to say. That long walk home was lonesome as the cloudless sky.

Chapter Twenty-Seven

BACK TO THE MARKET

BROOKLYN, NEW YORK—SEPTEMBER 1919

ELAINE

By the time Elaine reached the kitchen, Stephen had already charmed Kay Baggot. She set two bowls of steaming soup on the painted table for them. When May joined, Kay only raised her eyebrows slightly. "You'll be eating here then, Missus?" she asked, and ladled up another bowl.

"I most certainly will, Kay."

Elaine picked up her spoon and made a mental note not to slurp her soup. The broth was thick with noodles and chunks of chicken. As Stephen lifted the bowl to his lips, Elaine gave him a sharp kick under the table.

May took a small sip of soup. She paused and looked at both of them. The overhead light reflected off the jeweled comb in her hair. "As I told your sister, we're planning a picnic for my father's birthday, and I know my father is counting on you to be guests. It will be only the immediate family and Aunt Lydia."

Elaine watched Stephen's face erupt in a smile. "A picnic, Lainey! Can we go?"

She had never been on a picnic before. She pictured baskets of sandwiches, fruit, and cupcakes.

"We'd be honored to attend." Could life get much better than this—her own book and the promise of a picnic to come? Still, the thought of Pop pierced her like a sliver. The more she tried to pluck it out, the more it festered.

"Now that the birthday is resolved, we need to talk about some other things. It's time you returned to school, Elaine."

"But—"

Stephen cut her off. "Then we wouldn't have any money."

Mrs. Gossley paused, soup spoon to mouth.

Why did Stephen have to share everything? Didn't he remember the threat of the Orphan Asylum? She would never bring him with her to the Gossleys again.

"But your father—" Mrs. Gossley looked as if she were about to say more. Instead she swallowed her soup. "You could still work for my father after school."

Elaine took a deep breath.

"The pay would be the same."

Birthdays in the Gossley family took days of planning. May asked Elaine to accompany her to Wallabout Market, saying she couldn't trust anyone else to get the things they needed just right. They set out on a morning as crisp as autumn apples, baskets over their arms. Elaine thought of her own birthday that was coming in the next month. She would be fifteen, capable enough to take care of Stephen on her own.

In mid-September, the market was a different place than in spring. Booths were beginning to fill with knobby winter fruits in greens and golds and bundles of orange carrots. Bins of apples in yellow, red, and green shone like jewels in a dragon's hoard.

Many of the summer vendors were gone, but the cloth and lace merchants remained, as did the bookseller and the bakers. There was an energy in the air that came with autumn. May walked with purpose, commenting on everything they passed, sprinkling in instructive advice as she saw fit.

"Pink is not a color for redheads." She nodded toward a woman with dusky pink wraps draped over one arm. "You should never wear it. But green and gold suit you." May picked up an apple and sniffed it. "Apple pie is my father's favorite dessert. We'll bake three. Look for the ones with smooth skin and firm flesh." She began to examine the red and green pippins. "Let's fill your basket. I'll save mine for the bread and cheese."

Elaine helped her sort through the piles of apples. It was different than when she had come to the market with her mother. May was always instructing, always intent on a task. While her own mother had been—and here Elaine had difficulty coming up with the difference—softer, she supposed, and more playful.

They made their way to a stall offering huge wheels of cheese. There were rich golden cheeses, crumbly white sheep's cheese, and a strange blue-veined cheese that made her nose wrinkle.

"What's that?" she asked, pointing at a twist of cheese that hung like rope in the stall.

The vendor, a small woman with a dark fuzz of mustache, grinned at her. Three of her teeth were missing. "String cheese with nigella seed." She peeled away a strip as long as her forearm and handed it to Elaine. "Have a taste. Half the fun's in peeling it."

The small, dark seeds flecked the cheese like ants. Elaine took a careful bite. Other than salt, there was little flavor.

"We'll take some," May said. "Wait for her to wrap it up, and then get a loaf of dark rye." She pressed some money into Elaine's hand. "I'll be across the street at the cobbler's." But she didn't leave. Instead her eyes roamed Elaine's face. "I trust you, Elaine. Never forget that." Then May Gossley walked away.

Elaine stared at the money. It was more than she spent on food in a week. Mrs. Gossley's words made her face flame. It had never occurred to her that May wouldn't trust her. When the cheese was wrapped, she carefully counted out the coins and held them out to the old woman.

The woman smiled and ducked her head. Elaine noticed the tremor in her hand as she took the change, the way the collar of her dress was worn thin from too many washings.

Elaine dropped a few extra coins in the change tray. Then she walked away before the woman had a chance to say anything.

Maybe May was right.

As Elaine walked, she tried not to be amazed at the amount of purchases gathering in her basket. Food from the Gossleys now supplemented the main part of her and Stephen's diet. Everything she earned was saved toward rent.

"If it isn't my red-haired friend!" Elaine looked up into the face of Pete, the pigeon man. "You're looking more grown up."

"Thank you." She tried to answer in a very grown-up voice. "How are your pigeons?"

"They're grand. Perhaps that brother of yours would like to visit them." Pete took a sip from a steaming mug of coffee.

Elaine peered into the crates. The pigeons were cooing, and their smell of feathers and birdseed reminded her of glue. "He's in school just now, but I know he'd like to see them again."

"Well, bring him by on a Saturday, and we'll send one off with a message. I'll let him write it." And he turned his attention to a lanky young man who was cooing to the birds.

That would be a way to bribe Stephen to stay in school all week, she thought as she hurried over to the bread stall. She'd promise him a chance to visit the pigeons if he didn't miss a day.

The cobbler shop was a narrow wooden building with a window full of shoes, dwarfed by the brick grocery warehouse next to it. When Elaine pushed open the door, a bell tinkled. She inhaled the smell of leather and polish. Old shoes came in worn and broken, and left with a new life. The cobbler was wrapping May's parcel, a pair of tan kid leather boots.

"There you are, Elaine. These boots are as good as new now. Never discount the value of a good shoe." Elaine looked down at her own scuffed shoes that peeked from under her skirt. "It's time we headed back. I have a meeting with the Bureau of Social Hygiene this afternoon." May adjusted her hat in the cobbler's mirror.

A wind had begun to blow from the river, from the direction of the naval shipyards. Elaine drew her shawl closer. The basket of fruit was heavy and she switched arms, careful not to drop the cloth bag with bread and string cheese. The smell of chocolate wafted in from the Rockwood Chocolate Factory, making her mouth water.

"With proper social hygiene, we can keep unfortunate girls out of the penitentiaries." May continued her brisk pace. "Most of them are ignorant and weak immigrant girls with no proper education or home life."

How much did May suspect about her home? A mix of shame and anger rose in her throat like bile.

"The immigrants I know are strong."

"Physical strength is no match for will. These girls are weak willed. We provide second chances and help them find jobs so they can survive."

Elaine shifted the parcels from arm to arm and tried to keep up without dropping anything. "Maybe they want to do more than survive."

May looked at her, but the sun was in Elaine's eyes, and she couldn't tell if the expression was a smile or a grimace.

Chapter Twenty-Eight

DRAKE BROTHERS BAKERY

BROOKLYN, NEW YORK—SEPTEMBER 1919

ELAINE

Elaine stirred a soup made from carrots, potatoes, and scraps of ham from the Gossleys' kitchen. She'd said she was taking the scraps home for their dog. At the kitchen table, Stephen struggled to read while Elaine knew he really wanted to play in the vacant lot with the other boys. He'd been in school every day that week after she'd promised a visit to Pete and his pigeons on Saturday.

The potatoes were almost tender when the door burst open. Pop strolled in accompanied by a wiry little man who was hardly taller than Elaine.

"Pop!" Stephen exploded from the table so fast he knocked the chair over backward, then clamped on to Pop around the waist.

"Now isn't this nice—a family to come home to." The small man took off his cap and twirled it in his hands

Elaine didn't move. Pop hadn't been home in over a week.

She was aware of the tick of the clock on the windowsill, the bubbles starting to rise in the soup, the way the window over the sink was steaming. Slowly, she added a pinch of salt. She didn't turn. "How's my big girl?" His words rolled over her like a breeze she could ignore. From the corner of her eye, she saw him look at his friend. "Did you know she's employed by a rich family up Clinton Ave? Elaine and Stephen, this is Tim Meeks."

Pop didn't offer an *I'm sorry I haven't been home.* Nor a *How are you managing?* There was no word of explanation. When she turned toward them and saw Pop's face, Elaine prodded the empty space inside herself. She felt nothing.

"Nice to meet 'cher. Smells like there's soup?" Mr. Meeks looked hopefully toward the pot on the stove.

Elaine's lips drew tight against her teeth. Did Pop expect they'd have enough for a guest? How could he assume they'd have anything at all when he hadn't been home in two weeks? She turned back to the stove and stirred the soup until it splashed, burning her hand.

"Take a load off." Pop offered Mr. Meeks one of the three chairs at the table. "We've something to celebrate tonight." He rubbed his hands together, and Mr. Meeks dropped his cap onto the table, nodding. Elaine heard something hard also land on the table. She turned and rested one hip against the stove, sucking on her burned hand.

Tufts of hair bristled from Mr. Meeks's ears. She focused on those. She would not cry.

"Don't I even get a hello from my own daughter?"

"Hello, Pop."

"She's not much for talking, is she?" Mr. Meeks spoke as if she wasn't in the room.

"Mr. Meeks, here, has gotten me a job at Drake Brothers. He's a foreman, and I start in the morning."

"The bakery?" Her voice was a whisper. She had walked past Drake Brothers earlier today. She would not let hope get a foothold. "You'll have to be up early then."

Elaine ladled out four bowls of soup. There was barely enough for a bowl each if she skimped a little on her own. Two brown bags rested on the table.

"Let a man celebrate his victory," Pop said.

Mr. Meeks reached into one bag and pulled out four white rolls. Then he scrabbled his hand into the second bag and pulled out a bottle of Jack Daniels. "I like to do my share." His gap-toothed grin stretched from ear to ear. Elaine looked at Stephen, but his eyes were fixed on the soft rolls.

"Thank you, Mr. Meeks. We haven't had white rolls in a very long time," Stephen said.

Mr. Meeks took a big slurp from his bowl of soup. "They're from the bakery. But our biggest lot is pound cake, fifteen tons every day." He continued to spoon soup into his mouth while he talked and took bites of roll at the same time. When he chewed, his nose hairs quivered.

Elaine stood watching as the three males began to eat, until Pop noticed. "Here, take my chair, darling. I'll just perch on the crate over there." He nodded to the empty milk crate in the corner. Wordlessly, Elaine slid onto the wooden chair and took a bite of a soft white roll and felt it dissolve against her tongue.

Mr. Meeks continued, "It's all set up for efficiency, see. Fourth floor, all the mixing's done. Then the dough's sent up to the ovens on the fifth. Shipping's on the bottom floors where a wagon can pull right up to get loaded." He picked up the bowl and noisily drained out the last of the soup. "And on the roof's a laundry where our uniforms is washed every day, God bless 'em. Good soup, by the way."

"I'm going to be in shipping to start," Pop added. "Then move up to mixing. Maybe end up a foreman like Tim."

Stephen grinned; he was probably already imagining Pop as a foreman.

When she cleared the table, Pop took her chair back. Both men lit up cigarettes, something else they didn't have the money for, Elaine thought bitterly. She swirled the dishes in cold water first and then used the last of the hot water on the stove to wash them properly. Stephen stayed at the table like one of the men. He scooted his chair as close to Pop's as he could, and Elaine knew there'd be no more homework done that evening.

"And now for that celebration, Mr. Fitzgerald." Mr. Meeks twisted the top off the bottle. "To Drake Brothers' newest employee." He offered the first sip to Pop. "Got to fill up before the New Year. Prohibition's gonna suck the life out of us."

Elaine caught Stephen's eyes. "Don't forget you have school in the morning," she said as she walked into the bedroom.

"She sounds more like her mother every day." And the two men laughed. Elaine punched the pillow on her bed. What right did he have to mention her mother? Couldn't Pop get it right even this once?

She stretched out on the bed and lay still, but her mind ran in restless circles. Groaning, she rolled to her side. The blue *Hansel and Gretel* was under the bed. She reached for it now. Her favorite illustration showed Hansel and Gretel on the step in front of a small house. The witch, disguised as a very old woman, met them at the door. Elaine wished she could step into the picture and lead the two children away into the woods, to safety. The trees leered with the faces of goblins.

It wasn't long before Stephen crept in with her.

"Read to me, Lainey."

He looked so much like Hansel in the illustration that Elaine couldn't say no. In the main room, the two men got louder, their voices sloppier. Then the door slammed and a few minutes later opened again. Elaine listened for the clink of bottles.

In her dream, the witch slammed the door of the candy house. It startled her to wakefulness. Thick dark filled the room. Stephen's breathing was soft and regular beside her. There really wasn't room for both of them on the narrow bed—her right arm was heavy and numb where Stephen had rolled across it. She could slip out and into his bed across the room, but the warmth of another body was nice. She rolled Stephen to his side and slid her arm out, feeling it prickle. In the front room the men laughed, but it was as if from a great distance. She forced herself to imagine the Gossley picnic. She'd wear a new white dress and a hat with a rose. Howie would notice, like he used to. He'd call her his copper-headed princess.

The front door slammed. Elaine checked the wind-up clock by her bed. It was three a.m. She slowly reached one foot out of the bed so as not to wake Angus. Still in her work clothes, she tiptoed over to the bedroom door. Pop was asleep, head pillowed on his arms at the table. The room stunk of whiskey, stale cigarettes, and urine. Bottles littered the table and floor. Pop snored and snorted. It wouldn't matter how loudly she walked, still she crept over to the table, picked up the bottles, and threw them into the trash. Then she made sure none of the cigarettes were still burning and scooped them into the trash too. She went back into the bedroom and set the alarm for five thirty a.m. Then she placed the clock right by Pop's ear. After changing into her nightgown, she considered both beds, but curled back in with Stephen.

—◦═◉╌◦╌◎═◦—

*T*he two children had been walking a very long time. They huddled as close together as they could in the bleak forest. They might have been going in circles for all Hansel could tell, but he didn't want to mention it and frighten his little sister.

Dawn was just beginning to light the sky when the path grew wider. By now, the children were very hungry and tired indeed.

"Look, Gretel, there's a clearing up ahead." But neither of them was prepared for the sight that met their weary eyes. There, glowing in the middle of the forest, was the most

amazing thing the children had ever seen: a house made all of candy. The walls were thick slabs of gingerbread and the roof was white with frosting. Candies of every shape and color festooned the frosting roof. As they drew closer, they could see the sugar pane windows shine. They were lined with red licorice, and the door was smooth brown chocolate. Hansel and Gretel had come upon something better than either had imagined, even in their happiest dreams.

"Perhaps," said Gretel, "we should take a bite."

Chapter Twenty-Nine

PRIESTS AND PIGEONS

BROOKLYN, NEW YORK—SEPTEMBER 1919

ELAINE

The Gossleys' kitchen was the picnic command station. May directed operations like a general on the eve of battle.

"Why does there have to be so much fuss about an old man's birthday?" Mr. Seward asked Elaine.

"I thought you wanted a picnic."

"A picnic is the proper way of celebrating a birthday. Outside in the fresh air, with friends and family. But a picnic should be a simple thing, no fuss."

"Mrs. Gossley's trying to make sure you have the things you like," Elaine said.

"Hmm … trying to show what a devoted daughter she is, more to the point. Not that she isn't, but I don't like being one more of her causes."

Despite his gruffness, Elaine could tell he was pleased by the way he kept bringing the subject up.

"And you and that little brother of yours, Stanley—"

"Stephen, sir."

"Stephen, he will be there?"

"He wouldn't miss it. We've never been on a picnic before."

Mr. Seward put down his teacup with a clatter. "Never been on a picnic? Well, this will have to be an exemplary picnic then. What's your favorite sweet?"

"It's your picnic, Mr. Seward."

"Young lady, I asked you a question as your employer and I expect an answer. What's your favorite sweet?"

On her tenth birthday, her mother had made a spicy gingerbread cake. They had eaten it warm with cream. The image of her mother's hands working a wooden spoon in the chipped bowl arrived with sudden force. Her eyes watered.

"Gingerbread." The word was a papery whisper.

"Gingerbread," Mr. Seward repeated, leaning in to catch her answer. "I haven't had decent gingerbread in years. May!" He tinkled the small silver bell that was always next to his chair. "May!"

But it was Mrs. Theilen who answered the summons.

"Tell my daughter that I want gingerbread for my birthday!"

She looked surprised. "But we've made your favorite, sir, apple pies."

"I want gingerbread and apple pies. It's my birthday, damn it!"

Mrs. Theilen rolled her eyes at Elaine. "Yes, sir. I'll tell her straight away."

"That's settled; let's get back to the paper. See what scandals are happening in the world today." Mr. Seward leaned back and closed his eyes.

It was almost noon when Elaine heard the front door open and familiar whistling in the hall. When the whistling stopped right on the other side of the door, the words blurred on the page. There was something wrong with her breathing. She let the paper fall into her lap and then combed her fingers through her hair.

"What happened next?" Mr. Seward asked.

She didn't answer. She had prepared for this moment. Respond coolly with polite interest to whatever Howard said. Don't show enthusiasm. Don't ask where he'd been, why he didn't try to contact her.

The door pushed open and sucked all the air from the room. Howard paused on the threshold, his oversized grin flashing like lightning across his face.

"Beg your pardon, Grandfather, but can I borrow Elaine for a minute? I have something to show her."

Mr. Seward lowered his brows. "Go ahead." Then he closed his eyes again.

Elaine exhaled. This wasn't how the scene had played out in her head. She stood stiffly. "Hello, Howard. It's good to see you again." Then she added, "It's been a while." Her palms began to sweat.

"Come on, this can't wait." His eyes danced.

He was ignoring or didn't notice her reserve. Elaine couldn't tell.

"I won't be long," she assured Mr. Seward, and followed Howard out the door.

As soon as she left the room, Howard grabbed her arm and whispered, "I've got a gift for Grandfather you won't believe. Come in the kitchen."

No mention of where he'd been the last few weeks. No questions about how she was. Elaine let him lead her into the steamy kitchen. The pressure of his hand on her arm confused her thoughts. In a corner, a caged black bird with an improbable yellow beak pecked at a nut.

"It's a mynah bird!" Howie led her to the iron cage. "They can talk if you teach them. I got this fellow from a friend who's already taught him to say five or six different things. I thought he could keep the old man company."

Elaine eyed the bird. Its feathers were glossy black, the beak strong and hooked, and its eyes followed her every movement.

"Give me a kiss!"

Elaine jumped. Howie howled with laughter.

Kay scooted closer to the cage. "He's cheeky. What do you feed him?"

"Fresh fruit, nuts, and these pellets." Howie produced a bag from his pocket.

"Shut up!" the bird shrilled.

"They're mimics," Howie said. "He can meow like a cat when he wants."

"I'm sure Mr. Seward will like him." Elaine felt her words march out stiff as wood stakes. There was something wrong with her mouth when she tried to smile.

"I've got to get back to school. Feed it some pellets will you, princess? And keep my secret!" Howie winked at her, and then pecked Kay's cheek, which made the cook giggle.

"Don't you worry about it, Elaine. I'll feed the nasty thing." Kay shook her head.

"Give me a kiss! Give me a kiss!" the mynah shrieked at Howie's retreating back.

Saturday morning, Stephen was up early, full of the promise of the market and pigeons. Pop was already up and out. So far, so good, Elaine thought. He'd come home Friday night tired but happy, with a chunk of pound cake and complaints that his arms ached from all the heavy lifting. The fine weather had held, and the world was gilded with autumn light. Elaine had put aside a little money to buy her own present for Mr. Seward, although she had no idea what it would be. On the way, she told Stephen about the mynah bird, imitating its voice when it asked for a kiss and yowled like a cat, while her mind reworked every word Howard said. It was no good trying to analyze them. There was nothing worth mining.

Stephen was intent on finding the pigeons right away. He grabbed Elaine's arm and tugged.

"Hurry up. I've been waiting all week!"

They threaded their way between carts of apples and pumpkins. An Amish farmer was selling fresh cider. You could watch the apples sluice through the press and come out as a pulpy mass. While filling glass jars with the cloudy liquid, the farmer handed out samples. Elaine and Angus each took one.

When they got to Pete's stall, he was engaged in conversation. Elaine pulled Stephen back.

"He's trying to make a sale. You don't want to interrupt."

"But we could just look at the pigeons!' He wrestled his arm free from her grip.

The pigeons cooed and shuffled in their crates. Pete carried Lucky on one thick shoulder. His flannel shirt and apron were as always streaked with pigeon droppings. The young fair-haired man had his own carrier by his side. He turned in their direction as Stephen approached the crates. Elaine was startled to see the white clerical collar of a priest.

"I was hoping you two would pay me a visit." Pete beamed at them and turned to the priest. "These two youngsters have taken a fancy to the birds. Promised 'em we'd send off a pigeon post today."

The priest looked pensive, taking them both in.

"I think I've seen you two before at Sacred Heart."

Elaine blushed. "We don't attend services very often, Father."

"No, no, not at Mass. It was in the sanctuary, in front of the statue of Mary—several months back. I recognize you both by your hair." He had a thin, rubbery smile under a long, bony nose. The smile split his face in half, making it look almost handsome. "I'm Father Kearny, Michael Kearny."

Elaine found she was smiling too. "I'm Elaine Fitzgerald, and this is my brother, Stephen."

Stephen looked up, right into the priest's eyes. "Hello. Do you need an altar boy?"

Chapter Thirty

PIGEON POST

BROOKLYN, NEW YORK—SEPTEMBER 1919

ELAINE

Where did Stephen come up with these ideas?

"I'm sorry—he didn't mean anything—"

Father Kearny ignored her and squatted down so that he and Stephen were eye to eye. "How could you know that? It just so happens that one of my altar boys has moved away. We like to have two for Sunday services, and I was looking for another to take his place. How old are you, Stephen?"

"I'm nine."

"Altar boys have to receive some training first. It takes a while, and their families are expected to attend the parish where they're serving." Now he glanced up at Elaine.

"We haven't got any family," said Stephen, "except Pop, and he's not home much."

"Where's your mother?"

"She's dead."

Elaine recovered enough to say, "We've been planning on coming. We used to go to Holy Family."

Father Kearny straightened up, his thin smile disarming his face, but his eyes rested thoughtfully on Elaine. "Who looks after you then?"

"We live with our father."

A look transferred between Father Kearny and Pete, and in that glance Elaine saw the thin gleam of a knife's edge. Her future and Stephen's poised on that edge the way Pop balanced an apple on the sharp kitchen blade. A swift flip of the wrist, a flash of silver, and the apple was sliced.

"Well, I see no reason why Stephen can't come to the new training that starts next week. It's Saturday afternoons at three. But I'd like to meet with your father first."

"He works a lot." Elaine studied a discarded tin on the ground. Champagne-flavored Piper Heidsieck Chewing Tobacco. She flipped it over with the scuffed toe of her shoe.

"Can I, Lainey?"

When she looked up she was trapped between Stephen's hope and Father Kearny's keen brown eyes. "We'll have to talk it over with Pop. But you probably can."

"Maybe I can meet your father at work?"

Stephen's eyes sought out hers. It was as if he spoke the question out loud.

Elaine spoke for both of them. "We'll talk to him when he gets home tonight."

"He'd be a fine altar boy," Pete put in. "Father Kearny's got pigeons himself." Pete nodded at the crate by the priest's feet.

"A hobby I started as a boy, and I still love it. Pete got me started."

Elaine hadn't known that priests had hobbies.

"Would you like to see my birds?" Father Kearny managed to include them both in his glance. Opening the crate, he reached in and drew out a fat gray bird with green-tipped feathers. "This one's Gabriel. Flies like an angel. Sometimes,

Pete and I send messages back and forth from his house to the church for fun. I lived near Pete when I was a boy and made a few pennies cleaning his cages."

"That's right. Pigeons kept 'im out of trouble. Otherwise, who knows what he would've been up to? My farm's about twenty-five miles away. A good flight for pigeon post."

"We're sending a message today, right?" Stephen asked.

"Now I promised you, din' I?" Pete walked over to a second crate.

"Why don't we use mine?" Father Kearny suggested. "We'll give Gabriel a chance to stretch his wings. He can fly back to the church. Stephen and Elaine can pick up the message there."

"If you've got time, Michael."

Elaine wondered why Pete didn't call him Father.

Father Kearny opened a small metal tube attached to a band on the bird's scaly leg.

"You use this paper, here." Pete unrolled a small piece of cigarette paper and handed Stephen a stub of pencil. "You got to write small. Then stuff it back in the tube."

"What are you going to write?" She itched to write something herself, but it was Stephen's treat.

He screwed up his face and the tip of his pink tongue poked out between his lips. Hurriedly, he scrawled something on the tiny paper. When Elaine bent to read it, Stephen covered the paper with his hand and rolled it up quickly. "You'll have to wait to read it."

"Now why don't you both let the bird go," Father Kearny suggested. "You can each use one hand. Hold him gently. Then, you throw him up into the sky like this." He demonstrated, flinging both hands up into the air.

A small crowd had gathered around the pigeon stall to watch. Elaine slipped one hand under Gabriel. The bird was surprisingly light and still. "How long does it take him to get there?" Elaine asked.

"Gabriel will get there before you do. He doesn't have to obey any street signs or even follow the roads. Ready now?" Father Kearny counted to three. They swung their arms upward and opened their hands, releasing Gabriel toward the sun. The crowd clapped.

"I'm off to meet the bird." Father Kearny shook both their hands solemnly. "We'll be waiting when you get there. And I'll expect to see you, Stephen, next Saturday at three."

Two customers were already talking to Pete about his birds. Elaine grabbed Stephen by the sleeve. "Keep your mouth closed about our family. Do you want to end up in an institution? And what was that business about altar boys?"

"Jimmy Corbett in my class is one, and he tells me all about it. Besides, you remember, Lainey, Mom always promised me I could be one."

She hadn't remembered, not until he told her. When Mom was alive, they went to Mass each Sunday. Stephen had loved to watch the boys in their vestments light candles and assist the priests, so much so that Mom had promised Stephen that one day he could light the candles and help with Mass. He remembered things about their mother that she'd now forgotten. What else did he recall? It was a strange feeling knowing the past wasn't the same for both of them.

"I'm sorry, Mama," Elaine whispered. "Of course he can go."

The gold light that minutes before had gilded the landscape now looked tinny. For the first time that day, Elaine noticed that half the people at the market looked as poor as she felt.

"Come on. We have to go to church to find Gabriel." Stephen nudged her.

She elbowed him back.

Forgetting all about Mr. Seward's present, they hurried toward Sacred Heart.

When they reached the church, Elaine puzzled over where to find Father Kearny. Where would a priest keep pigeons? There was the church itself, banded brick and stone arches, with its deeply sloping roof and corner tower; the school, Sacred Heart Institute; then the rectory and convent.

"Up here!" Father Kearny's voice came from above. He waved at them like a gargoyle from the roof of the gymnasium. "Take the fire escape up. Lucky for me, gymnasiums have flat roofs!"

Elaine paused at the bottom of the metal fire escape. "Should we climb up?" she whispered to Stephen.

"Come on!" Stephen was already a few steps ahead of her, head cocked up to smile at Father Kearny, but Elaine looked down at the open space between the steps.

From the roof, all of Wallabout glowed red. Light reflected off the brick buildings and danced off the leaves of the maples. The roof of the gymnasium was flat as Father had said, and was bordered on each side by a short brick wall. A door opened from inside the building onto the roof. There was a clothesline for laundry and four wooden pigeon coops.

"This is my favorite place. The world looks glorious even when you know it isn't so pretty face-to-face." Father Kearny stood by her side. "Come see my pigeons."

Stephen was already over at the low wooden coops. They were tidily constructed with perches for roosting, screened fronts, and dishes to hold water and seed. Several fat birds cooed from inside, but Gabriel perched on a rail on top of a coop.

"This is my landing station for pigeon post. Let's see what we have." He picked the bird up gently and flipped him on his side to reach the leg. Gabriel didn't seem to mind the handling. "Would you like to do the honors?" He looked at Elaine.

Elaine glanced at Stephen. "No, let my brother do it."

"Careful, now," Father Kearny coaxed, as Stephen, his hands trembling, opened the small cap that pulled straight off the end of the tiny cylinder. Father Kearny handed Stephen a pair of tweezers. "Remove it with these."

Carefully, he pulled out the small roll of paper. "Read it, Lainey."

Elaine smoothed out the roll and read her brother's cramped hand. "Happy birthday, Mr. Seward."

Stephen looked at Elaine expectantly. "Do you think he'll like it? A birthday card carried by a pigeon?"

Chapter Thirty-One

THE PICNIC

BROOKLYN, NEW YORK—SEPTEMBER 1919

ELAINE

On the Sunday afternoon of the picnic, white clouds like a small fleet sailed the sky. Elaine was up early to heat water for baths. Pop had gone out around seven with Mr. Meeks and never returned, but she was used to his ways.

She'd grown enough that the hem of her dress was now a fashionable three inches above her ankles. She'd spent much of last week adding a cape of fabric to the bodice of her best dress. It covered the way the fabric now pulled tight across her chest and mimicked the style she had seen in dress shops on Myrtle Avenue. She added a sea green ribbon to her hair that matched the dress. If Mr. Seward didn't regularly rail about short hair on women, she'd have cut it into one of the new short bobs.

There was no hope of Stephen looking fashionable. As long as he and his clothes were clean, it would be enough. She'd spent two dollars of the rent money to buy him new shoes last month. His feet grew faster than the rest of him, and they'd been covered with blisters where they rubbed against the tight leather.

With hauling water and washing, there was no time for Mass. She hoped Father Kearny wouldn't hold it against them. And there had been the problem of Mr. Seward's gift. It was fine for Stephen to give him a rolled-up piece of pigeon paper, but she wanted a special gift that was only from her. So, late the previous night, after Stephen had gone to bed, she'd sat down with one of his pencils and a notebook. Stephen's schoolbook was an anthology of poems, stories, and essays. She poured over each poem until she found one by a poet named Walter de la Mare that wasn't too long, or too complex to understand. Then, after attempts that kept her up half the night, she'd written the best poem she could based on the model. When her head became too fuzzy to think clearly, she folded the paper and put it in the pocket of her picnic dress. She'd find a time when she could read it to Mr. Seward privately. It was the best she could do.

When Elaine and Stephen arrived at noon, picnic baskets and presents were being loaded into one of two cars in the driveway. May directed while Mr. Gossley helped his father-in-law into one of the cars.

Stephen's hand crept into hers and she was glad of the contact. "Lainey, do you think we're really supposed to be here?"

"Of course. We're invited, aren't we?" But no one took any notice of them as they approached the drive. People she didn't recognize sat in the wicker chairs on the porch. Just when she felt like turning and running away, Howie emerged.

In a navy blue flannel blazer with patch pockets and brass buttons, paired with pants pressed to sharp creases, this was a different Howard than the one she ate with in the kitchen. As soon as he spotted them, he came running down the steps.

"Elaine, Stephen, over here. Wait 'til the old man sees the bird!"

"I want to see the mynah!" Stephen dropped Lainey's hand. Had he remembered to stuff the pigeon post in his pocket?

"And so you shall! Follow me!" Howie led them around to the kitchen entrance where they almost collided with Mrs. Theilen, her arms piled with blankets. On the kitchen table, a towel draped a large cage. From under the towel a muffled voice implored, "Save the bird! Save the bird!" and then it wailed like a siren.

Howie edged up a corner of the towel. "Take a look."

Stephen thrust his head under.

"Attack! Attack!" the bird shrilled. Stephen squeaked and jumped back. Elaine laughed so hard that tears sprang to her eyes.

"We're going to Fort Greene Park. You can ride with me in the second car." Howie picked up the birdcage. "The old man's already gone off in the first car with my father."

Elaine grabbed Stephen by the hand and climbed into a new Nash sedan with Howie, an elderly lady introduced as Great Aunt Myra, and May. Happily squashed between Stephen and Howie with the noisy mynah on his lap, Elaine tried to relax. The bird kept up a running commentary of "Bless my buttons!" and "Save the bird!"

"Don't you children look nice." May was all brightness and bustle. "Mr. Parks, Father's solicitor, will be driving us."

Elaine noticed every detail. Mr. Parks was short and solid like a fire hydrant. In a bold-striped jacket and with his rollicking laugh, he resembled a carnival barker. Elaine liked him immediately.

With the top down, they glided past the familiar stores on Myrtle Avenue, past the Sunday strollers dressed in church clothes, and past a gang of children playing kick the can. And everyone glanced their way. Howie's thigh was pressed hard against hers. Did he feel the same pulse of heat that ran from her hip to her ankle? If he did, he didn't show it. But he didn't move his leg away.

The road into Fort Greene Park was lined with chestnut trees turning to gold. Beyond them a white granite pillar, taller than any tree in the park, balanced an urn on its tip.

"What's that?" asked Stephen.

"It's the Prison Ship Martyrs' Monument," began May.

"And there are dead people buried under it." Howie laughed ghoulishly.

"Dead people?" Stephen's voice went up a notch.

"Dead people from the Revolutionary War, in a crypt under the monument."

A thrilling shudder ran up Elaine's spine.

"Everyone out. Croquet lawn up ahead." Mr. Parks bounced out of the car and held the door open. The croquet lawn was a wide green tabletop bordered by trees. From the far end of the lawn, they could see Mr. Gossley waving. Mr. Seward, in his wheelchair, was surrounded by a patchwork of picnic blankets and baskets. Howie helped his mother from the car, and then offered Elaine his hand, but Stephen sprang down by himself, dashing off toward Mr. Seward.

There were at least fifteen people sprawled on the sea of blankets. Every blanket had a picnic basket filled with cold fried chicken and ham, cakes, and apples. There were cups of cider and the loaves of bread she had bought at the market. Elaine soon learned May's sister and her five young children had surprised them all by coming on the train from New Jersey. Howie's cousins ran in and out between the picnickers, laughing and chasing a large blue ball. Mr. Seward presided over them all with a bottle of root beer in one hand and a chicken leg in the other.

Elaine watched from the edge of the crowd. Where was she supposed to sit? Stephen was already shouting in a game of keep away. Howie was talking to his aunt Sarah, who balanced an infant on her lap.

"Elaine, come sit over here," Mr. Gossley called to her from his father-in-law's side. "Arthur has been asking for you."

Relieved, Elaine joined Mr. Seward and Mr. Gossley.

"Have you had anything to eat yet? How about the ginger-bread?" Mr. Seward asked.

When Mr. Gossley handed her a plate, she was sure nothing had ever tasted so good. As cloud shadows ran across the blankets, it was easy to imagine that she and Stephen were part of this large family, two more of the children out celebrating their grandfather's birthday.

"Time for presents!" When May called, Stephen and the other children came running. A tower of wrapped packages emerged from the trunk in Mr. Park's arms and, one by one, each present was opened and exclaimed over.

After the last gift was opened, Stephen stepped forward. "Happy birthday, Mr. Seward." Reaching into his pocket, he pulled out the crumpled roll of paper. He took Mr. Seward's freckled hand in his own small one and pressed the paper into his palm. Then he closed the fingers over it so that the paper wouldn't drop and be lost in the grass.

Mr. Seward crinkled his leathery brow. "What's this?"

"Pigeon post! It says, 'Happy Birthday' and it was carried by a real pigeon named Gabriel."

"Pigeon post, eh, delivered by an angel?" Mr. Seward roared with laughter. Tears stood out in his sightless eyes. "I have never had a birthday greeting delivered by a bird before. Thank you very much."

"And speaking of birds—" Howie's lips twitched. "I've got the very thing for you!" He pulled the towel off from the cage and swung the bird up as high as his head. This made the mynah squawk and whistle. "Give me a kiss!" The cousins shrieked with delight.

"Is that my grandson asking for a kiss from his grandfather?"

Howie turned red. "No, sir, it's a mynah bird that wants kissing."

"Then kiss the bird, son. Kiss the bird!"

"Kiss the bird!" everyone cheered.

Howie shrugged his shoulders and made a mock bow. He leaned in to the cage and made a loud kissing noise.

The bird squawked, "Attack! Attack!" The audience clapped and shouted. Howie set the cage on Mr. Seward's lap.

Mr. Seward wrinkled his nose. "Smells like birdseed. Never expected I'd have a talking animal living in my house."

But Elaine could tell he was pleased.

May lit candles on a three-layer red velvet cake, but the wind had drifted in from the bay and blew them out each time. So they sang "Happy Birthday" without candles. Elaine waited until the talk turned to the annual croquet game before she dared approach Mr. Seward.

"I have something for you too," she said. "It's not very good, only something I wrote myself."

"Let's hear it then."

Elaine unfolded the paper she'd kept in her pocket all morning. In a small voice she began to read the poem. It was the first time she'd ever read anything she wrote out loud to someone else.

Mr. Seward listened with his eyes closed. When she had finished, he was quiet for a few seconds. Elaine was sure she'd made a fool of herself. What had she been thinking? She wasn't a poet.

Mr. Seward cleared his throat. "I think it the nicest birthday present I have ever received. Thank you. I suppose you will give me a copy of it, even if I can't read it myself?"

"Really?" Elaine blinked back tears. "I know I'm not a real poet."

"Really."

She refolded the poem and put it in Mr. Seward's freckled hand. "Here you go."

He tucked the poem into the pocket of his tweed coat. "I will keep this close, Elaine."

With those words it felt as if Mr. Seward had crossed a line from employer to friend. Someone she could count on.

"Come on, Lainey! It's time for croquet!" Stephen was at her elbow holding a wooden mallet.

"Yes, come on! You're on our team." Howie was right behind holding two mallets, extending one in her direction.

"But I don't know how to play."

"What, you've never played croquet?" Howie swiveled his head from Elaine to Stephen. "Well, you'll both have to learn, and fast—I hate to lose."

Chapter Thirty-Two

IN THE BRAMBLES

BROOKLYN, NEW YORK—SEPTEMBER 1919

ELAINE

The leaves rustled in the chestnut trees, and shadows swept more quickly across the lawn now. Shivering, Elaine was glad for a chance to move. Stephen had eagerly grabbed a mallet and with a satisfying *thunk* struck a wooden ball. If only she could be more like her brother, less interested in what people thought of her.

Mr. Parks captained their team and proved to be a more patient teacher than Howie, who was only as helpful as suited his mood. The rest of the time he was in constant motion, giving advice, running between the players, his face a signpost for his team's status.

When Elaine had whacked her ball through the third wicket, it rolled into Howie's ten-year-old cousin Laurie's and stopped.

"Too bad I'm going to send you away!" Gleefully, Laurie put her small foot on her ball and smacked it against Elaine's with all her might.

Elaine's ball shot to the side, and following a dip in the lawn, rolled down a ravine into a thicket of barberry bushes. She groaned. She was already well behind the rest of her team. Elaine ran down the slope, and as she pushed the spiny branches aside, their small, round leaves fluttered to the ground around her like tiny red wings. The yellow ball was just beyond her reach. Maybe if she got down on her hands and knees and used her mallet to increase the length of her arm . . .

"Need some help?"

Elaine turned at the sound of Howie's voice. "Yes, please! I can't quite reach it."

"Allow me." He crouched down and crawled sideways into the bushes, snagging the ball with one long reach.

Elaine brushed the hair from her face. "Thanks. I'm so far behind the others—" She grabbed for the ball, but Howie pulled it away.

"It's going to cost you, you know." His eyes laughed at her. Red leaves glittered in his hair.

"What do you mean?" There was a strange catch in her voice.

He pinned her in place with his eyes. Her pulse sped, as if she'd been running. A rush of heat.

He moved closer.

"A kiss. I think that's a fair price." He kept the ball slightly beyond her reach. "I've been thinking about it all day. Every time I look at you."

It wasn't that she hadn't imagined kissing him, especially nights in her small bed on Steuben Street while she lay awake listening for Pop to come home. But now panic seized her. Should she protest? Was that expected?

Stepping forward again, Howard slipped one hand behind her head. "Come here." He drew her toward him, all the while looking straight into her eyes.

The ground dropped away. Even though his eyes made her dizzy, she couldn't look away, even when his face drew so close that everything blurred except one tiny red leaf caught in a curl right above his eyebrow. His lips were softer than she expected and slightly salty. Elaine closed her eyes and let her head rest in his hand.

In the stories she read, girls swooned when they were kissed. This didn't happen. Even with her eyes closed, her mind kept working. She smelled his cologne, spicy and sharp, felt the warmth of his breath and the slight stubble of his cheek as it moved against hers. Were his eyes open? Was she doing it right, this kissing thing she had read about?

Howard pressed closer, and her thoughts broke apart. She was one large nerve ending, breathing hard and fast. One hand tangled in her hair, the other ran down her neck. Elaine pushed away.

Howie laughed and handed her the croquet ball. "Your ball, Madam."

Not daring to look him in the eye, Elaine reached out and took it.

"Come on. They'll be wondering where we are." And he grabbed her hand, pulling her up the ravine, back into the circle of the party, and left her beside his mother.

May continued talking to Great Aunt Myra. No one looked at Elaine, even though she was sure her face was changed. With both hands she smoothed her hair, ran a finger across her lips. Overhead, boiling clouds turned the sky the color of wet cement. A few fat drops sent the picnickers gathering blankets and baskets.

Elaine searched for Stephen while her thoughts churned. As they hurried to the cars, she looked for Howard, but he had disappeared into the crowd.

The drops of rain had only been a stutter. For now, the sky held back. Nevertheless, Mr. Parks spread blankets over them as they got into the Nash. This time Stephen slid into the car first, leaving Elaine against the door. At the last minute, Howard appeared and climbed in on the other side of Stephen. He didn't look at her.

"Perhaps we should drive you two straight home if it's going to rain." May drew her blanket up closer.

"No, we'll be fine. I promised my father I'd stop by the market for bread on the way home," she lied. She didn't want Howie or his mother to see where they lived.

"Lainey—" Stephen began, but she jabbed him sharply with her elbow.

May hesitated. "Well, if you're sure."

"Really, I'm sure. Thank you so much for inviting us." Elaine found she could keep up a conversation while thinking about something entirely different. She wondered if Howie was thinking about her. He didn't seem to be. Leaning over the front seat, he talked baseball with Mr. Parks. What were the odds the Yankees would beat the Athletics, and would the Reds or the White Sox win the World Series? Elaine noticed every detail. Howie's red birthmark now brighter in the cold, his eyelashes long, like a girl's. Would everything be different between them now?

By the time they reached Clinton Avenue, Stephen was asleep on her shoulder. She shook him awake. And once they were out of the car, Howie disappeared. Mr. Seward came back to their car on Mr. Gossley's arm to thank both Elaine and Stephen for attending his party. Elaine walked away from the house as slowly as she could, with Stephen whining that he was cold. Moments later, fat drops pelted down.

They were halfway down the block when she heard footsteps behind. She turned at her name.

Howard winked. "See you." Then he turned and jogged back toward his house.

Elaine stood for a moment in the rain, while Stephen tugged at her arm. A strange new warmth spread through her body. She began to hum.

There were no lights on in the flat when they arrived home. There was no fire in the stove, no sign that Pop had been home at all. Elaine shivered. Her dress stuck to her skin and water squelched in her shoes.

"I'm hungry!" Stephen's voice sliced through her head.

"You had food all day at the picnic! I'm going to change my clothes."

"Where's Pop?"

Hands on hips, she looked her brother over. Rain had plastered his hair to his head and the tips of his ears were red with cold. There was almost no food in the house and no warm water. She didn't want to deal with this now. She went into the bathroom and grabbed a towel. "Dry yourself off!" Then she slammed the bedroom door.

In the chilly room, she peeled off her wet dress and stockings and draped them over the metal headboard. A draft rattled the window and crept in over the sill. Teeth chattering, she pulled on a sweater and her heavy brown skirt. Then she sat down on the bed and stared into the dark. She'd have to make sure Stephen did his homework. The next day was Monday, and she'd have to be at work herself. But Howard would be waiting for her. There was still a pile of dirty clothes on the floor and dishes in the sink, which meant she'd have to heat water before she did anything else. Instead, she pulled *Hansel and Gretel* from under her bed. She'd read to herself for a few minutes. It would make up for returning to her black-and-white world, where she only subsisted until she was at the Gossleys' again.

—◦═◉─◦─◉═◦—

The candy house shimmered in the moonlight. Gretel took the first bite. She was so hungry, and the house looked so delectable. She reached up toward a sugar pane window and broke off a piece of the red licorice trim. Following her lead, Hansel cracked off a gingerbread shingle. Soon their mouths were bulging with the unexpected delight. But it wasn't long until the chocolate door swung open and an aged woman poked her head out. "Nibble, nibble, little mouse, who is nibbling at my house?" Gretel couldn't speak, as her mouth was full of sugar. She tried to rub her sticky fingers clean on her skirt. Hansel looked at his own chocolate-stained hands. "We have been lost in the woods and without food for a day and a night."

"Then you must come in and rest yourselves," the old woman offered. Above them, the owl in the tree hooted, spread wide wings, and sailed off deeper into the woods. The children, filled with sweets and the promise of warmth, followed the old woman into her house, where a fire burned merrily. They never heard the chocolate door slam shut.

Chapter Thirty-Three

THE MIRACLE BOY

SAN JOSE, CALIFORNIA—AUGUST 1955

Molly

"Explain to me again why we're doing this." Mom looked at her mouth in a compact mirror and blotted her cherry lipstick.

"You know why. The Craters have invited us to dinner as a way of saying thanks," Uncle Stephen said.

All four of us were sweating in Uncle Stephen's car. I wanted the windows rolled down, but Mom was afraid it would mess her hair. We compromised—two windows down, two up. We were going to have dinner with Robert the miracle boy and his family. I wondered how someone who had received a miracle would look. Would there be any signs of the miraculous?

It had been a very long time since we'd had dinner at anyone's house. Mom had actually dressed up for the occasion, twisting her hair into something French at the nape of her neck. Her gardenia perfume bloomed in the heat. Nothing could ever make Uncle Stephen look dressed up. Clothes wilted the minute they touched his body; the crispest shirt collapsed to wrinkles.

Every time we left the house, we snuck out through the garage or the backyard. Once we were in the car, we were separated from the pleas of the faithful remnant in front of the house. As Uncle Stephen backed out of the driveway, I'd stared straight ahead, not wanting to make eye contact with so much hope and devotion.

The Craters lived in a big house with a real front porch, and Uncle Stephen had told us they had two other children besides Robert. Mr. Crater met us on the porch with a baby boy in his arms. He was a big man—all muscle—and he carried his son like a football.

"Hello. Hello. So glad you could come." He nodded to all of us. "This is Roger. He's nine months old today, and this is Richard." A boy of about four or five with bright white hair wandered out. His hair was so startling that I stared for a moment or two longer than was polite.

"Hi." He looked at us and then stuck a thumb in his mouth. I was thinking *Roger, Richard, Robert.*

"Take your thumb out, Richard. Big boys don't suck their thumbs." Mr. Crater looked annoyed. Richard obediently removed his thumb, wiping it across his stomach.

Inside, the heat-saturated air was cooler. A large ceiling fan spun in lazy circles. Mrs. Crater bustled out from the kitchen, wiping her hands on her apron, and we did the whole hand shaking routine again. She was a small, birdlike woman with the same white-blond hair as her son's, cut close to her head. In her case, it reminded me of feathers on a newly hatched chick.

I was wondering where Robert was when a thin boy about my age came down the stairs. You could tell he was part of the family by looking at the white stubble that was filling in on his head like a newly seeded lawn.

It is difficult to search a face for signs of a miracle. I didn't really know what I was looking for. But it seemed to me that the miraculous should leave fingerprints; a face would never look the same. Robert Crater's face was beautiful. Perhaps it had always been that way. Perhaps it was the miracle. His skin and hair were so pale they reflected light, and his eyes were a lighter blue than the sky. I suddenly was aware that my own hair was sweaty and stuck to my head, and last year's skirt too short.

Mrs. Crater had made an impressive meal of pot roast and potatoes, Jell-O with slices of mandarin orange, and chocolate cake for dessert. Even in their cool house, it was almost ' too hot to eat, but we kept passing the dishes around anyway and smiling politely. I stole glances at Robert across the table. When I glanced up, his eyes would skitter away.

At the end of the meal, the children were excused to go play. Angus immediately leapt up to join the middle R, but Robert and I stayed at the table, too old to be included in the definition of children, too young to be included in all the conversation.

"Things have been different around here since the miracle." Mr. Crater leaned in when he spoke as if we were part of a conspiracy. Mrs. Crater, with the littlest R now on her lap, nodded. "I hadn't gone to church in years, but you can bet I'm there every Sunday now. This boy is destined for great things. That's why God spared him."

A faint blush was starting to spread up Robert's neck.

"I tell everyone that my son was spared by a miracle."

Uncle Stephen cleared his throat as if he was about to speak, but Mr. Crater kept going. "I call it bearing witness."

"We can't even begin to tell you how grateful we are." Mrs. Crater's blue eyes filled with tears.

"But it really wasn't me."

Mr. Crater cut right through Uncle Stephen's words. "Of course it wasn't you. God has set aside our son for a special purpose. And you won't let us down, son, will you?"

By now, the flush had spread to Robert's face and his ears. I hadn't noticed his neat, flat ears before, but now they were a most unbecoming shade of purple. I was suddenly glad that I was not a miracle recipient. Mom looked uncomfortable too. In fact, she looked like she was winding up to say something. I had to cut her off.

"Did it hurt?" All eyes at the table turned my direction. I sank down into myself. "Being cured, I mean." This time my voice was almost a whisper.

"No, my head felt strange—warm all over." Robert looked at me, embarrassed.

"To whom much is given, much is expected, eh? Remember that, son." Mr. Crater turned back to Uncle Stephen. "We've taken out a life insurance policy on him."

"What we were wondering," Mrs. Crater chirped up, "is what you think we should do with him. We need to protect Robert for God's purposes. I've been keeping him in so that nothing can happen to him."

The words that had been building up in Mom finally burst out like steam from a kettle. "That's the most ridiculous thing I've ever heard! This boy has been protected from one thing or another his whole life! When does he ever get to be a boy?"

Now everyone at the table was staring at her. Mrs. Crater's mouth was opening and closing like a goldfish's. Robert's eyes were circles of surprise, but he was smiling his angelic smile.

Uncle Stephen stepped in to smooth things out. "I'm sure God has his reasons for healing Robert. We don't always know what they are. He may be called to do amazing things, but I don't think growing up as a normal boy would stop that."

Mr. Crater shook his huge head slowly from side to side. "He is holy ground, Mr. Fitzgerald, holy ground. I thought you, as a miracle worker, would understand this."

Uncle Stephen tried a different tack. "Well, let's take Jesus for an example. He was the holiest man that ever lived, and God did mighty things through him."

"Amen." Mr. Crater nodded his head this time.

"But he grew up like a normal boy, helping out in a carpenter's shop."

I looked across at Robert and thought I spied a gleam of hope in his eyes. This boy was desperate.

"Maybe Robert can come over to our house sometimes and hang out with Angus and me."

Mom drew her penciled eyebrows together so tightly that they made a bridge over her nose.

"Why, that would be nice." Mrs. Crater smiled and wiped some drool off little R's chin. "It must be someplace where he's safe, where folks understand Robert's situation with God."

"That poor boy," was the first thing Mom said when we got in the car to go home. "To have parents like that." She clucked her tongue.

"Miracles can do funny things to people," Uncle Stephen agreed.

"Oh, it wasn't the miracle," said Mom. "It's them—pretending they have a direct line to God. In my experience, he's too busy to answer the phone."

Chapter Thirty-Four

THE RIVER

BROOKLYN, NEW YORK—OCTOBER 1919

ELAINE

Monday morning the sky was a grimace, waiting for sleet—a preview of winter. Overnight the temperature had dropped to hover at that point just above freezing, too cold for pleasure, too warm for snow, the point where all of Brooklyn shivered for most of the winter. Elaine's mind had insisted on chattering most of the night. And now, barely awake, it began again with questions about Howard. It had been a week since the picnic, and she hadn't seen him once.

She dragged the covers off a sleeping Stephen, and then checked for what she already knew in her heart. Pop had not come in during the night. Maybe he slept somewhere else last night and was drinking his tea in Tim Meeks's kitchen, ready to hurry off to his job.

After heating the tea water, she called Stephen to hurry up and then climbed on a chair to get down the sugar jar, a place to keep her pay where Pop wouldn't look. Two dollars and twenty-five cents left. Bread, milk, and eggs for the week. When she got paid again, she'd have to decide whether to put the money toward rent or food. Slipping the money into the pocket of her skirt, she finished dishing up the sticky oatmeal.

After seeing Stephen off to school, she headed south along Myrtle to Clinton as businesses opened for the day. Wind tugged her umbrella and bit at her cheeks. Her stomach curled at a whiff of coffee brewing and the scent of chocolate from the Rockwood factory.

She'd taken special care with her hair that morning, twisting it into a bun as she recalled the feel of Howie's hands on the back her of neck. With her hair up, she could easily pass for sixteen, even when the damp air made tendrils curl and frizz around her face.

As she walked, her thoughts fell in rhythm with the tap of her shoes. Pop and Howie, Howie and Pop. Pop had been gone this long before; he'd always appear again as if nothing had happened. But now with his job at Drake Brothers, there was more to lose. Was he still showing up for work?

When she was little, he was the only one who could comfort her. He sang and made up stories, carried her on his shoulders to the market, and brought home candy in his pockets. But sometime after Stephen was born, when her mother was having miscarriage after miscarriage, he changed, stopping off for a nightcap on the way home. When Claire and her mother died, it was as if the last strings holding him to them were cut. Where was Claire now? Aunt Agnes said babies who weren't baptized got stuck in a place called purgatory. They had to be prayed out. If Claire's escape depended on Elaine's prayers, her little sister was still in that gray, forsaken place, wailing for her mother. Guilt settled on her shoulders. Who else remembered to pray for her baby sister?

And then Elaine was on the Gossleys' back porch, heart galloping out of control. Howie was probably waiting to see her before he left for school. Would he kiss her again, right in the kitchen? If he did, she'd kiss him back, right in front of everyone. With a deep breath, she closed her umbrella, gave it a shake, and walked in. The scent of fresh-baked rolls enveloped her.

"Go ahead and take one." Kay nodded her head at the pans lining the table. "You look like you haven't slept a wink."

Elaine gratefully closed her hand around one of the warm rolls as she listened for Howie's clatter in the hall. But the house was strangely quiet.

"Mrs. Gossley's down with a cold and Mr. Howie's already off to school." She shot Elaine a quick look that Elaine chose not to interpret. "Go on in. Mr. Seward's expecting you."

A weight dropped from nowhere onto her chest. She was tired. Her throat felt sore. It didn't matter; she'd see him at lunch. She rapped on the door to the morning room. When there was no answer, she walked in. Mr. Seward sat with his feet up, his head thrown back, mouth open. The newspapers were piled, as usual, on the table next to the silver teapot and two empty cups.

Quietly, Elaine unwrapped her shawl, pulled up a chair, and poured herself a cup of tea. Mr. Seward's breathing was regular and deep. She reached for the *Herald Tribune*, took a bite of roll, and chased it with a sip of tea. The steel worker's strike had turned violent. Police in Pennsylvania had clubbed down hundreds of the striking workers. She flipped through the other papers. Every headline had something to do with the steel workers' strike. What would it be like to want something so badly that you'd be willing to be beaten for it? She chewed thoughtfully, tallying the things she wanted. She wanted a family again, for Pop to come home and take care of them; she wanted to go back to school; to live in a house like the Gossleys'; and to do something important with her life. Her odds were even greater than the steel workers'. She also wanted Howard to kiss her again. This time she'd be ready.

An hour passed, and Mr. Seward still slept. May hadn't

appeared and given her any work to do. Elaine wandered into the kitchen.

"It doesn't look like there's much for you to do today. Perhaps you should head home. I'm sure Mrs. Gossley won't mind."

If she left now, she'd miss her chance to see Howie at lunch. He'd probably get there early since he missed her this morning. "Is there anything I can help you with?"

"I wouldn't say no to having you peel some apples. I'm making applesauce this afternoon when the baking's done."

For the rest of the morning she peeled the grainy skins from green apples. If she was careful, she could undress the apple with one long curl like a snake shedding its skin. Elaine inhaled the routine of the kitchen.

Noon came and went. No sign of Howie. The box of apples was empty. Three bowls overflowed with their shed skins. Through the steamy window, she could see the back walk bordered by golden trees. Each day more gold spilled to the ground. Soon the branches would be bare. Where was he? Maybe he had extra work to do, a test to study for. Maybe he'd gotten into trouble again. Elaine turned over his words. *I've been thinking about it all day. Every time I look at you.*

Kay returned to the kitchen with Mrs. Gossley's lunch tray. "You've been a great help to me today. Mrs. Gossley says to take the afternoon off, but be back tomorrow." She cut two thick slices of warm dark bread and spread them with butter and honey. "A little something for the walk home, and take some of the chicken left over from the picnic. I'm sure that brother of yours is hungry." She handed Elaine a plump bag of fried chicken. "Now, shoo. Go enjoy yourself."

That was how Elaine found herself walking down Clinton Street at one thirty on a chilly Monday afternoon. The sleet had stopped, and the umbrella hung from one hand, her bag of food from the other. After the holidays she hoped to try school again like Mrs. Gossley suggested. But that depended on Pop. For now, she had an entire afternoon to herself, a bag of chicken for dinner, and no one depending on her. Her feet led her toward the river.

The Brooklyn Navy Yard covered much of the banks of the East River in the Wallabout Basin. But to the north of the Yard, there were muddy paths that all the children knew. Here eager swimmers made their way to the river's edge when the heat and humidity of summer became unbearable. Elaine followed one of these, through weeds and brambles, to the riverbank.

Today, thick tongues of fog unfurled, lapping at the water of the East River. Across the river, Manhattan was only a moving shadow. To the north, the Williamsburg Bridge connected the two worlds, the largest suspension bridge on earth. Elaine remembered her parents' stories of fireworks lighting up the night sky in the middle of December, when the bridge had opened in 1903, a year before she was born. She had never crossed the bridge to that other world beyond Brooklyn.

To the south, she could see the steel girders of the Manhattan Bridge fade into white. The river damp enclosed her, made her teeth chatter, yet she lingered, straining into the mist. It was as if she was called by a voice just beyond hearing, just out of reach. There wasn't a name for this longing. It was an ache composed of sadness and hope, as real but as insubstantial as the fog. It was easy to believe that the far bank was an illusion, that life in Brooklyn was all there was. But, if she stared hard enough, she could see the ghosts of buildings and trees, a rumor of life beyond what she knew. By now, the dampness had reached her bones; her whole body shook. She turned from the river, and with the wind and fog at her back trudged the long blocks home.

There would be time today, before Stephen came bursting through the door, to do some laundry, but instead, after she heated water for tea, Elaine opened the Hansel and Gretel book. She could hear the shuffling of the forest. Trees with faces and gnarled limbs peered from the pages. While she traced the intricate lines of bark, Stephen charged through the door looking for food.

Dark was coming earlier now. Elaine had saved the surprise of chicken for a special dinner. She laid out enough for Pop, hoping he'd come whistling in and tell them stories of the day's work at Drake Brothers. She even made Stephen wait until six o'clock, the time they had always eaten dinner when her mother was alive. It would be right after Claire was fed and rocked to sleep. However, six o'clock came and went without Pop. Elaine served up the warmed chicken with potatoes and bread. As they chewed, Elaine though about the fact that if they kept only the front room heated, they could move the beds in there, saving some money.

Rain tapped the window. Elaine's eyes slipped shut while Stephen talked. Did Howard miss her? Was he looking out the window right now at the same rain and wondering what she was doing? A pounding on the door jolted her fully alert.

"Maybe it's Pop?" Stephen looked hopefully at the door.

"Why would he knock at his own door?" But the same flutter of hope stirred inside her like an animal awoken from sleep. They rarely had visitors at all. Cautiously, she opened the door an inch or two. Mr. Meeks, hat in hand, stood on the landing.

"Come in." Elaine swung the door open wider, hoping to see Pop right behind him. But Mr. Meeks came in by himself, reeking of whiskey as he brushed past.

"I've got some hard news." He looked at the ground rather than at Elaine or Stephen. His scrawny shoulders were hunched as if he were bearing a burden too heavy for him. "Your father was injured. They took him to the Brooklyn Hospital."

A chill, like the river fog, seeped into Elaine. She began to tremble. "What happened to him?" she asked as she grabbed her shawl from the back of the chair.

Mr. Meeks twisted his hat and shrank further into himself. "There was this fight, see, down at Clancy's. Some sons of mothers hit him over the head with a chair and he went down hard."

Stephen began to whimper.

"Can you take us to him?" Elaine had never been to the Brooklyn Hospital before, but she knew it was near Fort Greene Park, where they'd had the picnic.

"It's this way, see. I was coming to get both of youse yesterday, but that blow to his head was bad, and I wasn't feeling too good myself, and the thing is"—he collapsed with a thud on one of the wooden chairs—"he's gone and died."

For a moment there was only silence. Elaine looked at the small man slumped in the chair. His words made no sense. She wanted to shake him. Pop was late or on a binge.

She felt as if her head would explode.

"Lainey? Lainey?" Stephen's voice was a sledgehammer.

She couldn't think. "Stephen, shut up!"

Startled into silence, Stephen gulped and wiped at his nose.

"The police took up a collection to get you through." Meeks reached into his pocket and brought out a roll of bills and set them carefully on the table. "And don't worry none about the hospital bill; they took him as a charity case."

Her pulse pounded in her head. "Why did the police give us this money?"

Mr. Meeks looked away.

"What happened?"

His watery eyes circled back to her, blue pouches underneath, tender as bruises.

"He was a stoolie. That's why they let him out the last time he was in. Some of the guys found out."

A stool pigeon? Pop?

"And they'll take care of the body for you. It might be best—"

"Pop's no snitch!" Stephen kicked at Mr. Meeks's shin, and missed.

Elaine's stomach was a cold sea. Pop was gone. What did it matter what he'd done? Where would they go? Who would take care of them?

"I suppose you got relatives to take you in?" Meeks asked hopefully, sidling toward the door.

Relatives? One aunt dead, another married and moved to the Midwest, and her aunt Flo with kids of her own and no husband. She wanted to wail like Stephen, to lie down on the floor and sob. They'd manage; they'd been managing all along. She eyed the roll of bills. How much was there? The important thing was to take care of Stephen. She needed to make this man go away before he asked any more questions.

"Well, if there's nothing more . . . he was a fine gentleman, your father. Wanted to help the law." As he talked, he inched closer to the door.

Elaine, feeling like it was someone else's hand, reached out and opened the door. Someone else's words flowed out of her mouth. "Thank you. We'll be fine. Yes, I'll get in touch with my aunt." Then she closed the door, drew Stephen on her lap like her mother used to do, and, dry-eyed, began to plan their future.

Chapter Thirty-Five

SET APART

SAN JOSE, CALIFORNIA—AUGUST 1955

Molly

The first time Robert came to our house, I kept a close watch on him to see if he really was a different kind of species, a miracle boy.

He had an elusive air about him that made him seem apart. And it was his very elusiveness I found intriguing at first.

Apparently, Robert had been asking to come ever since we had dinner at their house. Mom had agreed, somewhat reluctantly, I thought, especially when she heard Uncle Stephen would be at an all-day teacher meeting to prepare for the coming school year.

I knew Robert would have to cross the front lawn, where a handful of the faithful still lingered. Angus and I watched from the window as an old man reached out to touch his arm as he walked the path to our front door. Robert smiled. He didn't pull away like I would have.

Angus and I had barely begun one of our perpetual summer Monopoly games. These games could last for days, the board left open on our kitchen table, and usually involved Ari and several other friends. But I hadn't heard from Ari or any of my friends since the news of the miracle broke. I wondered how long I'd be ostracized. With a pang, I thought about Jesse's words. *Boys don't like girls who are different.* Apparently, friends didn't either.

Robert was thrilled to join in our Monopoly game. He claimed the shoe and began amassing property as quickly as he could. One thing I liked about him right away was that he played the game like Angus and I did—to win. I had no time for people who played a half-hearted game. I threw in everything I had each time, and then tried not to feel too bad if I didn't win. But I never managed not to care.

Angus had added his final hotels to Park Place when Mom appeared in the kitchen doorway. She leaned against the door jamb without speaking for a few minutes, watching us play. A newspaper ad for back-to-school specials at Sears dangled from one hand.

"What happened to your report card?"

All three of us turned to look at her. My stomach clenched.

"It's August. It should have been here months ago. I'm calling the school tomorrow."

"No one will be there," I said.

"Then I'm calling Mr. Pedersen at home."

My whole body began to vibrate. There was going to be no easy way out of this. "You can't call the principal at home. He isn't the one who sends out the report cards."

She straightened up. "It's his school and he should be responsible for what's happening or not happening in it."

The problem was, I knew she would do it. Angus was counting money and Robert was reading something in the rule book. Neither of them felt the warning tremors.

"Don't call anyone. I have it."

"Then why haven't I seen it? Since when have you become the kind of person who keeps secrets?"

The color was rising in her cheeks. Angus and Robert both looked up.

"What secrets?" Angus asked.

Mom ignored him and kept her eyes glued to me.

"I learned from you!" Something was unspooling inside me. "And why are you asking now? Any other mother would have asked two months ago."

She took a step forward. "Don't try and make this about me. Did you or did you not hide your report card from me?"

I glared at her, noticing how when she was really mad, the area around her lips went white.

"I want to see it now."

Angus and Robert looked at each other. Without a word, they both got up and left.

"Fine." We locked eyes. There was no escape now.

I stood and stalked into my bedroom. Flinging open the closet door, I burrowed behind my clothes to the back shelf. The envelope was lying unopened next to the biography box. I dumped the box on the floor and the Polaroids scattered with the dust bunnies. Let her figure out her own life. Tears pricked my eyes.

She was waiting outside my bedroom door. I handed her the unopened envelope. She ripped it open with one finger.

"You're grounded."

"I might as well be already. No one wants to come here with all the crazies in the front yard." I couldn't stop myself. "People already thought we were strange. Uncle Stephen didn't have to prove it to them!"

She pulled out the report card. I knew there was only one grade that mattered to her.

"You got a C in English." Her voice sounded incredulous. "There's a note from your teacher. She says that you had an A, but you didn't turn in the final project."

Her eyes met mine.

I didn't say anything.

"I'm waiting for an explanation."

"It wasn't good enough. I learned that from you. If it's not perfect, it doesn't count. That's why we don't count."

"Is that what you think? I want you to be perfect?"

Tears were leaking down my cheeks now. I scrubbed them away with the heel of my hand.

She let her hand drop, reached out to touch me, and then drew her hand back. "I only want you to be better than me."

"I'll never be better than you."

For a moment we locked eyes. Hers were soft now, softer than her words.

"Oh, Molly, you already are."

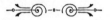

The fire burned bright inside the candy house, and the old woman bade them sit at the table and eat their fill. Hansel and Gretel could hardly believe their good fortune. All the while the old woman watched them with her flint-hard eyes. They could do with a bit of fattening up. She fed them tender lies. How easily they slipped down the children's throats. Then she gave them soft beds with real feather mattresses and tucked them safely in.

The round moon crouched by the window, guarding the children while they slept. An owl hooted in the dark. Perhaps tomorrow or the next day, it would show them the path home.

Chapter Thirty-Six

ORPHAN

BROOKLYN, NEW YORK—OCTOBER 1919

ELAINE

Every night at dusk that first week after Pop died, Elaine found herself listening for his whistle on the stairs to their flat. Some days she was sure she heard it; the door would burst open and he would saunter in. She pictured them sitting around the dinner table while he told stories about trying to tame Harry Ames's cantankerous horse. Then she'd tell him how hard it was trying to figure everything out by herself, and she'd ask him what to do next. He'd tell her not to worry because he had a plan and would take care of everything. But it had never been that way.

Orphan was an ugly word. Hollow and cold on the tongue, like a bone with all the marrow sucked out. Now, like Hansel and Gretel, they were alone. And the woods felt dark and treacherous.

There had been no service for Pop, but Elaine had agreed, when Tim Meeks asked, to put him in the same grave with her mother and baby Claire. A grave she hadn't visited in the last six months, but one that was always there, imprinted on her eyelids.

On Saturday, Elaine walked with Stephen to his first altar boy class and shopped for food while he was busy. Then, in the gathering dark, they walked home.

"Remember that you don't say anything about Pop to anyone—not at the church, not at school."

"I know." Stephen kicked a stone for several steps. "When Father Kearny asked, I said Pop was working overtime. Mom wouldn't like me lying to a priest." The rest of the way home, he told Elaine about everything he learned.

She nodded as he talked, but her thoughts were elsewhere, planning how to make it through the next week and the week after that. Her mind could never rest. At night she lay awake thinking about their future. How long could they escape notice? She'd told May that it would be easier to start school in January, after the holidays, and that she was studying to catch up with her class. That bought her a little time without questioning.

Their rent had gone from fifteen to twenty dollars over the last six months. All over Brooklyn, rents had skyrocketed. The newspapers were filled with stories of renter strikes. Mr. Seward called the landlords profiteers, but said the Socialists were no better, trying to gain political office off people's misery. All Elaine knew was that her salary alone wouldn't be enough. She'd have to take in sewing on the weekends, and maybe Stephen could get a delivery job after school.

Most of the time she thought about Howie. May said he was in the middle of midterm exams and very busy. When Elaine couldn't sleep, she pretended she was part of the Gossley family, wore new dresses, and went to school every day riding in a fine car. And thinking about these things helped her mind drift into a more comfortable place where sleep was a possibility, unless she thought about the kiss. Then she lay awake staring into the dark, wondering if it would happen again. And if she wanted it to. Now every time they met, however briefly, the kiss hovered between them like a tiny moth Elaine couldn't ignore but was powerless to capture.

After Howie passed his exams, the Gossleys talked about college. Howie wanted to be an architect and design skyscrapers like his uncle Sherman. His father's brother had an office in Manhattan, and he'd invited Howie to visit him for a day to see what an architect really did. Ever since, Howie could talk of nothing else. He was coming home for lunch more frequently again, and Elaine looked forward to their short times together, but the moth was always there, always a distraction.

"Come keep me company while I eat, Princess." Howie poked his head into the morning room where Elaine and Mr. Seward had just finished the papers.

"Can I?" Elaine looked up at Mr. Seward, who merely grunted in response. Elaine took that as an affirmative and left the room to the mynah's calls of "Retreat! Retreat!"

"There's a dance at school next week," Howie said with his mouth full of soup. "None of the girls are as pretty as you."

Elaine looked down at her bowl. She didn't want him to see her smile.

"I suppose I'll have to go. When are you going back to school?"

Tucking the smile away, she looked up. Her answer would have to be careful. "Maybe in the spring, but I hear it's better to start in the fall. That way you're with the rest of the class."

"But you'll be a whole year behind then." He wrinkled his brow. "Maybe I could keep you caught up."

"Would you? I like to study. I wouldn't be much trouble to teach."

"I bet you wouldn't. Who wouldn't want a pupil with as many fine points as you have?"

This time Elaine was not quick enough to disguise her blush.

Howard laughed. "But in exchange, I want some information. What did you give my grandfather for his birthday that made him so pleased?"

"It was nothing." Had Mr. Seward shown it to anyone?

"*Nothing* wouldn't make him so happy. He liked it way better than the mynah." Howie caught her arm. "What was it?"

"Nothing much. A poem I wrote."

"A poem? The old man got all worked up about a poem?" Howie studied her face and dropped her arm. "You'll have to recite it to me sometime." His smile this time didn't reach his eyes.

The next afternoon, he arrived at lunch with a math book and dropped it on the table. "Show me what you know."

Elaine slowly opened it. "It's been a long time since I've done sums, but I used to be good at them." What if she'd forgotten how? The problems blurred and swam on the page. When the text settled, she realized the book was just a little ahead of where she'd left off in school.

"I think I can do these." She pointed to the first problem set in the book. "And the rest with some practice."

"Right, then. Have them done by Thursday, and I'll check your answers." He grabbed some bread, then gathered up his coat and cap.

Elaine hugged the book to herself. If he didn't care about her, he wouldn't bother tutoring her, would he? And he didn't bring up the poem this time. She breathed a sigh of relief.

Her evening ritual changed. While Stephen did his homework, Elaine puzzled out math problems at the wooden table. Math was like anything else: the more you practiced, the better you got. All that mattered was that Howie became impressed with her progress. Would he ask her to the dance? He'd said none of the other girls were as pretty. When her studying was done, she began to work on remaking one of her mother's dresses, so she'd be ready when he asked.

Meanwhile, missing Pop was a dull ache, nothing like the knife twist of her mother's death. Pop had really left them when their mother died. Any mourning now was for herself and for Stephen, for how life had thrown them a curve ball.

Friday afternoon, as Elaine was leaving for home, Howie surprised her in the Gossleys' entry. In a pinstriped suit with a cherry red tie, Elaine was sure he was the handsomest man she'd ever seen.

"How do I look?"

She cocked her head to one side. "Not bad. Why aren't you at school?"

"Half day, and what do you mean, not bad? Is that all you have to say?" He ran his hands down the legs of his trousers. "I bought these for the dance tomorrow."

Elaine smiled. She'd finished the hem on her dress last night.

"Want to see a picture of the girl I'm taking?" He dug in the pocket of his coat and pulled out an envelope. "Sally Wilson." He drew out a small photo. "Her father's a friend of my old man."

It was uncomfortably still in Elaine's chest. Had her heart stopped beating? She leaned over his arm and stared at a photo of a sweet-faced girl with dark hair cut in the latest bob.

"She's pretty." The words hurt her mouth.

"What color flowers should I get her? Don't all girls like pink?" Howie put the photo back in the envelope and returned it to his pocket.

How could she have been so mistaken? Was he really asking her to pick out flowers for his date?

"You don't know anything about girls. Not all girls like the same things. If you paid more attention to anything but their looks, you'd know that!"

"No need to go for a full attack. I merely asked a simple question." He smoothed his hair in the entryway mirror. "We won't be able to study today. I've got to clean the car if I want to take it tomorrow."

"I have other plans anyway," Elaine lied.

"Oh, you do, do you?" Howie looked at her quizzically, but when Elaine didn't say anything more, he shrugged. "Well, I'll see you Monday for geometry."

Howard still loitered in the entry. Elaine pictured him with Sally. Her chest ached.

"You're an idiot, Howard Gossley!" She yanked open the front door.

"Girls," he said. "Never understand them."

Chapter Thirty-Seven

WINGS

SAN JOSE, CALIFORNIA—AUGUST 1955

Molly

The wind had been grinding its teeth all day. It was a wild, warm wind, nothing like I'd ever seen before in a Bay Area summer. It was the kind of wind expected in the fall, a wind to strip the leaves from trees, baring them for winter. But here it was, kicking up its heels in the middle of an August afternoon. Along with the wind, the sky had changed, swelling to a purple bruise. Mom said it reminded her of thunderstorm weather, something we never experienced in San Jose.

I should have known what a strong wind would do to Angus. It was the signal he'd been waiting for all summer. But I had been preoccupied with my own things, and hadn't been thinking about Angus and Robert at all. Robert had arrived around noontime; Mrs. Crater had dropped him off on her way to get her hair done. Just like always, she reminded him of his special status in the eyes of God and man and then kissed him on the cheek before she drove off with a screaming little R in the backseat.

As it turned out, Robert preferred spending time with Angus rather than with me. It didn't seem to bother him that Angus was so much younger. He was enthralled with Angus's bedroom/workshop. I guess his parents didn't let him touch any tools at all, ever.

His preference for Angus didn't bother me. For all his good looks, I found Robert Crater, after an hour or so, kind of boring. He talked about sports, especially baseball—something that held little interest for me—incessantly. As I watched Robert follow Angus, I wondered if the elusiveness came from the fact he had been sick so much of his life, or if he really believed all that stuff his parents told him.

By this time in the summer, there were only a few people in our yard each day. Without anything miraculous happening, I couldn't understand why they bothered to come unless it was to hear Uncle Stephen talk. He was still sleeping on our couch, although he claimed he had a lead on another apartment. He faithfully came out every day and said at least a few words to the people huddled in the bright sun on our front lawn. They were mostly old folks, ladies who always wore headscarves and men with skin as wrinkled as elephant hide. Occasionally, there would be women with babies to be blessed, but they didn't stay long in the relentless sun. Today, with the strange and turbulent weather, there were only three or four people. I was so used to them now that I hardly paid attention. I guess that's why I didn't notice the blue Chevy Bel Air was back in the neighborhood. In its own way, it was one of the faithful hoping for a miracle.

Besides, the world was full of distractions. President Eisenhower had announced last month that we were going to launch satellites to circle around the earth. I wasn't sure what purpose the satellites would serve, but lately Angus was taken by any idea involving flight. For weeks it was all he would talk about. It was a novelty while the miracle began to feel familiar.

Being grounded hadn't changed my life much. I missed my friend's pizza party at the bowling alley, but circumstances being what they were, I might not have gone anyway. Uncle Stephen had finagled Mom into letting me have a small celebration dinner for my birthday. This wasn't how I'd pictured my fifteenth birthday. Dad sent me a new journal and a charm bracelet with a silver book on it, with a promise that before school started he'd take Angus and me to the beach. But the date was vague enough to keep my hopes tamped down.

The backyard was the safest place to be, now that the faithful occupied the front lawn. The grass might be brown and crunchy underfoot, but miraculously, the beheaded flowers had survived. There were new buds on the geraniums. Even the roses bloomed.

When Angus and I were little, on windy days like this we'd take an umbrella outside to see if we could get airborne. I wondered if he was thinking about those days too.

I found Angus and Robert on the back porch laughing together. When they saw me, Angus whispered something to Robert, who shot me a sidelong glance and said something that made Angus double over laughing.

"What's so funny?" The wind slapped my hair against my face.

"Mind your own beeswax!"

I took a step toward Angus, hot words sputtering on my tongue, and then I noticed Robert smirking.

That smirk was the proverbial last straw. I was alienated from my friends. I might never be what Jesse called a "normal" girl, and I was trying to figure out if I cared. Ninety-nine percent of the time, I didn't.

I turned on Robert. "Why are you hanging around with a little kid?"

"I'm not a little kid," Angus said.

Robert stared at me. I stared back.

"Maybe it's because no one else believes you're special," I suggested.

Like the wind, my frustration had whipped into a frenzy. Nothing about this summer was working out the way I'd planned. My classified ad had failed. I was no closer to discovering the secret of Mom's past, and Dad showed no signs of coming back.

"People like you can't understand." Robert's voice was calm, fuel to my fire.

"Then if you're so special, prove it!"

Robert's eyes slid sideways to Angus. He gave a nod, and they both walked inside. It didn't matter; I was glad they were gone. I wanted to be alone.

I decided to check on the little vegetable patch I'd planted early in the spring. As the summer progressed, I'd become increasingly neglectful.

On close inspection, I could see orange and red humps protruding through the tangle of weeds in each row. A few vegetables, despite my neglect, were ready to harvest. I pulled out carrots and radishes, shaking off clumps of dirt, and piled them on the ground. The tomato vines were brown and limp. I could almost hear them gasping in the sun.

A lone crow screamed in the top of the sycamore.

Our backyard was enclosed by a fence of six foot high cedar boards. It was a great relief not to be under observation, or in the house with the drapes closed. The crow swept down and landed on the fence, his feathers askew like a man in an ill-fitting suit. His caw was relentless.

From up above, someone called my name. It sent a shiver down my spine, with all the talk of miracles that summer. I looked up. Two seagulls were spinning in the updrafts, white wings pearlized against the purple sky. Then I heard it again and turned to look behind me. In the empty field behind our house, Angus and Robert perched like two weathervanes on top of the Browns' old barn. They stood at least twenty feet off the ground, and Angus was wearing the wings.

Chapter Thirty-Eight

CHANGE OF PLANS

BROOKLYN, NEW YORK—OCTOBER 1919

ELAINE

It was Saturday afternoon, and Stephen had been pleading with Elaine all day to visit Father Kearny and his pigeons. Soon enough winter would fall upon them, and then pigeon post would be over until spring. After spending the morning sewing, her legs were as restless as her thoughts, so she agreed.

Father Kearny had invited several children from the parish. By the time Elaine and Stephen arrived, the others already stood huddled in the chill wind on the roof. The priest ceremoniously lifted Gabriel from the coop. Elaine, hands buried in her armpits for warmth, pressed close to Stephen. The tips of her nose and ears stung.

Stephen leaned back against her. "Lainey, my head hurts."

"I'm up here freezing to death so you can see your stupid pigeons. Stop complaining or we'll leave right now."

"But it does hurt. You never listen. I wish Pop was here."

"A lot of good he'd do you. Stop being such a baby."

Father Kearny's voice cut through the wind: "We've one last post. I'm sending three of Pete's birds. They'll be flying twenty miles today, and be back by this time tomorrow. I thought some of you might want to write the post."

At least five hands popped up. "Let me! I've never had a chance before."

"It's my turn!"

"We'll let chance settle it. Each of you draw a paper, and the three with the marks on them will get to write this time." He pulled a paper sack out of his coat pocket. Stephen squirmed with anticipation.

The pigeons were not distraction enough for Elaine. Howie was probably buying flowers for Sally right now: pink roses. The cold bit through Elaine's warmest shawl. Stephen would be fine if she climbed down from the roof and waited in the warm church. When the bag was passed her way, she almost didn't take it. But at the last minute, she dipped her hand in and drew out a paper slip. It was marked with an x. Maybe she should give it to Stephen. His slip was blank. But the image of her words being carried through the sky caught her.

She looked out over Brooklyn. Today was her birthday, and she'd never felt so alone. Below, some of the trees had lost their leaves, but others flamed scarlet in the late afternoon light. For a moment the lowering sun turned the East River to gold. Elaine knew what she would write, even before Father Kearny passed her a pencil stub.

Once her post was sent, she told Stephen to see himself home after class. He was almost ten now, and she couldn't take care of him all the time. Besides, her own head ached, and she wanted to lie down. Had Howie and Sally left for the dance yet? The wind scoured the streets. Overhead, seagulls cried and spun on the updrafts. As soon as she got into the apartment, Elaine lay down on her bed and closed her eyes. The next thing she knew, someone was pounding on the door, and she sat up in a now dark room.

Father Kearny's voice rang out. "It looks like your brother's not feeling so well."

Elaine forced herself out of bed and met them in the front room. Stephen was pale, his eyes glazed.

"Look here." Father Kearny lifted Stephen's chin. A blotchy red rash covered his neck. "It's on his arms too. It looks like the measles. Is your father home?"

"No, he's out just now." Her own head still pounded, and her throat was sore.

Father Kearny looked around the flat. "You don't have much heat in here."

Stephen slumped down on a chair. Father Kearny directed his gaze at Elaine, eyes sharp enough to pierce right through her. "And when was the last time you saw your father?"

"He's working late." She crossed her arms and looked away. "I can take care of Stephen."

"On a Saturday, is he? Didn't you tell me your mother died of the flu this year?"

Miserably, Elaine nodded her head.

"Let's get a fire going in the stove and make some hot water." Father Kearny busied himself making tea.

Elaine sank into the other chair. She was so very tired. All the while Father Kearny made conversation. The words floated somewhere above her head.

"Your brother will make a fine altar boy. He's bright and helpful, but most important, he has a good heart." He clattered three mugs on the table and sat down opposite Elaine.

"Now don't lie to me." His eyes bored into her. "What's happened to your father?"

"He's died," Stephen croaked.

Elaine wanted to slap him, but she was too tired. Instead she began to cry, great gulping sobs she couldn't stop.

Father Kearny pulled out a large handkerchief. Then he rummaged in the cupboards, sliced potatoes into thin wedges and fried them in lard. He left for a few minutes and returned with sausage to add to the pan. All the while Elaine sat in the chair. Her nose ran, and she wiped it with the back of her hand. Her legs were too heavy to move. Stephen had fallen asleep with his head on the table and woke up just enough to eat when Father Kearny brought over the sizzling pan.

"I can't leave you like this, you know. I have to report it. You're only kids, for Pete's sake. It isn't right you should be living on your own."

"We won't go to an orphanage. We're fine." Elaine glared across the table.

Father Kearny met her glare head on. "I'll be by in the morning to look in on you. Tonight, I want you both to go straight to bed."

Too tired to protest, Elaine helped Stephen into his bed, washed his hot face, and then lay down herself. Her thoughts were askew. She needed a plan to get them both away.

True to his word, Father Kearny arrived in the morning with tea and muffins for breakfast. Stephen was now covered head to toe with fierce red spots. His skin burned. After careful inspection, Elaine decided she had no spots at all. Her throat was still sore, but as usual, she coped.

"Most people don't die of the measles if they're looked after properly. He needs rest, food, and someone to take care of him," Father Kearny said after sending Stephen back to bed. "Tell me, how have you been surviving?"

"I've got a job. I work at the Gossleys, and we've some money left from Pop's friends." Each word was a betrayal.

"May Gossley?" Father Kearny's eyebrows went up even higher. "She's involved in half the charity cases in town. Does she know about this?"

Elaine shook her head.

"Well, perhaps she should." Father Kearny looked thoughtful. "I've got a few contacts in the parish. I'll do what I can to keep you and Stephen together. I'm off to Mass, but I want a promise from you before I go."

Elaine merely looked at him.

"Promise me you'll come get me right away if your brother gets worse. I want you to give him something to drink every hour to keep the fever down, and I want you to stay with him."

"But I have to go to work tomorrow." Elaine's voice felt faint and far away.

"Leave that to me. I'll let the Gossleys know. You're not looking any too well yourself, and they won't want you bringing disease into the house. Do you have spots?"

"No."

"Have you had the measles, then?"

"I don't know. Not that I remember."

He shook his head. "You mind what I say." He left sausage and milk on the table after making Elaine promise. Elaine tried not to think about the Orphan Asylum. If she could get her head clear, she could make a plan. They could go west and get jobs, or— She crept back into their bedroom and lay on the bed, unable to think what came next.

Elaine bolted up. The room was filled with a thin gray light. Someone was knocking on the door. It had to be the social worker come to take them both away. Most of the night she'd been up, bathing Stephen's face and giving him sips of water. He slept quietly now. If she ignored the knocking, maybe social services would go away. But the knocking became pounding.

Head spinning, she cracked open the door and peered out.

The opening filled with Kay's broad smile. "Get your things. You're both coming with me."

"Where? Why are you here?'

Kay pushed into the room. "Father Kearny came by last evening. Mr. Seward said to fetch you both with all your things and come to the house. The missus was afraid of you bringing the measles, but he told her he'd hire a nurse if need be and there'd be no more discussing it."

Kay peeked in the bedroom where Stephen slept. "Is it true your father's dead? And you never said a word."

"What will happen now?"

"You'll get looked after with proper meals and rest until he's better—that's what will happen. You want your brother taken care of, don't you?"

Elaine looked at Stephen.

"If he dies, you'd never forgive yourself." Kay's words bored into Elaine's throbbing head.

Without protest, she gathered up their few belongings. Kay cleaned up the dishes and they both shook Stephen awake.

"There's a car outside. You can't be walking like this."

"We're going in the car?" Stephen's face lit up. "Did you hear that, Lainey?"

She didn't answer. How long would it be until the Gossleys called one of May's charities or another to collect them?

❧

*B*ut life in the candy house was not as sweet as it appeared. *After the children had slept and been fed a fine break-fast of sweet cream and cakes, the old woman pinched their cheeks and their thin arms between her knobby fingers.*

"This will never do," she said. "You need fattening up if you are to stay in my house." She led Hansel into the pantry. "Look in the larder and tell me if we have any butter. My eyes are not as good as they once were."

Hansel obediently opened a small door and peered into the darkness. The old woman, with surprising strength in her sinewy arms, shoved him from behind. He stumbled forward into the pantry, and with a final click she locked the door.

"Here you'll remain until meat grows on your bones."

Poor Hansel didn't know what to do. In desperation, he called out for his sister.

When Gretel heard his muffled pleas, she tried to run to him, but the old woman detained her with an iron grip.

"Little bird, do you wish to be caged as well? Things can only go worse for your brother. Now fly about my house, cleaning it from top to toe!" The old woman thrust a scrub brush and bucket into Gretel's small hands, a bucket soon filled with the poor girl's tears.

While Gretel worked on hands and knees to polish the old woman's floors, Hansel, who still was a resourceful boy, devised a plan. The old woman's eyesight was poor. Each day, when she came to check for fat on his bones, she pinched his one finger and arm. Counting on her poor vision, Hansel stuck a chicken bone through the small grate in the door. The old woman would pinch the bone instead of a finger and shake her head in dismay. "Little bird, my chicken is not ready yet for my stew."

And Gretel laughed, though her poor back ached and her hands were cracked and red.

In this way, the children, who were in mortal peril, tricked the old woman, day by day, into sparing their lives just a little longer.

Chapter Thirty-Nine

THE GINGERBREAD HOUSE

BROOKLYN, NEW YORK—NOVEMBER 1919

ELAINE

Elaine startled awake, her panicked thoughts flapping like trapped birds in the dark room. Where was Stephen? She didn't hear him breathing. Then, memories flooded in. They were safe at the Gossleys. No need to fret about food or rent. And inside her, where the worry had been lodged, there was a hollow, empty space.

It should feel like stepping into a fairy tale. For the first time, she had a room to herself, with a rose-colored bedspread and a delicate dressing table with a mirror. From the small window, she looked out through the winter limbs of a chestnut tree into a small grass yard.

Stephen was right next door in a smaller room that had once been a gentleman's dressing room. While his fever came and went, Stephen spent the first days of their new life in bed. Kay looked in on him, but it was mostly Elaine who brought him soup and bathed his forehead. Mrs. Gossley forbade

Howie to come near either of them until the disease had run its course. Elaine was excused from all her duties in the rest of the house. She wasn't used to long, leisurely days, but she passed the time reading *Hansel and Gretel* and books from the Gossleys' library out loud to Stephen.

At the end of the second week, when the measles rash was completely gone, May asked to meet with both of them in the morning room.

"Elaine, I'm surprised you never said a word to me. I shouldn't have heard about your father's passing from Father Kearny."

Elaine looked down at her own reflection in the polished table. "We managed."

"Managing is not enough. You're both still children. You need a stable place to live, and now that Stephen's well, you both need to be in school."

Was she was hinting it was time for them to go? "I'll make sure he goes to school."

"That's too much for you to bear alone."

Would she send them to the Orphan Asylum?

"Please," Elaine whispered.

"My father would like you both to stay on with us."

Stay here, close to Howie? The fairy tale was coming true.

"Mr. Gossley and I agree that this may be the best thing, staying here until you are old enough to be on your own."

An uncertain smile nudged its way across Elaine's face. She glanced out of the corner of her eyes at her brother. He'd stopped swinging his legs. A grin lit his face.

"Can we, Lainey?"

But a sliver of uncertainty worked its way into her thoughts. Did she really want someone else telling her what to do? She bit a fingernail. The sliver dug in deeper. What if they forgot their own parents?

"Elaine, you would still be employed after school, and I'm sure Stephen could help with the yard work. I wouldn't want you to think you were merely charity cases."

So, that's how it was to be. Elaine looked up. They'd live with the Gossleys, but still be employees of a sort. She wouldn't have to become someone else's daughter.

"Thank you. We won't be any trouble at all."

"I consider myself a good judge of character. We'll enjoy having you here. This week would be a good time for both of you to return to school."

"This week?" It had been too long. How would she ever fit in?

"The sooner the better. You don't want to get any farther behind than you already are." May lifted the small gold watch that hung around her neck and checked the time. "I've asked Mrs. Theilen to see about getting you some new things to wear. I plan to register you this afternoon."

Just as she feared, Elaine didn't fit in at school. Ahead in reading, behind in math and science, she couldn't talk fashion and didn't know the popular movie stars like Lillian Gish. Her goal became to slip through the days unnoticed.

May tried on and discarded projects like hats. How soon would the Gossleys tire of them? Some days Howie played the role of big brother, asking her about her day at school or teasing her about her new clothes. Other days, his stares made her think of the picnic kiss, something she now worked at forgetting. He was class president, a competent if lazy student, and one of the most popular boys on his campus. There were days when Elaine only caught glimpses of his back retreating down the drive.

It was easier for Stephen. No doubts about their new living arrangements appeared to trouble him. He continued altar boy classes, although the Gossleys themselves rarely attended church, and when they did it was the Episcopal one. The only difficulty Stephen encountered was having his own room.

For the first weeks after most of the house had gone to bed, he crept into Elaine's room and curled on the foot of her bed. He was so quiet that she rarely knew he was there until she woke in the morning. Then they ate hurried breakfast and together walked the few short blocks to school.

After school, Elaine read to Mr. Seward or helped Kay in the kitchen. Her evenings were spent in schoolwork, trying to catch up with the others in her grade. The weekends were the most difficult time of all. Howie was rarely at home, and Elaine, with more free time than ever before, found herself reflecting.

She missed her mother more than ever. Elaine listened to the girls in her class talk about weekend shopping trips to Manhattan. She watched the way they walked with their mothers, leaning in close to share a confidence, the way their mothers smoothed a stray hair or straightened a bow. And she longed for that careless intimacy.

CHRISTMAS, 1919

On Steuben Street, Christmas meant a special dinner and a single gift. At the Gossleys', Christmas was complicated. May took decorating seriously. She attacked the holiday with the same single-minded force she turned toward poverty or illiteracy. They strung garlands, ordered Christmas cards, and hosted charity teas.

A week before Christmas, Mr. Gossley staggered home under the weight of a ten-foot Christmas tree. Howie and his father spent an evening clipping candleholders to the stately limbs while Mrs. Theilen, with a bucket of water at her side, fretted about setting the house on fire. It felt disloyal to be enjoying such a splendid Christmas. Caught between two worlds, her lost family and this house full of cheerful strangers, Elaine longed for old times with Mom and Pop on Steuben Street. Not even Howie could make her laugh.

The only place Elaine felt at ease was in the routine of reading to Mr. Seward. As the steel worker strike flowed into its twelfth week, Mr. Seward raged that Bolsheviks engineered it to undermine the economy. Every time Elaine read the headlines, he'd grow red in the face.

"The only one with enough gumption to do anything about these confounded aliens invading our country is Mr. Hoover. He should be president instead of Wilson."

Elaine smiled, happy to lose herself in his rants.

Second.

SPRING, 1920

By March, Elaine was ahead of most students in her grade. She'd made a friend, Sarah Mueller, and joined a choral singing group. She bobbed her hair with May's full approval, and Mr. Seward never quite forgave her. Life on Steuben Street was fading.

Stephen's latest passion was baseball. He followed every game the Dodgers played, idolizing each and every player. But his favorite was an outfielder named Zack Wheat, who the fans called Buck. On May 4, the Dodgers beat the Braves at Ebbets Field in front of a sellout crowd, and Howie, with two friends from school, was there to see it. For days after Stephen followed Howie around begging for another play by play. That May, it had became legal to hold baseball games on a Sunday, which Howie declared was better than church any day.

Even when he had to miss some of the live radio broadcasts, Stephen was at church. And Elaine attended faithfully to watch him assist Father Kearny as an altar boy. She wondered if God knew that she attended Mass more for Stephen's sake than for the sake of her own soul, and if he did, did he mind? Each altar boy was required to memorize the words in Latin, and so Elaine and Stephen spent long evenings at the kitchen table while Stephen stumbled over the Latin words *Suscipiat*

Dominus sacrificium de manibus tuis . . . Every week she worried he'd forget the words.

When she asked Stephen if he was nervous trying to remember everything, he looked at her strangely. "If I make a mistake, God won't get mad at me, Lainey."

Obviously, Stephen understood all the church business better than she ever would.

Chapter Forty

AGAINST THE WIND

SAN JOSE, CALIFORNIA—AUGUST 1955

Molly

Fear shot through me like an electric shock. "Angus, what do you think you're doing? Get down here right now!" But the wind swallowed my words as soon as they left my lips. I ran through the fence gate that opened onto the empty land behind our house. The barn was several yards off.

Sometimes, as smart as he is, my brother had no common sense. I could see rope hanging from a roof rafter. They must have used that rope to lift the enormous wings. The two boys teetered on the ridgeline; I planted myself right in their line of vision and cupped my hands around my mouth. "Down! Now! Before you kill yourself!"

I could see them conferring. I wanted to run back to the house to get Uncle Stephen, but if I left, Angus might jump. I had to hold my ground. When the wind shifted direction, I heard Robert's voice as clearly as if he was standing next to me.

"I'll do it. Let me try the wings!"

I shook my head no, but the conversation didn't involve me.

"I'm going to prove it to you!" he shouted at me. "God wants me alive." He reached out and tugged at one wing.

For another long minute, the two boys argued while I screamed at them to come down. And then screamed for Uncle Stephen, for the faithful, for God to do something. By that point Angus was shrugging off the wings. The wind caught them like a giant sail. He slipped sideways and grabbed the roof ridge with one hand. I ran toward the house. The back door was locked. I pounded with both fists. Kicked the door and screamed.

When I looked to the barn, Robert had turned his back toward my brother and spread his arms. Angus had now righted himself on the roof and fought against the wind to strap them on. They stretched at least six feet from each shoulder, and a wooden bar went straight across Robert's chest. He leaned forward.

What had I done?

The roof of the barn was higher than the second story on a house. The faithful, the man in the blue car, and anyone else out in the noonday sun must have seen them too. I screamed. My feet rooted to the spot with fear.

A glint of sun winked off Robert's white hair. He spread his arms wide. A shadow rushed past me from behind, as Robert, face still titled toward the light, leapt from the roof of the barn.

APRIL 1920

ELAINE

"Mind if I come in?" Howard leaned against the doorjamb of Elaine's room.

At the sound of his voice, Elaine looked up from her book

and self-consciously tugged the covers higher. How long had he been standing there?

"Of course not, come in."

"Good. Saw your light was still on." He sat on the side of her bed and kicked off his shoes. "It looks like everyone else has gone to bed. Is it that late?"

"Almost midnight. I was reading." She looked pointedly at her book, but pulled her feet up so there'd be more room.

"I went into town this afternoon to see the Woolworth Building. It's the tallest building in the world—seven hundred ninety-two feet. Amazing."

Elaine laid her book across her knees. "I wish I could see it."

"I'll take you there one day. It was designed by Cass Gilbert. I'm going to design buildings like that someday."

The small circle of light etched Howie's face with shadows. Even in the dimness, Elaine knew his eyes were glowing; she could hear it in his voice.

"Of course you are—the finest buildings in the world."

He laughed. "I wish everyone believed in me like you do."

"How do you know I don't take pity on all boys with big dreams?"

"Oh, I'm a boy now? That's not what Sally thinks."

"That's because she doesn't know you as well as I do."

"Nobody knows me as well as you do." Howie rested one arm on her tented knees. "One day I'm going to design sky-scrapers for a living in Manhattan, and then I'm going to study in Europe. Want to come with me?"

For a breathless second, she let herself imagine his request was real.

Howie leaned across her knees and ran his fingers through her bob. The book slid into the covers. "This suits you, you know. I bet you're the prettiest girl at your school."

Elaine closed her eyes. She liked the play of his fingers in her hair, brushing against her neck. She inhaled the scent of cigarettes, aftershave, something warm and musky.

"How many boys are after you? Besides me, that is?"

Elaine lowered her knees. His eyes sought out hers.

"Come here." Howie pulled her toward him until his eyelashes brushed her cheeks and ran his finger over the outline of her mouth. She tasted salt on his lips, felt his breath on her cheek. His lips parted with a low groan.

The second kiss was like she imagined it would be.

On the surface, their relationship didn't change. But Howie became a frequent late-night visitor. He painted a future she learned by heart, describing buildings in such detail that Elaine felt as if she walked inside them.

"I bet you didn't know that the first steel frame building was the Wainwright in St. Louis."

"Not until you told me."

He lifted her chin, balancing it in the palm of his hand, and looked directly into her eyes. "It takes steel to make a really tall building. I'm going to design one taller than the Woolworth, just see if I don't. I'll get a job working for McKim, Mead, and White or Carrère and Hastings until I start my own firm." Then he frowned and cocked his head to one side. "Why do I always want to kiss you?"

"Because I'm irresistible?" Elaine rubbed her hand against the stubble of his cheek while she imagined what it would be like to be an architect's wife in a fancy dress at the dedication of a building.

No matter what happened in the world of school, Howie's heart belonged to her. When he asked her about her plans for the future, she had little to say. Her future was bound to his, and his was bound to her. She didn't need to imagine anything else.

Chapter Forty-One

GRADUATION

BROOKLYN, NEW YORK—JUNE TO AUGUST 1920

ELAINE

Howie was accepted at Cornell, the college of his father and grandfather, and was expected to pledge to a fraternity. While Mr. Gossley took to reminiscing over meals about parties on the hill, even though Howie wouldn't be leaving until mid-August, May fussed over the appropriate clothes for a college man. Because the college allowed both women and blacks, she was pleased with Howard's choice.

Elaine listened as if they were describing a foreign land. No one she knew went to college. And Cornell was in Ithaca, miles from Brooklyn.

The high school graduation ceremony took place on a Saturday in early June. May said it was for families only and that Elaine and Stephen shouldn't expect them back for dinner. Howie left the house wearing a new black suit with spats and a white rosebud in his lapel. The Gossleys and Mr. Seward returned hours later without him.

Elaine lay awake expecting that he would stop in her room as he often did, tell her about the ceremony, describe the parties afterward. The handkerchiefs she'd embroidered with his name were wrapped in fine tissue and ready next to her pillow. At two, she heard footsteps in the hall. They never paused outside her door. She lay on her back staring at the ceiling, counting the fine cracks in the plaster, while her hand, as if it had a life of its own, searched the blanket and closed around the tissue-wrapped present. She balled it in her fist, and without sitting up tossed it under the bed. It was natural to want to celebrate with his friends. He was doing what anyone would do. But college became her enemy. It was a rival, a siren, seducing him away from her. Long after Howie resumed his nighttime confidences, the handkerchiefs collected dust in the empty space beneath the bed.

"I'm going to try out for field hockey. Dad played all four years."

"Will you still remember me when you're away at school?" The word *college* still stuck in her throat.

"Of course I will. Didn't I say that nobody knows me better than you?"

Elaine pressed close to his side, resting her chin on his shoulder. "When will you come home?"

"Only on holidays, I expect. Ithaca's halfway across the state, and I won't have a car the first year."

The car argument was still a point of contention. Mr. Seward insisted that the train was all that was necessary for a freshman, adding that a car might be considered for his second year depending on his performance. Howie countered that everyone he knew was taking a car for the freshman year.

"If that's the case, it should be easy for you to get rides home." Mr. Seward was immovable.

"Perhaps after the first semester—" May suggested.

"May, since the car will be purchased with my money, I will be the one to make that call." And Mr. Seward closed his eyes to signal the end of the conversation.

Now Elaine tried to memorize Howie's face in the light from the streetlamp—the red birthmark mapping his cheek, the upward tilt of his mouth even when he wasn't smiling, the way his hair curled over the tops of his ears. Life at the Gossleys' would go on, but with all of the color and energy gone. Just as her life had always gone on.

"Maybe I could visit you sometime." Elaine sought his eyes, but they were hidden in the shadows. Could he hear the thin wire of hope that vibrated in her question?

"Maybe. I think they have a family day in the fall."

Howie was receding right in front of her. It was possible, she had learned, for someone to be there and gone at the same time. Or there and already leaving. Despair crested like waves. She turned her face toward the window.

"What's so interesting out there?" Howie peered over her shoulder.

Elaine's shoulders began to shake.

"Are you crying?"

Elaine couldn't speak. Instead, she buried her head on his shoulder. Her sobs were loud and guttural. She cried for all the leavings in her life, but for herself most of all.

Howie stroked her hair. "It's only July; I'm not leaving until August." Lifting her face with one hand, Howie brushed his thumb across her cheek. Elaine dug her fingers into his shoulders, clinging to him with the strength of the drowning.

"Stop." He brushed her eyes with his lips. "You're too pretty to cry so much."

She shook her head. The wall, the one she'd so carefully constructed after Pop's death, was shattering.

Howie's next words were a soothing mumble against the hollow of her throat. Trembling, Elaine locked her hands behind his neck and pulled him down.

In October 1920, exactly forty-two days after Howie left—fifteen days before her sixteenth birthday—Elaine accepted she might be pregnant. If accepting meant giving a name to the fear that almost swallowed her whole. She had suspected something was wrong by the end of September, since she hadn't bled that month or the last. It had been easy to believe she was ill. The sight of certain foods made her stomach turn and smells were even worse. She'd picked her birthday at the end of October as a deadline. By then her body should have righted itself. But her birthday came and went. The only change was that her breasts ached. There was no denying what was happening inside her now. There was no one to talk with, and nothing else she could think about. Most important of all, Stephen mustn't find out.

Taking some of the good writing paper from the morning room, Elaine composed a letter to Howie in her most careful penmanship. But the words in her head didn't work on the page. *I'm in the family way.* She crossed out the words and tried again. *We are going to have a baby.* These were words that couldn't be let loose into the world without seeing how they were received. Without watching Howie's eyes, she'd never know what the news meant to him. She tore the paper into tiny fragments and buried them in the trash.

Daily, she ran her hand over her bare stomach, checking for any signs of swelling. It remained flat. Her breasts were larger, but that might be natural at her age; she didn't know. She avoided Stephen and even her few friends at school.

After that first night in July when she had felt like she was dying, she'd slept with Howie two more times. It was their own private miracle. Now they were bound forever.

She would tell him the truth in person when he came home.

Chapter Forty-Two

INTO THE FIRE

BROOKLYN, NEW YORK—NOVEMBER 1920

ELAINE

Elaine expected Howie for the Thanksgiving holidays. She'd prepared her speech and imagined his surprise turning to joy. Of course, his family would have to help them out until he finished school. She also imagined a darker version: May refusing to help, Howard dropping out of school, and the three of them—Howard, Elaine, and Stephen—having to make do in a cheap apartment. It was a good thing she'd had lots of practice at making do.

An unexpected snowstorm kept Howard in Ithaca over Thanksgiving, and he celebrated at a friend's home. Now he was expected to arrive on December 20 by train. She'd received one postcard from him in early November, which she carried in her pocket and worried until the edges were bent and frayed. It showed the front of the library building, a piece of architecture he admired, and had a few scrawled lines about how wonderful college life was. He'd signed it *Your Friend, Howard Gossley*, as if she didn't know his last name.

On December 20 the Gossleys prepared for the trip to the train station. Mr. Seward elected to remain at home, likely because the temperature was a frosty 28 degrees. Stephen was attending a school friend's birthday party. And so Elaine appeared alone in the hallway in her hat and coat.

"May I come?" Her heart tap-danced in her chest. She'd let her bob grow out a bit and wore her new navy blue coat, an early Christmas gift from the Gossleys.

"Well, that would be nice. I'm sure Howard will be pleased to see you." May adjusted her fur-trimmed hat.

But by this time, Elaine wasn't sure at all. She tugged on her gloves. Her clothes were tight. Soon her condition would be obvious to everyone.

They rode to the station in silence, Mr. Gossley intent on navigating the icy streets and May wrapped in thoughts of her own. In the backseat, Elaine breathed deeply, and went over one last time the way she would make her announcement.

They drove to Brighton's Prospect Park station, where trains from the Manhattan Street Bridge and the Fulton El arrived. As always, the station teemed with people. Elaine walked wooden legged behind the Gossleys to the platform. Would Howie notice right away? The coat strained a bit over her stomach.

As the train pulled in, Mr. Gossley checked his watch. "Awfully punctual for the BMT—ice and snow too."

"Do you see him?" May was on tiptoe, straining to see over the sea of winter hats. As the first passengers disembarked, Elaine gripped her hands together. A mother with a toddler in her arms and two more children clinging to their father's hands, an elderly woman leaning on the arm of a rotund man, two giggling college girls. Elaine strained forward. Then she heard May call out.

From a car farther up the platform, passengers poured out.

Howie was unmistakable. He wore a gray fedora and a charcoal overcoat. In one hand, he carried his traveling valise; the other was firmly supporting the arm of a dark-haired girl.

If her legs had worked, Elaine would have run then. She looked for a way out through the swirling mob. May rushed forward to throw her arms around Howie. Howie, his quick smile lighting his face, grabbed his father's hand and shook it.

"Mom, Dad, you remember Sally."

Sally Wilson. The girl Howie had taken to the dance his senior year in high school. Up close she was even prettier than her picture. She had the pale skin, blue eyes, and dark hair of the black Irish. Two dimples framed her smile.

"Sally's ended up in Ithaca too. She's studying pre-law. I told her you wouldn't mind giving her a ride home."

"My parents couldn't make it to the station today. My little sister is sick, and my father had to work. I so appreciate this."

All the while Elaine stood frozen, a smile etched on her face.

"Elaine, I didn't see you back there." Howie pushed past his parents and threw an arm around her shoulder. He turned to Sally. "Sally, this is Elaine. I've told you about her. She's like a kid sister to me."

"Hello, Howie." Elaine watched from a great distance as her words dropped from her lips. She pictured them sinking unnoticed like a stone into a pond and settling in the muck of the bottom layer. The surface of the water barely disturbed.

They gathered up bags and fought their way back through the crowds to the waiting car. Elaine realized with horror that she would be stuck in the backseat with Howie and Sally. Howie helped Sally into the car and then reached for Elaine's hand. She jerked it away to climb in by herself. For a moment a puzzled frown creased his face, but it quickly disappeared as Sally talked of classes and Ithaca.

Elaine heard none of it. She was too busy trying to breathe. Sally laughed easily, talking animatedly with her gloved hands. An overpowering fragrance of roses made Elaine break out in a sweat. Her stomach roiled. To keep from losing her breakfast, she fastened her eyes on Sally's hands. Like small gray doves, they flitted against the dark leather of the car as she spoke, lighted on Howie's arm, and finally came to rest in her lap. Then Howie reached out with his two bare hands and enclosed them. Sally smiled into his eyes.

After they dropped Sally off, Howie turned to Elaine, his eyes still dancing.

"How's school? Have you won the prize in mathematics yet?"

"Not yet." Elaine placed a hand on her stomach.

"You don't look too good. Has Grandpa been working you too hard? By the way, you'd love Ithaca. It's a dream town. You should see the buildings."

Elaine scooted into the far corner. "I got your postcard. Thanks."

"What? Oh, the postcard. Glad you liked it. You'll have to catch me up on everything at home." He leaned forward over Mr. Gossley's shoulder. "What do you know? I made the field hockey team."

Elaine hurried to her room as soon as they arrived at Clinton Avenue. There was nothing to say now. Her carefully rehearsed speech crumbled to dust. Curling on her bed, she poked her stomach and wondered about the life inside her. She would not tell Howie. Not now. Not ever. She wanted her mother. She prayed for a miracle.

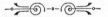

The day finally came when the old woman could wait no longer. Hansel was not so fat as she would like, but she had Gretel heat the oven in preparation for a feast. She laid her plans carefully. Once Hansel was in the oven, she would push the girl in too.

But Gretel had her own plans. She had learned a thing or two from all her travail in the forest. Restraining her panic, as one would corral an unruly dog, she listened to the old woman's instructions. The brick oven was large and fired with wood. Its opening gaped like a maw ready to swallow them whole.

Chapter Forty-Three

FLIGHT

SAN JOSE, CALIFORNIA—AUGUST 1955

Molly

For one beautiful moment, the wind caught his wings. Instead of dropping straight down, Robert was lifted, blazing white against the purple sky. The faithful later said his face was radiant like an angel's. I was too busy screaming to notice.

The next moment a gust caught the corner of one wing. It lifted him higher. Would the wings really save him? Then he was tipping sideways, twisting like a leaf.

I bit my lip until I tasted blood. I ran a few steps forward, but by then the wind had released him and he was plummeting headfirst toward the ground. Robert landed with a sudden ferocity, not on the hard-packed earth but half in the arms of a stout man, who fell over backward with the weight of him. They were both buried under the crumpled wings.

I ran to the tangled bodies. Several of the faithful were running alongside me. Whatever had happened to Robert, it was my fault for goading him into it.

I was the first to arrive. Robert and the stranger were completely covered by the enormous wings. Angus was screaming from the rooftop. With my eyes half-squinted shut, I lifted the heavy fabric. Robert, arms and legs jutting at strange angles, looked like my first doll after the neighbor's dog got hold of it. No one would ever naturally lie in this position. His lips were slightly parted to reveal a pool of blood in his mouth and a thin line of red drool that trickled from his chin. His limp body was splayed across a large man who was gasping for air. I didn't know if Robert was alive or not.

An old man with skin wrinkled as a walnut carefully lifted the wings away from Robert and the stranger. He was speaking in Spanish, and although I couldn't understand a word of what he said, the sound of his voice was comforting. He put a hand on Robert's neck and turned toward the rest of us.

"The boy, he is alive." He spoke that much in English.

At that news, a cheer went up from the remnant of the faithful, and I felt my heart lurch into beating again. Somehow, Uncle Stephen was by my side.

"I've called an ambulance. How badly are you hurt?" he asked the stranger.

"I think my back's broken." The man gasped.

Then Angus was there, and he was crying, and Robert still wasn't saying anything or moving.

"Pray for him!" a lady called from the back of the group.

And so Uncle Stephen did. He put one hand on Robert and one on the stranger, and thanked God that they weren't dead and prayed that they'd be healed. I looked at Robert's leg; the bone was poking like an umbrella rib clear through the skin.

I wondered if he'd survive.

I wondered what would happen when Uncle Stephen discovered it was my fault.

DECEMBER 1920

ELAINE

Elaine talked to Maudie Jenkins at school. Her sister had been in the family way and then she wasn't.

"It's awful." Maudie's round eyes grew even rounder. "They stick something long and sharp up inside you. Then you bleed and bleed. My sister almost died."

In the end, it wasn't the pain or the money that decided Elaine. It was the memory of the babies her mother had lost and how she had cried for each one. How could she kill the tiny life inside her? If she did, she worried she wouldn't see her own mother again in heaven.

But what about Stephen? What would she tell him? It was as if her little brother, forgotten for the last few months, had suddenly reappeared in her consciousness as a giant. Perhaps this was her punishment for forgetting about him. Now, Elaine spent as much time with him as she could, knowing that she would be leaving soon.

She had avoided Howie as much as possible during his visit home. For the most part, it hadn't been difficult. He'd been out with Sally as often as he'd been in. But he'd noticed her rebuffs and seemed to be hurt by them.

One night he knocked on her bedroom door. "Can I come in?"

Elaine panicked. Try as she might, she had found it impossible to hate Howard Gossley.

"Yes."

He entered tentatively and sat on the edge of the chair by her dressing table. "I miss our talks. I suppose you've got other things on your mind now."

"You're the one with things on your mind. Things like Sally. Besides, all you miss is your midnight grope."

Howie blanched. "That never should have happened, but

we were both young and didn't know any better, I suppose. I wanted to make you feel better, and I didn't know how. You are beautiful. I meant everything I said."

He had never said he loved her. He had never promised anything. Elaine massaged her forehead. She had been so sure.

"You've been a good friend to me, Elaine. I meant it when I said no one knew me as well as you."

"And what about now? Who knows you now?"

"College is different. Feels like you know everybody in your frat. And Sally. Sally's a great girl. We've got the same ideas about things."

Elaine wanted to wail. To pummel him with her fists. "I thought we had the same ideas about things."

Howie smiled. "We probably do. But you're still a kid. You've got lots of school ahead of you. I need to start taking responsibility for my life, getting serious. We can still be friends though, can't we?"

Elaine closed her eyes and tried to block out Sally's name still ringing in her ears. "I've got something serious—"

"Sally's coming to dinner tomorrow night. You should get to know her. I think you two would really hit it off." He paused. "I'm sorry. What were you saying?"

The words were stillborn in her throat. "Nothing."

He stood up and stretched. "You're too young to be so serious. Enjoy life while you can." He turned toward the door and then stopped. "You'll keep in touch with me, won't you, when you go off into the big world?"

Elaine didn't say anything. There was a strange fluttering in her stomach that she couldn't control.

Chapter Forty-Four

THOUGHTS LIKE QUICKSAND

BROOKLYN, NEW YORK—DECEMBER 1920

ELAINE

She'd leave after Christmas. Elaine counted the money she'd been hoarding ever since moving in with the Gossleys. She'd learned of a place she could stay temporarily with a class-mate's older sister. She stared out from her bedroom window into the growing dark and tried to imagine what life would be like without Stephen. A bitter and rainy winter loomed, much like her mood. Of course she couldn't take him with her. His chances in life were better if he stayed with the Gossleys. As long as she could recall, she'd been his protector. He'd been the reason she kept going no matter how bad things were. Telling him she was leaving would be like trying to reassure a wounded animal. There was no way to explain to an animal that you were there to help. To keep down the hurt, abandon-ment, and fear he might feel, she needed a story to tell him. He mustn't know how weak his sister was.

She'd find a job, and then when she couldn't work anymore,

239

go to one of the charity houses like Woodward or Hope House. How hard could it be? She'd made do before and she could again. After the baby she'd find a place where Stephen could move in with her, if he still wanted to.

Turning from the window, Elaine caught her face in the mirror. The same face. It should look different. But the rest of her body was betraying her now. Running her hand over her stomach, she felt the swelling. It was impossible to button her skirts anymore, and dresses wouldn't be able to disguise her shame much longer. She'd tried to eat as little as she could in hopes that her stomach wouldn't grow too much. But that wasn't good for the baby, she was pretty sure. The baby. It was difficult to think of the thing inside her as human. What would she do with it when it came out? Would she keep it?

"Lainey!" Stephen's voice echoed in the hall outside her room. It was time to help with dinner. Taking a final look in the mirror, she knotted her shawl over her shoulders so that it hid the way her dress strained across her breasts.

That Christmas, 1920, was the Christmas of electric lights. Mr. Gossley, claiming that he could take no more of Mrs. Theilen's nagging about fires, bought electrified lights to string on the tree. Stephen was mesmerized. But the only thing Elaine noticed was that Howie left before New Year's to get back for field hockey practice and parties in Ithaca. Sally left with him.

Elaine then spent her free time looking for jobs. Stephen remarked that she was getting fat. So she ate even less, although she was hungry all the time, and she kept praying for a miracle even when none looked forthcoming. It all might have worked if it hadn't been for Kay. Elaine had been helping polish silver for the New Year's celebration. The kitchen was hot and steamy. After working all morning, she felt in desperate need of fresh air.

"Kay, I'm going out to get some air. I'll finish when I get back," she called.

Then she stood to fetch her coat. The room spun. When she reached for the table, it seemed to have moved. The floor rushed to her face.

When she came to, she was on the couch with a cold cloth on her face.

"I've sent for the doctor, love. You've been looking peaked far too long, and it ain't natural for a young girl in good health to faint like that." Kay face was rumpled with worry.

"Don't be crazy, Kay. I don't need a doctor; I got overheated." Elaine struggled to sit up and immediately the room spun again.

"I'll not have the flu untreated in this house." Kay shook her head. "I've told Mrs. Gossley, and she agreed. Don't you move. He'll be along shortly."

There was no choice. Everyone would know her shame. Elaine pulled the blanket up to her chin. Underneath she laid her hands on her belly and prayed that the baby would die.

The doctor's visit was short and embarrassing. At the end of it, May was called into the spare room.

"Your young charge is pregnant. I'd say five months."

May's eyebrows rose to her hairline. Elaine kept her eyes on the rug and counted the flowers in the pattern. If she kept counting, she wouldn't hear the things they said about her.

"There must be some mistake. Pregnant?" May lifted Elaine's chin in one hand. Her breath smelled like coffee. "Elaine, is this true?"

Elaine closed her eyes and nodded.

"How did this happen? Who is the father?" May pulled her hand away. Elaine let her chin drop.

She didn't answer.

"Young lady, I demand that you tell me immediately. We take you into our home, treat you like a daughter, and now this!" May's breath was rapid, her face white as bone.

Forty-one, forty-two, forty-three. She'd counted the carpet roses from her feet to the edge of the room.

"When did your son leave for college?" the doctor asked.

May took a deep breath. Elaine watched as May's nostrils retracted and her mouth worked before she spoke. "My son is engaged. This girl is no better than she should be. Terrible upbringing. Her father was a drunk. What can you expect?"

Without meeting Elaine's eyes, May took the doctor's arm and they left the room together without another word. Engaged? No one had mentioned that. She was sure May was lying. Elaine waited in the empty guest room for something to happen. She pictured May telling Mr. Seward. Even he would turn against her now. No matter what, she couldn't tell them Howie was the father, that she'd never been with another boy. The minutes ticked by. No one came. Elaine crept to her room and stayed there through dinner. When Stephen came to find her, she sent him away saying she was sick. It was late when May reappeared.

"I can no longer have a girl of your character residing under our roof. I've talked it over with Mr. Gossley. We'll make arrangements for you, but you must be out at once."

A strange sense of relief mingled with despair. The worst was known. It was now out of her hands; someone else would make the arrangements. All Elaine wanted to do was sleep. But there was one last thing. "You can't tell Stephen. I'll tell him I'm going away to school. And you must promise me that he'll finish school."

May met her eyes. "You're a bright girl, Elaine. It's too bad you don't have better morals. You're in no position to bargain."

It had never occurred to her before that moment that Stephen might be cast out too.

"Stephen didn't do anything." She'd beg on his behalf if she had to.

"No, he didn't. We saved him in time."

May's eyes were chips of flint, dark and hard. Why had she ever thought this woman was beautiful? How could she have compared May to her own mother?

"I suppose there's no need for your brother to know what his sister's really like." May looked at Elaine with such scorn that she felt scorched.

Elaine closed her eyes. Stephen was spared. Nothing else mattered. She felt May hesitate a moment longer, then heard the sound of her door being drawn closed. She wouldn't think about telling Stephen she was leaving. She wouldn't think about May's words, that Howie was engaged. Those thoughts were like quicksand; they would pull her under and there would be no escape. Curling on her side, she drew her legs up to her chest and began to hum.

Chapter Forty-Five

WOODWARD HOUSE

BROOKLYN, NEW YORK—MARCH 1921

ELAINE

Elaine sat on the toilet and listened to one of the other girls talk to her from the other side of the door. The toilet stalls were the one sanctuary of privacy at Woodward House. But Catty, when she wanted to talk, ignored the unspoken rules and conversed even there. She'd immediately taken Elaine under her wing, and even if she did talk too much, Elaine was glad for a friend. Catty was seventeen, and it was the second time she'd been at the home. She'd had her first baby at fifteen.

"My first was a girl—the prettiest baby they ever had here. Sister Theresa told me so. I still gave her away."

Giving up on privacy, Elaine came out of the stall. Catty was fixing her hair in the small mirror. The few mirrors at Woodward House were kept small so they wouldn't encourage vanity. She spun around to face Elaine.

"Couldn't work with a baby to feed, could I? I'm going to

be an actress someday, and you can't do that with a kid." She crossed her arms and leaned them on the shelf of her belly.

"Then why are you here again?" Catty never took offense at direct questions. Elaine could ask her anything.

"First time was my pa. Nothing I could do about it. Good thing the baby looked like me. Pa has a mug like the wrong end of a pig. This time it was my choice."

Elaine let the warm water run through her fingers as she wondered at Catty's words. Why would anyone choose this?

"Distinguished gentleman. He wasn't much to look at either, but he bought me presents. Had a wife and kids of his own, but he was sweet, and funny when he was zozzled. Said he loved me, so I thought if I got in the family way it might help things along." She widened her enormous blue eyes and shrugged her shoulders.

Even with a stomach the size of a watermelon, Catty was beautiful. Blond ringlets framed a chiseled face. Elaine ran a hand through her own red hair that needed washing.

"What did he do?"

"Soon as I mentioned a baby, he run away with his bits in his hand." Catty laughed and checked herself in the mirror. "It was all horsefeathers! That's how stupid I am. I'm done with men for sure now, unless they're really good looking."

She explained childbirth in all its gory detail to Elaine, and then advised her to give up the baby before she even looked at it.

"Otherwise it's hard to forget. Find myself thinking about Lily more than I should. I named her after Lillian Gish. Don't know if the family kept the name, but it's how I think of her."

"You can name your baby?" Elaine hadn't considered this possibility before.

"Don't know if you can, but I did."

All the girls were required to attend hygiene and home and family classes, but each one considered them jokes. They already knew where babies came from, and it wasn't likely they'd be good candidates for marriage now. But, as Catty reminded Elaine, times were changing. Men of the twenties were more broad-minded. Not that it mattered to Elaine. For a moment she'd considered keeping the baby, but she'd never be able to take care of it and Stephen. The baby deserved a real home with a father and mother. As soon as she got rid of the baby, she'd save up money and then bring Stephen to live with her. Then her life would be complete.

The sisters had found her a part-time job as a housemaid, and she spent her evenings writing letters to Stephen. She never included a return address. If he knew she was still in Brooklyn, he'd come looking for her. But sending a letter with no hope of reply made her feel even lonelier. What if he forgot about her? Or worse, remembered, but didn't miss her at all?

Howie had forgotten her by now. She was sure of it. She tried not to think of him, but her old trick of constructing a wall didn't work anymore. As winter howled through Brooklyn, she imagined him in Ithaca sledding with friends and meeting Sally for a drink after classes. The pain was sharper than the baby's kicks. And May's words that he was engaged haunted her nights. It wasn't right that his life should go on when hers was ruined. But it would be even worse if he felt pity for her.

In late March, Elaine received her first letter. The envelope was typed and she didn't recognize the return address. Who would write to her if it wasn't Stephen? Howie? She couldn't afford to let her hopes go there. With trembling hands, she opened the letter in a bathroom stall.

March 20, 1921

My Dear Elaine,

I am entrusting this letter to my close friend and personal solicitor, Mr. John Parks. Blindness may have curtailed my ability to write letters on my own, but it is no excuse for keeping me ignorant of events in my own household.

I believe that you are carrying Howard's child, my great-grandchild. I do not have definite proof of this, but my suspicions are strong enough that I would like to see you after the child is born so that I can make provisions for you both. I will not notify Howard, as I think it is of the utmost importance that he completes his college degree. News that would interfere with that goal would be unwelcome. However, I do hope that at some time in the future, he is alerted to the existence of his child and knows that you are both taken care of. A man must know the consequences of his actions.

I have spoken to May about my suspicions, but as I expected, she is not objective when it comes to her son. She has hardened her heart against you. In my experience, mothers tend to have a blind spot concerning their boys.

I plan to set up a trust fund for both you and the child. As you know, I think very highly of you, and it would do my old heart good to know that you are able to continue your education. You cannot believe that there is any future for you and the child with Howard. He has obligations that befit his social standing. Not that I approve of his conduct. I would like to think that my great-grandchild will be provided for and would very much like to meet him or her while I am still able to do so. Please notify me immediately upon the baby's birth through Mr. Parks.

In the meantime, if there is anything you lack, please do not hesitate to let Mr. Parks know. I have enclosed a small sum to help with incidentals which a pregnancy may require, and plan to send more upon news of the birth. Stephen continues to prosper in our home, although he misses his sister very much.

With fondness,
Mr. Arthur Seward

Sitting on the toilet, Elaine read and reread the letter, her face hot with anger. She thought of flushing the money order down the drain. Footsteps came in. The door on the stall next to her opened and closed. Elaine felt sick. Obligations to his social standing? She howled with rage.

"The baby, it is coming?"

She recognized Svetlana's voice.

"No, the baby's not coming. Mind your business."

The toilet flushed. A door opened and closed.

Mr. Seward had been the only Gossley who really did know her, despite what Howie said. She'd spent more time with the old man than with anyone else in the family. She thought they were friends. He'd kept her poem. In his own gruff way, he cared about her and wanted to do right by her. She rested her head in her hands and counted the black-and-white tiles on the bathroom floor. A trust fund. She didn't even know what that meant. If there was money coming, it belonged to the baby. She and Stephen would manage on their own and not be beholden to any Gossleys.

On the other hand, why shouldn't she tell who the father was? Why shouldn't Howie leave college? Why shouldn't he be inconvenienced? Here she was, growing monstrous with his child, about to go through pain worse than any beating—at least that's what Catty said—while he spent his days worrying about grades and what flowers to buy Sally Wilson. Elaine worried the edges of the money order. It wasn't Mr. Seward's fault that his grandson was a fool, but it was his fault for thinking Howie's life shouldn't be disrupted.

Chapter Forty-Six

THE MAN IN THE CAR

SAN JOSE, CALIFORNIA—AUGUST 1955

Molly

We were all at the hospital, but Uncle Stephen had left a note for Mom. Angus and I sat in orange plastic chairs in the waiting room with Uncle Stephen while Robert's parents talked with the doctor. He said he wanted to perform surgery on Robert's shattered leg as soon as he regained consciousness.

The moment Robert's parents arrived, his father started in on the miracle boy story, explaining how Robert's life was more precious than the usual person's. Then his mother spied Uncle Stephen and ran over to him. Her hair was wound in tiny pink sponge rollers that covered her head and gave her a strange, hairless look. With one small hand she grabbed Uncle Stephen's arm while she begged him to come into Robert's room and pray. But a nurse barred the door from any miracle workers.

"What on earth happened?" Mom arrived like squealing

brakes. I could almost smell burning rubber as she tore into the waiting room.

Angus burst into tears again.

"The boys were trying out Angus's wings on the roof of the barn. Robert jumped and a stranger broke the fall," Uncle Stephen said simply. "It looks like everyone will survive."

Mom looked at Angus like he had just risen from the dead. I thought she'd be angry with him. Her words caught me by surprise.

"Where was Molly?"

My stomach flip-flopped. Was she thinking I should have done a better job of watching my brother?

"How could you have let this happen?"

Uncle Stephen put his hand on her arm. "Take it easy, Lainey. None of us saw this coming. Molly was the first one to the rescue. I called the ambulance as soon as I saw what happened."

"I didn't know how to stop him!" The tears that had been pushing against my eyes burst out. "I didn't mean for it to happen." I moved closer to Uncle Stephen. Angus burrowed into Mom's side.

"I thought we'd fly. Molly told us to stop. Besides, Robert said nothing could hurt him, and Molly told him to prove it," Angus said through sobs.

"You *what*?" Mom grabbed me by the shoulders. "How could you say such a thing?"

"That was before. I didn't know—"

Uncle Stephen covered her hands.

Mom expelled a deep breath of air through her nose. Her next words were slow and directed right at me. "Why wasn't I told about the wings in the first place?"

"I didn't think Angus would do something so stupid."

"Your younger brother is your responsibility—"

Uncle Stephen cut her off. "Angus is okay, Lainey. Robert made his own choice. Molly did the best she could. That's all any of us can do." He paused and looked her directly in the eye. "No one can save anyone but themselves."

Between sobs, I told about the shadow rushing past me right before Robert jumped, how a large man held his arms out as Robert came tumbling down, and how when he hit, Robert and the man were both buried under the wings.

She sat on the edge of a plastic chair and gripped her hands together until the knuckles turned white. "Who was the man? What happened to him?"

"He must be one of the faithful who saw the whole thing happening. We haven't seen him since they unloaded the ambulance," Uncle Stephen said.

Angus was still snuffling. He wiped his nose across the back of his arm. "Is it another miracle?"

A nurse came out through the swinging door. "Mr. Whipple is asking for his family."

We all looked at each other. There was no one else in our little waiting area.

Finally, Uncle Stephen spoke up. "If that's the gentleman who came in the ambulance, we'd be happy to see him. He saved a boy's life. Although we can't claim to be family."

We all followed the nurse into the white room, first Uncle Stephen with Angus under one arm and then Mom and I right behind. The man who had saved Robert sat propped up in bed.

I looked at him curiously. He was pudgy with dark, curling hair, and when he smiled like he did right then, there was something that made me feel at home.

Chapter Forty-Seven

ARTHUR

BROOKLYN, NEW YORK—APRIL 1921

ELAINE

The baby, a boy, was born on April 15th. The birth was long and difficult. Elaine believed she was dying. Every time the pain got too bad, she pictured Stephen's face. She screamed for her mother, and then bit down on the sheet and cried silently. Hours later, a healthy boy emerged. By then, Elaine was too exhausted to care. But the baby's cry moved her in a way she hadn't anticipated. Something in that wail ripped through her, shook her resolve to part with the tiny, crying thing. But the nuns were strict about the policy for adopted infants: any baby to be given up was whisked away. She caught a glimpse of a scrunched-up face and a thatch of pale hair swaddled in a blue blanket. The baby looked more alien than human, which she found a relief. She had half expected to see Howie's face staring up at her.

Elaine remembered what Cattie had told her about baby Lily.

"If I can't hold him, then I at least want to give him his proper name."

Sister Catalina paused pushing on Elaine's stomach. Sister Michaela and the baby were already out of the room.

"His name is Arthur."

The sister pushed again, and a wet red sack slithered out between Elaine's trembling legs. Elaine had no idea what it was. She turned her eyes away in revulsion. Maybe she'd lost part of her insides.

"I'll tell the other sisters your wishes. Of course, it's up to his new family—we can only suggest."

When Sister Catalina left, Elaine rolled to her side. Next to a small window was a picture of an angel helping two children across a rickety wooden bridge. The girl was older, the boy still had chubby little legs. It reminded her of Stephen when they were younger. For the last nine months she had never been alone. Now even baby Arthur was gone. Her body was sore and empty. She suspected some vital part of her had been ripped out during the birth and expelled, and that no one had the nerve to tell her. The alien baby didn't look anything like Howie or like her. She suddenly wondered if babies aged in heaven, or if Claire would be a baby for eternity. Beyond the window, new leaves uncurled on the ash tree like tiny fists opening to the sun.

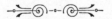

*I*t was her bleakest moment when the old woman bade Gretel to inspect the yawning oven. Was there nothing she could do to save her brother, to save them both?

"When I bring out the boy, you will put him in here. Or, if you do not, I will kill you first and then he will follow."

Gretel stuck her head inside the wide opening. "I don't understand how this oven works. Surely my brother is too large to fit inside."

"What, you foolish child? The opening is plenty large for

you and your brother both. I will show you how it's done." The old woman leaned her head inside the oven so that she could feel the fire's roar against her skin. And Gretel did something she thought she would never be able to do. With one strong shove, she toppled the old woman into the oven and closed the door. Then she climbed on a stool and got the key from the pantry to release her brother from his cage.

Chapter Forty-Eight

LIFELINE

BROOKLYN, NEW YORK—APRIL/MAY 1921

ELAINE

Only days after the baby Arthur was born, Elaine started back to work. By day, she continued to work as a housekeeper; in the evening, she took high school classes at Woodward House. After classes, she studied until lights out and then lay awake as long as she could, afraid of her own dreams, of seeing the squalling face of a baby or dreaming that she was back with her brother Stephen and then waking to find it wasn't true.

Mr. Seward had asked her to let him know when the baby was born. But there would be no baby to show him. At least she could tell him the baby was a boy, and that she had named him Arthur. If he wanted to set up a trust for someone he only suspected was his great-grandson, then he'd have to go through the nuns to find the family that adopted him. She'd cashed the money order, but she wasn't going to ask for more. She saved every penny from her job, and if she could stay on at Woodward House for a few more months to finish classes, she'd have barely enough to rent a room for herself. Stephen could join her as soon as she had a steady job. She'd promised him she would graduate early and find them a place together, and she meant to keep that promise.

After several agonizing attempts, she wrote Mr. Seward a carefully considered letter.

April 22, 1921

Dear Mr. Seward,

On April 15th, I had a healthy baby boy. I named him Arthur, after you. He was big—eight and a half pounds— and the nuns tell me he is handsome, but I never saw him. I chose to give him up for adoption so he could have a proper home. To find the family, you will have to con- tact the Sisters of Mercy at Woodward House. I'm sorry you didn't have a chance to see him either.

I hope you are well and thank you for the money you sent. Please watch over Stephen for me.

Sincerely,

Elaine Margaret Fitzgerald

Once a week, on her day off, Elaine wandered the market rather than stay and socialize with the other girls. The first time she went, she noticed that Pete was still there with his pigeons, and an idea began to take shape. It would involve a few lies, but they weren't big ones. The next week, she dressed as carefully as she could and went straight to Pete's booth in the market.

"Well, if it isn't Elaine. It's been a long time since I've laid eyes on you. And where's your little brother?"

"I'm off at boarding school, and Stephen is still with the Gossleys. I was wondering if you might do me a favor. I'd be willing to pay for it," she added quickly.

"And what favor could I do for you?" Pete stroked his stubbled chin while his eyes twinkled at her.

"I'd like to send my brother a pigeon post by way of Father Kearny. Stephen could pick it up from Father Kearny, and then send one back to you. I'd get it from you each week. It would be a game. I'd come every Saturday to pick it up. He loves to get mail by pigeon post."

Pete cocked his head like one of his birds. "Well, I don't see why not. It wouldn't be much of a letter, the paper's so small."

"That's okay. It's only a game." Her pulse drummed in her ears.

"Where is this boarding school of yours?"

She hadn't planned for this question. Looking out toward the river, she said the first place that came to mind.

"Manhattan. I come to the market on Saturdays and visit my brother and the Gossleys." Her words trailed off, sounding ridiculous even to herself, but it was the only way she could think of to get news from Stephen. And she was desperate.

"Write a note here." Pete handed her a slip of paper and stub of pencil. "I'll send one of Father Kearny's pigeons off today."

She scribbled a note, explaining Stephen could write her back and send it with a pigeon. She handed it to Pete. "Do you think Father Kearny will mind?"

"What, him? Nah, he likes any excuse to fiddle with the birds. He's got Lucky with him now. I suppose that school keeps you pretty busy."

"It does, but I'll be back next Saturday."

"The Gossleys must think highly of you, paying for a private school and all." Pete slipped the rolled paper into the small metal cylinder.

Elaine bit her cheek. "May's always fond of causes. I have to go now, but thank you so much."

Pete waved a thick hand in her direction. "You can help me clean cages next time you're here."

She felt his gaze follow her through the teeming market crowds.

All week she was torn between hope and fear. What if Stephen hadn't forgiven her for leaving? What if he didn't answer at all?

On Saturday, she hurried to the market as soon as she could get away. Pete was selling bunches of lettuce to a crowd. Elaine watched from the edges. Had an answer come for her? The pigeons were all in their crates. Her heartbeat filled her ears.

As the shoppers thinned, she edged closer. "Do you have mail for me?" The words, thick with anticipation, had trouble leaving her mouth.

Pete looked up, startled. "I didn't see you there." He wiped the mud from his hands on his great white apron. "Been saving it for you." Unzipping a leather pouch, he lifted out a pair of tweezers and a metal cylinder.

Elaine grew dizzy.

He handed both to her. "Thought you might want to take it out yourself."

She poked the tweezers into the tube and withdrew the small roll of paper. After handing the tweezers and tube back to Pete, she carefully unrolled the paper. Stephen's cramped writing made her eyes hot with tears.

Miss you, when are you coming home? School is good.
I'm taking piano lessons.

She wanted to run to him. Her breath came in short snatches. "You don't know how much this means to me. What can I pay you?"

Pete looked at her steadily. "Not a dime, but I still want you to help me with cages."

Slipping the paper into her bag, she nodded and got to work.

What Pete told Father Kearny, Elaine never knew, but pigeon post became her lifeline—that and books. The sisters said she had a talent for writing and research. Reading and the few lines from her brother made life at Woodward House bearable.

A few days after sending the first pigeon post, she'd also received her second letter.

May 2, 1921

Dear Miss Fitzgerald:

I regret to inform you that Mr. Arthur Seward passed away on April 27th. He has left instructions for me regarding you and the child he believes to be his great-grandson, Arthur. Arthur will inherit a trust at age twenty-one. You will have enough money to house you and allow you and your brother to complete college.

Please contact me regarding the terms of Mr. Seward's will.

Sincerely,
John Parks II

Elaine stared at the letter, willing the words to say something different. This was a world where people vanished out of your life forever in a moment, before you could even catch your breath. Just like her father. The same way baby Arthur had vanished. This pain was too sharp for tears, and she clutched her stomach as if the words had settled there.

Again, she reread the letter. A will. She didn't know how those worked, but there would be money for her and Stephen to go to college. College. It was too much to take in. Suddenly, the world was wider. She should have told Mr. Seward that Arthur truly was his great-grandson. Even without knowing for sure, he left her the money. And he left a fund for the baby. But the baby wasn't real. He had been in her and then he was gone. She had Stephen to think about, and she needed to tell him about their good fortune.

Mr. Parks appeared at Woodward House later in the week as the single rose bush by the door bloomed. Elaine hadn't seen him since Mr. Seward's birthday picnic, when Howie first kissed her. Mr. Parks was different now, serious in a suit and tie.

259

They sat in the front room, and as he talked his right leg jiggled up and down. The money, he told her, could only be accessed when she finished her high school studies. She told him that she was almost done and that the nuns were letting her stay until the end of summer so she could finish. He wiped his hand across his forehead, which had begun to sweat. They'd make plans then, he said, for living arrangements—and by the way, Howie was not to be told until he finished college. That was a condition of the will. Elaine nodded solemnly. She understood. What did it matter now? The future fluttered just beyond her reach. She could almost grasp it, and it smelled of hope.

Three days later, Sister Anne was waiting for Elaine when she returned from house cleaning. The look in her eyes made Elaine's heart beat faster.

"Your baby was returned. He's contracted scarlet fever, and the family doesn't want him infecting their other child."

Elaine looked into the sister's face. Tiny fissures had appeared above her lips as she compressed her mouth, and now her forehead furrowed into rows. She was still speaking, had just said something that was important. But Elaine wouldn't let the words in. It was only a child she had barely seen, who was stricken. But her palms were slick with sweat and her heart raced.

When Elaine didn't reply, Sister Anne rested her hand on her shoulder. "Not many survive at so young an age, but we'll do the best we can by him. He could use some mothering now."

Elaine looked out the window. A crow hunched in the branches of an ash tree, cawing the same note over and over. Summer was in the wind. She and Stephen would be starting their real life soon, a life she had been waiting for, for years. Without a word, she turned.

And walked away.

Chapter Forty-Nine

THE WAY HOME

SAN JOSE, CALIFORNIA—AUGUST 1955

Molly

"How are you feeling?" Uncle Stephen asked, pulling a chair up to the bedside. The rest of us huddled awkwardly in the doorway of Mr. Whipple's room.

"Sore. They tell me I've cracked a few ribs. Every time I take a breath, it hurts. And maybe I fractured my spine." But he looked awfully happy for a man with a fractured spine.

"Well, we appreciate what you did for the boy. It was heroic."

"I'd been watching the whole thing. I wish I could have stopped them."

Furrows appeared between Mom's eyes. "Where did you see all this from?"

"My car—"

"The blue Chevy Bel Air. You're Arthur," Angus cut in.

This was the man in the mystery car? Everything was in fast forward. I couldn't keep up. Was he a reporter, or a miracle investigator watching Uncle Stephen?

261

"That's right. I'm sorry if—"

This time it was Mom who cut him off. "You've been watching children in the neighborhood? I should call the police right now. Stephen, this man is some kind of pervert."

Uncle Stephen looked as puzzled as I felt.

"I'm sorry if I've caused you any alarm." The man continued: "I confess I've been watching your house." And here his round face burst into that smile that looked so familiar again. "I asked that my family be allowed to come in and see me."

Mom gawked. Uncle Stephen's eyes yo-yoed back and forth between Mom and the man in the bed.

My uncle cleared his throat. "There must be some mistake."

Angus inched a bit closer to me.

"Arthur Whipple is my adopted name. My birth name was Arthur Gossley. I'm Arthur, Mom. And Molly and Angus are my half brother and sister."

Mom's shoulders began to shake in a funny way. I grabbed her arm in case she was about to have some kind of seizure. The name Arthur Gossley meant nothing to me, but it appeared to have a powerful effect on Mom. I threw a worried glance at Uncle Stephen, but he wasn't any help. He was running both hands through his hair until it stood straight up in mangy tufts. Mom began to hiccup, which for all I knew was a prelude to spasming. What right did he have to call my mother Mom? I had only one brother.

"I don't know what you're playing at, but it's a sick game. Arthur Gossley died of scarlet fever." Mom's face was red and swollen. Her words, sharp staccato bursts.

"But I didn't die. The nuns saw me through. I grew up in upstate New York with a family by the name of Whipple. They're good people who couldn't have children of their own. They never planned to tell me I was adopted, but when I was ten years old, a lawyer tracked them down and said that their kid—me—had some money coming to him from a big-time architect named Howard Gossley."

Mom sat down with a thump on the straight-backed chair, and Uncle Stephen went over and put his arm around her. "But how could he know—"

Arthur held up a pale hand. "I finally met my father, Howard Gossley, when I was eighteen. He was a fine man, and we stayed in touch until he died last year."

"Died?" A little puff escaped from Mom like someone had knocked the wind out of her.

"He had a heart attack. Shame, because he was only in his fifties, but then I suppose you know that. So, I decided it was time to meet the rest of my family. I hired a detective and gave him the scoop. He did a little investigating, and then he discovered an ad in the *New York Times* classifieds. He gave me an address in California."

My heart gave a sudden lurch. "What did the ad say?" Had I drawn this crazy person to us? There had to be some mistake.

"I don't remember exactly, but it had a name, Elaine Fitzgerald Donnelly, and an address. I hoped you were looking for me." He looked at Mom.

"But I didn't place any ad. I thought you were dead."

"I saved it. It had your address and said to contact Molly. So I drove out as soon as I could."

Everyone looked at me.

"Molly?" My mother sounded like she was about to choke. "But how could you—"

Arthur kept right on talking. "I thought it would be better if I watched for a bit before I barged in. I didn't want to cause any problems. It took me a while to figure out you two weren't married." He nodded at Uncle Stephen. "Lots of husbands wouldn't put up with their wife's kid showing up on the doorstep."

I thought about the hair ring. Things were beginning to sink in.

Arthur looked over at me and Angus. "And I got kind of caught up watching my brother and sister here. When I was growing up, I used to pretend I had siblings. I was planning on introducing myself tomorrow, but then with the accident and all . . ." He shrugged and then winced.

Uncle Stephen was blinking his eyes and swiping at them with the palm of his hand.

Mom stood and walked out the door.

I started to follow. But Uncle Stephen grabbed my arm. "Let her be. It's a lot to process."

For a few seconds, no one spoke. We simply looked at each other.

What had I done? I'd been trying to fix our lives, and now it looked like I might have destroyed them. Placing the ad had been opening Pandora's Box. Did my father know Mom had a child with someone else? Did this mean he'd never come back now?

Angus broke the silence. "You're my brother? You don't look like it." He walked closer to the bed.

"I guess I take after my father." He laughed, and then grabbed his side as he turned a greenish shade of white. "How's the boy?"

"He survived, thanks to you," Uncle Stephen said. "He needs to have surgery on his leg. It was shattered pretty badly, and apparently he bit clean through his tongue. Things could have been a lot worse."

We fell silent again. I felt the minutes tick by on my skin. What if she wasn't coming back? Fear rose like bile in my throat. I locked eyes with my uncle. My fear was mirrored there. Even he didn't know what she'd do.

I stood. He shook his head.

"I'm sorry if I've caused any grief. I thought—" Arthur cleared his throat. "I hoped."

"You did the right thing," Uncle Steven replied.

"Is Mom coming back?" Angus's voice rang with a high note of panic. I put my arm around him

"She needed some fresh air."

Chapter Fifty

FAMILY

SAN JOSE, CALIFORNIA—AUGUST 1955

Molly

A nurse came in with a clipboard. "Mr. Whipple could use some rest. We're going to give him something to manage the pain and then we'll take him down for more X-rays. But family is welcome to wait for the results."

When none of us said anything, she wrinkled her forehead. "You are family, aren't you?"

There was a movement in the doorway. Mom hesitated. Her eyes were puffy, as if she'd been crying. Her hands covered her nose and mouth. Uncle Stephen looked at Mom; there were questions in his eyes, but there was hurt too. For the first time I realized this news might be as surprising to him as it was to me.

She offered the briefest of nods. My heart took a roller-coaster dive.

"Yes, we are. We're family," Uncle Stephen said as he pulled a handkerchief out of his pocket and blew his nose.

Arthur lay back on the pillow and closed his eyes, thick lashes fanning against his cheeks, while the nurse gave him more pain medication. Mom was staring at Arthur so hard that I don't think she heard a thing the nurse said. I searched for a resemblance between my elegant, red-haired mother and this pudgy, dark-haired man. And I knew then why his smile had made me feel at home.

The nurse ushered us out of the room, but Mom stayed behind.

ELAINE

She looked at this stranger in the hospital bed and searched for herself in him. Dark stubble speckled his pale face. His brown hair was already thinning. When she'd met his dark eyes, for a minute she'd lost her balance. They were quick and lively, and maybe that's how she'd known, even before he said anything. When he did speak, his voice most of all was his father's. Every time he spoke it was like peeling a scab from a wound.

She had spent years forcing herself not to imagine Howard Gossley, and then when she wanted to call his memory back, it refused to come until she heard Arthur's voice.

Could it be possible this man had spent nine months inside her body, hearing her heart beat, eating what she ate, totally dependent on her for survival? He'd picked the wrong mother—not that anyone could select his family.

The last time she'd seen this man, he was a light-haired baby with a rosebud mouth, and a solemn gaze that had met hers before he was whisked away. Did he know then that she didn't want him?

And yet.

Despite turning away, despite setting a fence around her

heart, she had wanted him with a visceral ache. This tiny life had been attached to her by the invisible cord that connected every mother and child. And they'd told her he was dying.

She'd turned her back. What kind of person did that?

Her pulse pounded in her temple.

His eyes opened as if he knew she was staring at him, drinking him in.

"Mom? Can I call you that?"

She bit the inside of her cheek. She wouldn't let this stranger see her cry. "I'm more comfortable with Elaine. You can't expect me to take all this in right away."

"Okay, Elaine. I know I have to be a shock. I've had years to wonder about my family. I can't expect that you thought about me."

"I was sixteen when you were born. I thought you'd died."

"It must have been hard. I don't blame you." He pushed himself up on the pillows. "I've always wanted to know who I was like. The Whipples are good people, but I'm nothing like them. They're farmers to the core. They don't have time for books or movies. But me, I've always loved words and stories. I used to read books under the covers at night. For a while I wanted to be a writer, but now I know I want to teach history."

He loved words. He wanted to teach history. Her boy.

"Well, I make my living writing, if that satisfies your curiosity." She swallowed. "Molly's like that too. Her brother—um, your brother—is more like their father." She twisted her hands. There was something she needed to ask. "Your father, Howard, did he have a good life?"

"I think he did. He and his wife traveled a lot. He never had any other children. He said his wife couldn't have them."

She thought of Sally and how she had once hated her. That feeling was gone now, smoothed and flattened by the current of years, just like her anger at Howard. They had all been so young. She hadn't been much older than Molly. What would Molly and Angus think about her now?

Arthur was still watching her face.

"All this"—she flipped a hand back and forth between them—"might take some getting used to."

When Arthur smiled, Elaine felt a curious lightening inside.

"I've got time."

Chapter Fifty-One

REVELATIONS

SAN JOSE, CALIFORNIA—AUGUST 1955

Molly

When Mom came out of Arthur's room, I couldn't read the expression on her face. I expected tears or shock, but she looked like the very same person I'd seen at breakfast that morning. How could she have carried this secret all these years without a mark on the outside? I thought of my hidden report card. Secrets didn't always reveal themselves.

Angus, Uncle Stephen, and I were sitting in the small waiting room at the end of the hall. With so much to process, I had very little to say. But the situation kept getting clearer to me. The hair ring. Woodward House.

"You had another baby besides us?" Angus looked at Mom. She didn't answer him. Her gaze was fastened on Uncle Stephen.

"I'm so sorry."

Uncle Stephen dug into his pockets. "Here, why don't you two go buy us some Cokes? I'm feeling terribly thirsty right now."

269

I know when I'm being pawned off, and I wasn't about to leave, but Angus had no hesitation. We didn't often get to drink soda pop. I stayed glued to my chair while Angus ran off to find a pop machine.

"All these years and you never said a thing." Uncle Stephen made room for Mom on the vinyl couch.

"Secrets are things you don't talk about. You should know that."

Uncle Stephen gave her a half smile, a dip of his head as if he understood something she wasn't saying out loud.

Mom continued. "You knew it wasn't a real boarding school."

"I had my suspicions, but not until I was older. The Gossleys never said a word to me."

"Arthur Seward must have left instructions for Howard to be notified," she said.

"Maybe he knew you'd never tell him." Uncle Stephen took Mom's hands in his own. "Why, your hands are as cold as ice, Lainey." And he began to rub them.

Mom looked like she was wearing a mask; her face was that stiff. "When I got word that Mr. Seward died, I never heard from anyone else in the family. I used the money to rent that room in the house Father Kearny found for us. I was working, and you were about to start high school."

"And then you had some money for college." Uncle Stephen turned to me. "Your mother worked very hard for a long time. She didn't start college until she was twenty-five years old, and I was thinking about becoming a priest."

"You, a priest?"

"Well, I soon realized it wasn't the life for me, and I decided I'd rather be a teacher. Then after college, your mother got a job, and then, later in life, she met your father and had you two."

I looked at Mom. "Why did you think Arthur died?"

Mom was staring at her hands as if she didn't recognize them. "He had scarlet fever. Not many babies survived scarlet fever in those days. He was almost a month old."

The only thing I knew about scarlet fever came from reading *Little Women*. The chapters always made me cry.

As she described life at Woodward House, I watched the way regret played across her features like shadows. But there was something in her eyes that I hadn't seen for a very long time: hope.

She leaned her head on her hand. "I've made an awful lot of mistakes in my life, Molly. Even after the sisters told me he was dying, I never went to see him, not even once. I couldn't take anymore sorrow. I needed to think about the future. One of the nuns gave me a ring made out of his baby hair. I assumed he'd died."

"The blond one in your drawer," I said.

For a minute fire flashed in her eyes, and then she sighed. "So you found that. I should have known. He had a funny thatch of blond hair when he was born."

Uncle Stephen slung his arm around her. "Lainey, you had some hard choices to make."

She shook her head. "Not too hard to see my own child." She began to snuffle into his shoulder.

I went over and put my hand on her arm. "But he didn't die."

Angus came back with two Coke bottles in his hands and one protruding from each pocket.

"I can't believe this is happening," Mom said, and she took a long swallow of Coke. I couldn't believe she was drinking soda pop. "It's like something right out of a story."

A story I never predicted when I started her biography box, and I wasn't sure I liked the way it was turning out. A person couldn't show up and expect to immediately be part of your family, even if he technically was.

"Does Dad know about him?"

"I told him before we got married and made him promise never to say anything." Her eyes filled again. "I told him the baby died. Because that was what I believed."

It was painful to see her that way. Angus put his head on her arm.

"Arthur saved Robert Crater," I reminded them all. I wondered if bringing Arthur to us with my ad cancelled out my role in getting Robert to jump. But that sounded like a question for Uncle Stephen, who knew much more about this kind of thing than I did.

"He did. We should be celebrating." Uncle Stephen raised his Coke bottle into the air. "To family!"

After two weeks in the hospital, Arthur was ready to be released, and that became a point of discussion for all of us. He'd quit his job, which he'd hated anyway, when he came out to California. His entire life had been put on hold when he came to spy out his family. We knew he had a serious girlfriend back in New York and that her name was Andrea, but that was all. Uncle Stephen believed it was our business to help him sort it all out.

Somehow, he managed to get in touch with Andrea, and she showed up at the San Francisco airport. It seemed she hadn't given up on Arthur, and she didn't hold his leaving against him once she heard the whole story. Uncle Stephen went to pick her up, and what was said on that hour-long drive back to San Jose, I never heard.

Andrea was small and dark, quick with energy and ambition. Just what someone as laid back as Arthur needed, Mom said. Andrea was willing to support him while he went back to getting a teaching degree, which pleased Uncle Stephen to no end. They would still live in New York, which I think made Mom feel relieved. She even bought a new dress for Arthur's wedding. It was jade green with a scalloped neckline, and when she tried it on for me, it made me think of spring.

And best of all, we'd be going to New York in early October for a wedding.

Chapter Fifty-Two

BURYING THE PAST

SAN JOSE, CALIFORNIA—SEPTEMBER/OCTOBER 1955

Molly

The doorbell rang late in the afternoon the day before we were to leave for New York. I hesitated before answering it, something I never used to do before the events of this summer. Although the remnant had mostly disappeared after Robert jumped from the roof, as if some question they had been waiting for was answered.

When I cracked the door open, Aricelia was standing on the front porch.

"Hi." Her smile flickered uncertainly.

"Hi." My fingers crushed the doorknob. I didn't open the door any wider, didn't move at all.

"I heard you're going to New York."

I nodded my head. "For Arthur's wedding." It still felt awkward calling him my brother.

"Well, I have something for your trip." She held up a bag I

hadn't noticed. "I'm sorry I haven't been there for you. I should have been."

My eyes blurred. My chest hurt. "You're right, you should have been." I made no move to reach for the bag, but I stepped out onto the porch, letting the door close behind me. She dropped the bag to her side.

"I know. I let other people decide how I should feel . . . and I guess I was scared." Her brown eyes shone, and she was biting her lip the way she always did when she was upset.

"People already thought we were weirdos—now they know."

"At least it's settled. My best friend's family is peculiar. Famous people's families usually are." She held out the bag again. "You don't have to forgive me, but at least take this."

I looked inside. There was a red notebook. As I drew it out, I noticed the cover was smooth leather.

"You always said writers get their start in New York. I thought you might need a new notebook for your start."

I ran my hand over the leather. It was almost too fine to write in. Almost.

"Open it up."

On the first page, in her loopy script, Ari had written:

> Remember me when you're famous.
> > With love from your best
> > friend, Aricelia

"Always," I said as my face melted into a smile.

It was close to midnight and we were catching an early flight, but I couldn't sleep. I got out my new notebook to explore a thought that had been nipping at me all day and wrote the question at the top of a new page. *What does it feel like to have a surprise sibling?* I didn't often know how I felt until I wrote things down as a way to think them through, and I couldn't rest until I got everything sorted out.

I found myself writing that having a surprise sibling felt muddy, like when I was little and played with finger paints. I'd take two of my favorite colors and mix them together, expecting a remarkable shade, but usually it was brown and murky. Good and bad mixed together felt the same way. I wasn't sure I liked the idea of a stranger having the same mother I did. I was pretty sure I wasn't ready to be Arthur's new best friend like Angus was. On the other hand, I liked the idea of our family—which had always seemed disappointingly small—being larger, and I liked the way Arthur made my mom's lips curl into a secret smile when no one else was watching. I wished the one triggering that smile was me.

The click of typewriter keys made me realize I wasn't the only one having trouble sleeping. Mom was at her desk in her worn flannel pajamas, hair in a ponytail, tapping away about some dead person from a biography box. She must have felt me staring at her back, because she stopped typing and swiveled around to face me.

"Molly, why are you up?"

I climbed onto the couch and drew my knees to my chest. "I couldn't sleep. I was trying to figure out how I felt about having a new brother."

She rested her head on one hand and looked at me between her fingers before she spoke. "And what do you think?"

"It's complicated."

"I think I'd say complex." She paused, thinking. "It takes a while for someone to stop being a stranger, even when he's my own child and even when I'm very glad he found us."

Then I asked the question that been lurking in the darkest corner of my mind.

"If Angus or I had been very sick, would you have left us?"

In a second she was up and had both arms around me. She smelled like lavender from the two sachets I bought her last Mother's Day, the ones she kept in her pajama drawer.

"Of course not, Molly. I was very young and very scared. More than anything, I wanted to be with my little brother. He was the only family I knew. I wanted to make a life for us. I couldn't give up." She brushed the hair from my face. "For years I thought I'd never be able to forgive myself. And then I had you and Angus, and it was like I was given a second chance. And now I find I really have been."

I burrowed deeper into her hug.

"It's going to take me a while to figure out how to be a mother to a grown man. But I like the idea of second chances."

For the next few minutes my sobs and Mom's crying blended together into one mournful sound. Then she started talking again while I wiped my nose on my pajama sleeve. She told me about all the places she wanted me to see in New York.

Then she made me promise to get back to bed because we'd all be getting up in a few hours.

As I looked at the pile of papers on her desk, I thought about how hard she worked, how she never gave up when there was a problem to solve, and how she kept most of her feelings close. She was like a wary dog when she met someone new, watching and sniffing, not getting too close right away, even when the person was a long-lost son. And then I had a startling thought without even having to write it down first: Maybe Mom and I were a lot more alike than I thought.

Chapter Fifty-Three

NEW YORK

BROOKLYN, NEW YORK—OCTOBER 1955

Molly

Arthur and Andrea picked an auspicious date for a wedding: Sunday, October 2. We arrived on the first and planned to stay through the fifth so that we could do a little sightseeing, not knowing that week would make Brooklyn history and be talked about for years after.

We spent what was left of our first day hunting through Holy Cross Cemetery for a grave. A woman in a small building right at the cemetery gates looked up the name of Mom's father, Michael Fitzgerald, in a ledger.

"He's in section F10. Right about here." She pointed with a chipped orange fingernail to a spot on the cemetery map. "But he's not the only one in the grave. There's four of 'em."

"All in the same grave?" I asked. I wasn't sure what to think about bodies being stacked in a single grave like sardines in a can.

"Four?" Mom had been quiet all the way to Holy Cross,

277

her eyes a million miles away from us. Now her face, under a brand-new pillbox hat in peacock blue, was puzzled. "What are the names?"

The lady snapped her gum and Mom winced. "Michael, Anna, and Claire Fitzgerald, and Timothy Meeks. Look like the Meeks man paid for the marker."

Mom looked up at Uncle Stephen. "I have no idea," he said, and scratched his nose.

As we walked, Mom explained, "He was the man who told us Pop died. Tim Meeks used to come home with him sometimes. I always resented the extra mouth to feed."

We wandered a bit until we found the right place, being careful not to walk across other people's graves as Angus had suddenly developed a concern about dead people germs. The marker was a cement slab smaller than the pillow on my bed. The names of my relatives looked like they had been scratched by hand in wet cement.

Crouching down, so she was almost kneeling in the grass, Mom opened her purse and brought something out in her hand.

I squatted down next to her

She unfurled her fist, and the tiny hair ring sat alone in the middle of her palm. She started talking, but not to us.

"You have three grandchildren: Arthur"—she dropped the ring onto the marker and reached back into her purse—"Molly, and Angus. I thought you'd want to know."

She pulled out an old photograph with scalloped edges. Angus and I were little, and we each held an Easter basket filled with eggs. Angus's mouth was stretched in a wide smile, but I looked stern, like egg hunting was serious business. She placed the photo, held down by a rock, next to the tiny ring. Then she stood up, brushed herself off, and turned to Uncle Stephen. "It's good to come home."

He slung an arm around her as we walked back to the rented car, and I tried to distract Angus from complaining about the dead people germs.

Arthur and Andrea gave us their two tickets to see the Brooklyn Dodgers play the New York Yankees in the final game of the World Series on October 4 at Ebbets Field, since they would be on their honeymoon. It was impossible to get two more. So, we drew straws to see which two of us would go. Angus and Mom won and headed out to see the game under a rare October sun.

I didn't mind. Uncle Stephen had promised to take me to Wallabout Basin to see where he and Mom grew up. Ever since Arthur arrived in our lives, Mom had begun to reveal pieces of her childhood, and Uncle Stephen had joined in with stories of his own.

Wallabout Market no longer flourished between Flushing and the East River. But many of the old buildings remained, and with a little squinting and a great deal of imagination, I could see Pop, with his cap set at a jaunty angle, going in through the doors of Drake Brothers Bakery. Fort Greene Park was still a lovely place for a picnic even in the autumn, as Uncle Stephen and I found out. We basked in almost seventy-degree sunshine and ate Chinese food right out of the box. The croquet lawn was still there, where Mom and Uncle Stephen experienced their very first picnic, and where Howie presented Mr. Seward with the mynah bird.

The two places I wanted to see most were Sacred Heart, with the pigeon coops on the roof, and the Gossleys' house, where so many wonderful and terrible days passed. Both were still standing. On the corner of Adelphi, taking up almost the whole block, Sacred Heart Church was in all its brick glory, still home to hundreds of parishioners.

"And there, Molly, is where the pigeon coops were kept, on the top of the gymnasium."

"Can we go up there?" I craned my neck, trying to see if any of the coops remained.

"Well, it looks like the fire escape's closed off now." Uncle

Stephen looked as disappointed as I felt on discovering the chain and padlock across the bottom of the fire escape. "But there is someone you might want to meet."

He led me down the street, past the church property to a new coffee shop. It was a small, bland building full of people chatting over cups of coffee and sweet rolls. At a corner table, near the back, sat a solitary old man wearing the distinctive collar of a priest. He rose when he saw us and extended a freckled hand. His eyes, sunk into a web of wrinkles, were the faded blue of flax. "I would have known ya anywhere. I thought it was Elaine coming through the door all over again, except your hair's a different color," he said, looking straight at me.

Uncle Stephen and the old man embraced. "Molly, this is Father Kearny, the man who was like a father to me."

I took his warm hand in my cold one and tried to imagine him young and excited to be working in his first parish. He pulled out a chair for me, and we sat down while Uncle Stephen went up to the counter to order some tea.

"I hear this uncle of yours has been causing quite a stir out West. You know he was the best altar boy I ever had?"

"He's still pretty remarkable. He healed a boy from a tumor by laying a hand on his head and praying for him," I said.

"And what did your mother think of that?" he asked.

I wondered why that was his first question, but because he was very old and a priest, I allowed for a certain eccentricity. I thought for a minute and remembered the conversation I overheard from the linen closet.

"She wanted to know about all the others who weren't healed."

"Ah, that would be our Elaine. And what do you think?"

I pushed some spilled sugar into a white ridge on the plastic tablecloth. "I think it's a good question. There are too many prayers that are never answered." I looked into his warm eyes. "I think being a miracle worker isn't all it's cracked up to be."

Father Kearny laughed so hard he began to wheeze and

had to wipe his eyes. "Maybe the question should be why God interferes at all. Miracles don't grant wishes. They aren't for our comfort."

"Robert Crater, the miracle boy, jumped off a barn wearing a pair of wings my brother made. He broke a leg and an arm. The bone stuck out through the skin."

"Why did he do that?"

"I guess he thought nothing could happen to him since God was saving him for something special."

He shook his bald head. "Saving us from ourselves is God's work."

"Did you really raise pigeons on the roof of the church?"

Uncle Stephen returned, balancing two cups of tea and three doughnuts, one for each of us. I kept my eye on the one with coconut.

"I certainly did, but it was on the roof of the gymnasium. Of course, that was years ago. Birds are all gone now. Your uncle had a particular fondness for pigeons. I remember that your mother once sent a pigeon post from the roof of the church. It was the most peculiar message I ever sent; I guess that's why it stuck with me all these years."

I leaned in. Mom sending a pigeon post. "What did it say?"

"Just one word: *wonder.*"

I rolled that over in my mind while Uncle Stephen talked about teaching school and becoming a local celebrity. But still I couldn't understand why she'd written *wonder* and sent it by pigeon. I was gradually coming to the conclusion that there was still a lot about Mom I didn't know, more than enough to fill one biography box. And that was surprising. It simply didn't seem like parents should have so much life behind them.

Uncle Stephen tried to talk Father Kearny into visiting us in San Jose, but he only laughed. "I'm a New York boy, born and bred. I don't plan on dying on some foreign soil. But I will put in a few good words with the Big Fella for you when we meet up."

Chapter Fifty-Four

ROOM FOR MIRACLES

BROOKLYN, NEW YORK—OCTOBER 1955

Molly

It wasn't easy to make our way to the East River. Businesses marched in tight procession along the waterfront, not to the mention increased security at the Navy Yard, but we managed. We followed a worn and muddy path through weeds and discards to the river's edge. I could see Manhattan on the far shore; its tall buildings scalloping the skyline gleamed in the October sun. We stood between two bridges, the famous Manhattan Bridge to the south, and to the north, a span Uncle Stephen called the Williamsburg Bridge.

"Did you used to come down here when you were growing up?'

Uncle Stephen kept his gaze fixed on the gentle swells of the river. "In summer, kids who couldn't afford the trip to Canarsie or Coney Island came here to swim. I did it a few times myself, but never when your mother knew about it. She said she didn't like the crowd, they were hooligans, and she was probably right." He smiled. "She usually was."

We listened to the river lapping on the banks. A pair of ducks glided by. "There's a river that rushes inside all of us, Molly. It bears us along for good or ill unless we paddle hard. Your mom was the best paddler I knew until you came along."

"Me?"

"You changed everything. You brought Arthur to us."

"I almost killed Robert too."

"But you didn't. Robert made his own choice. And I suspect you've learned something about the power of words."

I looked at Uncle Stephen, his spare frame silhouetted against the current. The sun glinted off the water, and I had to shield my eyes.

"You're not content to go where the river takes you. You've lived in New York and California, and you're a miracle worker."

Uncle Stephen took my hand in his bony one. "I was caught in the current, Molly. I figure the only true evidence of miracles is transformation."

"You mean what happened to Robert?"

"Robert may have been the impetus, the first stone in the river. It seems to me that miracles spread transformation everywhere they travel—the rings keep widening like when a rock breaks the surface of the water. Take your mother, for instance."

"Mom?"

"Your mother thought she knew the ending to her story a long time ago, but now it's transforming into something different than she ever expected, like all good stories do. It's like I've always told you about writing and storytelling—every story should leave a little room for miracles."

I brushed the hair out of my eyes. The smell of the river surrounded me, damp and musty, the smell of mud and living things all mixed up together.

"She always claims that her story didn't have any miracles."

"We don't always know what a story means up front. In fact, we can't know until we experience the beginning and the end." He picked up a smooth, flat stone and sent it sailing out across the water. It skipped five times, leaving a widening trail of circles, before it sank. "I was looking at that *Hansel and Gretel* book the other day, the one that was your mom's. Most people don't remember the ending. They think the story ends when the witch is pushed into the oven."

"The children find their way home again."

"Yep. That's the part most people forget. The children find their way home and their miserable father is waiting for them. The stepmother has died. Some people would say it was a miracle the two children survived. In real life, it can take years to find your way through the woods. Your mother, Arthur, and I aren't the family any of us expected."

I liked it when Uncle Stephen talked philosophy, even when I wasn't completely sure what it all meant. "Do you think you'll ever perform another miracle?"

"I don't know if I'll ever be in the way of another miracle, but it seems that once you open yourself to the possibility of miracles, they start showing up all around you."

I chose a flat stone the gray-green of the river. It flew out of my hand and sank without a single skip. "That's not what the investigators said. They said that 'the occurrence of the miraculous is rare.'"

"Rare and common all at once, I expect. Here, Molly, pick a stone that's not too heavy, but not too light either."

I closed my hand around a smaller stone, felt its smooth warmth fill the hollow of my hand. With one flick, it skimmed the surface of the water, kissed it twice, and dropped.

A tremendous honking interrupted my concentration. It sounded like every car in Brooklyn was leaning on its horn.

"What's going on?" I asked.

Uncle Stephen ran a hand through his wild red hair. "I guess we'd better go find out." We hurried up the muddy path back toward Flushing Avenue, that unexpected October sun still warm on our backs.

People were out in the streets. A lady leaned from a second-story window beating two pot lids together. I began to worry that the whole town had gone mad or that we'd been invaded by the Communists like my teacher was always predicting.

"What's all the commotion?" Uncle Stephen shouted through the rolled-down window of a car stopped at the corner.

"Haven't you heard? The Bums just won the Series!"

The children, having discovered that the wooden trunks in the old woman's house were full of precious stones and jewels, filled their pockets and set out once more to face the dark forest, for both of them still longed for the promise of home. A dove, perched on a branch right outside the candy door, cooed and chortled. It fluttered to a branch just a few yards beyond them. The children did what all children in fairy tales know to do; they followed the bird into the woods.

The dove was soon joined by a second and then a third bird. As the children trudged through the woods' perpetual twilight, daylight began to filter through the branches of the trees. The path grew straight and wide. Holding hands, Hansel and Gretel followed the dove to the very edge of the forest. Now their journey became a familiar one; although the rest of the story could not be predicted, the children had found their way home.

Chapter Fifty-Five

FINDING THEIR WAY

BROOKLYN, NEW YORK—OCTOBER 1955

Molly

In the dark, I rolled over to the edge of the bed, leaned down, and quietly as I could unzipped the outer pocket of my suit-case. Tomorrow we were flying home, and I didn't want to risk waking Mom up. It had been a long day. Our new dresses were hanging side by side in the hotel closet, and Angus was sleeping in the room next door with Uncle Stephen. From the bed next to mine, Mom's breath was a steady snore, a low rumble.

I'd crammed my journal into the outside pocket of my bag. I pulled it out, along with a small flashlight. But it was dark, my hands were slippery, and the flashlight crashed to the wooden floor.

Mom snorted. I froze.

Her form, backlit by the faint glow of a streetlight, rose from the covers. "Molly, was that you?"

"Sorry, Mom. I dropped my flashlight. Go back to sleep."

"Well, I'm awake now." She leaned toward me but didn't turn on the light. "What are you writing about?"

"How did you know I was going to write?"

"I know you. You've been keeping those notebooks of yours for years. Of course you'd have one with you."

That caught me by surprise. I'd never suspected she paid attention. "I wanted to write about the trip, so I wouldn't forget."

She may have surprised me, but I had a surprise as well. In the bottom of my suitcase was the cigar box, still only partially full of her biography. I'd added a few notes to it after my day with Uncle Stephen. I planned on giving it to her in the morning. I smiled with secret satisfaction as I waited for her to tell me to sleep now. But she caught me off guard again. Was this the way it was going to be now, each of us surprising the other from here on out?

"I never heard all about what you and your uncle did yesterday." She yawned. "Tell me one favorite thing, and then we'll go back to sleep."

I lay on my back, supported by three fluffy hotel pillows.

"Before we met Father Kearny, we saw the church where he used to keep his pigeons. I'd like to send a message that way."

Mom's chuckle was soft and low. "It was pretty extraordinary—the idea of messages being sent by birds. I always loved pulling the rolled-up paper out of the little tube and waiting to see what it said."

A question had been rumbling around in my brain all day. I thought about how it's always easier to have conversations in the dark. "Father Kearny said he remembered one of your posts."

"He did? What did it say?"

"He said it was one word . . . *wonder*. Why did you write that?"

She was quiet so long, I thought maybe I shouldn't have asked.

"I'd forgotten about that. It was the day your uncle got sick, right before we moved in with the Gossleys. Things had been difficult; most of the time I was exhausted. But there was something about being up on that roof, above the city, that made me feel like all the struggle was down below me. Seeing the pigeons, knowing they could take a secret message and carry it through the sky—that felt extraordinary. There wasn't much extraordinary in my life."

While I was still thinking about what to say, she added in a quiet voice, "It felt like wonder was possible, like being inside a poem." She turned onto her side and slid back down under the covers. "It's been a long time since I thought about that feeling. Stephen told me you two went down to the river. That was another one of my favorite places."

"We did. He said it's where all the kids used to go swimming."

"He always wanted to do that, but I never let him. It was my job to take care of him, and sometimes I tried too hard."

I could almost hear her thinking in the silence between us.

"Molly, I shouldn't have expected you to keep your brother off the roof. I'm sorry for what I said. He would have tried the wings himself no matter what you said. Now, tomorrow's going to be another long day, and we need to get some sleep."

Then I heard her roll over away from me.

"That's okay." I don't know if she heard me, because the words came out small and feeble, a newborn revelation just finding its legs.

I lay on my back staring into the dark, my whirring brain fuzzy now with fatigue. The more I thought about it, the harder it was to separate ordinary and extraordinary. Uncle Stephen's miracle was extraordinary, but we still didn't know, and might not know for years, if it would be recognized. The best thing was that he still was here with us, a part of our family whether he was a miracle worker or not. I thought about his words, the ones I'd planned on writing down. *Once you open yourself to miracles, they start showing up all around you.*

I would like to able to say things changed at that one moment in time, when Mom finally met the son she'd abandoned. If I had been writing the story, they would have. But that's not how it happened. I have learned that most change involving people is as gradual as glacial melting, sometimes unperceived for years until you look back at the way things used to be. Like miracles, a series of events are set in motion with much of it spreading underground. There was a loosening in Mom, as if a sliver of ice had melted, changing the shape of her interior landscape in ways that were only beginning.

Of course, Arthur wanted more from her than she could give right away; he had been waiting so long. In that expectation, he was disappointed. I think he wanted more from Angus and me as well. And in this I surprised myself; I really was more like Mom than I realized. I could be friendly up to a point, but a dam of reserve was always in place. What did he know of our growing up, our longing, and our secrets? Angus, on the other hand, had always had more of Uncle Stephen's open good will. He was thrilled to have another relative, even a half brother twenty-five years older.

We didn't hear from the Craters again after the incident. I don't know if they blamed us for a lack of supervision, or do I know if they continued to believe that Robert was a miracle boy, set aside for some great purpose. Years later, when I had graduated Stanford and was starting my first job as a journalist, determined to be a serious writer, a newspaper story caught my eye. Robert Crater, the 1955 miracle boy, was a featured guest on a new TV game show, *Hollywood Squares*, hosted by Bert Parks. I'm not convinced that *Hollywood Squares* is the great work his parents had in mind.

From the bed next to mine, a soft snore rose and fell. Behind the curtains it was the earliest hours of the morning. Life was waking up. Light was seeping in through the cracks.

⊸⊷◉⊶ AUTHOR'S NOTE ⊶◉⊷⊸

The 1918–1919 influenza pandemic killed more people than any other flu outbreak in human history. The virus, which often led to pneumonia, killed over 600,000 in the US and 20,000 people in New York alone. My grandmother was one of them. She died in the third wave of the virus, in the spring of 1919, and it was her death and the stories my father told me about life afterward that set me on the path to writing this novel. She left three children behind. My father was ten years old when he, along with hundreds of other flu orphans, flooded the orphanages, and when they were full, the streets and alleys of New York. I grew up hearing stories about what it was like to survive as a child on the streets of Brooklyn, about Wallabout Market, the Brooklyn Navy Yard, and Prospect Park.

There are a number of theories about the geographic origins of the Spanish flu. One theory is that the virus began in a small farming community of Haskill County, Kansas in the spring of 1918, but other theories point to Europe or East Asia.

WWI, which ended November 11, 1918, had a profound influence on the spread of the virus. The deadly second wave, when the flu was at its peak, was in October 1918. During that time, the death rate for 15–34-year-olds was twenty times higher than in previous years. (Taubenberger, "1918 Influenza: the Mother of All Pandemics," *Emerging Infectious Diseases*, Vol. 12, No. 1, January 2006)

The locations in Brooklyn are accurate to the best of my ability. As far as I know, pigeons were never kept on the roof of Sacred Heart Church. I did take certain liberties with history to make dates work with my timeline. After all, this is a work of fiction! For example, the McDonald's on Meridian Ave in San Jose didn't have its grand opening in 1955. It opened in the early 60s and was still serving up burgers from the original building until 1999.

While the story has its roots in my own family story, the individuals and families in the novel are all products of my imagination. Any errors in historical detail are mine alone.

Why Hansel and Gretel?

In fairy tales, the woods are dark and dangerous places where anything might happen. There are many tales of children lost, abandoned, or sent into the woods at the request of a parent or evil stepmother. "Hansel and Gretel" is one such tale of abandonment and against-all-odds survival. Author and fairy tale expert Terri Windling put it this way in her blog post *Into the Woods, 10: Wild Children*: "The heroism of such children lies . . . in the ability to survive and transform their fate—and to outwit those who would do them harm without losing their lives, their souls, or their humanity in the process."

In late 1800s New York, up to 30,000 abandoned or orphaned children filled overflowing orphanages or lived on the streets. The vast number of orphans was due in part to the overwhelming number of destitute immigrants. By 1900, there were 16 million Irish immigrants alone. During these years, childbirth was still the number one cause of female mortality, leaving impoverished fathers with young children.

Then the Spanish flu arrived with its scythe and black cloak.

Many children became half-orphans, abandoned by one parent after the other died. For these children, the streets of our cities were the woods of the grimmest fairy tales, dark, full of predators and danger. Against all odds, many of these immigrant children survived their sojourn through the woods without losing their humanity. Many, of course, did not. Surviving childhood is not always easy, or is it guaranteed.

Children still struggle in the woods today. Some are still locked in the witch's house by parents' addictions, cruelty, or dire circumstances. There is still a need for tales of hope, stories that say circumstances, no matter how dark, need not define you.

⊷❧⟶ ACKNOWLEDGMENTS ⟵☙⊶

This book has been more than ten years in the making. During those years, there have been many voices of encouragement that kept me going and pointed the story in the right direction. The seed of the story was planted by stories my father, Joseph Doyle, told about growing up on the streets of Brooklyn and working in Wallabout Market. My mother, Lillian Fitzpatrick Doyle, introduced to me fairy tales, and they've inhabited my writing ever since.

A grateful heart to:

Sandra Bishop, who believed this story was meant to be a book and championed it from the start. David Bennet, of Transatlantic, who stepped in to support her vision.

Early readers who offered encouragement, insight, and feedback: Martha Swedlund, Jennie Sphor, Stephen Wallenfels, Randy and Gretchen LeBarge, Nancy Smith, Claire McQuerry, Fiona Kenshole, Renee Riva, and Caitlin Blasdell.

My critique group: Mary Cronk Farrell, Stephen Wallenfels, and Jeanette Mendel. They are some of the smartest, kindest, and funniest people I know.

Jillian Manning for her excitement at acquisitions, Sara Bierling for smart editing. I'm so thankful she understood the importance of the Hansel and Gretel retelling. And Jacque Alberta for bringing her thorough research, wise insights, and for loving Molly and Elaine as much as I do.

Terri Windling and her work on fairy tales in Endicott

Studio and her blog *Myth and Moor*, which inspired the Hansel and Gretel retelling.

A tour guide, a lifelong resident of Brooklyn, whose name I have shamefully forgotten, who showed me around the old neighborhoods of Brooklyn and made my settings come alive.

Suzanne Selfors, Megan Chance, Kyle Reynolds, and Sara Nickerson for the gift of encouragement, laughter, and good food when I needed it most.

And to my family: Dennis McQuerry, my stalwart companion in all; Brennan, Kristen, and Asher; Claire and Duane; Roger Doyle Knox; and Richard Doyle. It is your story too.

⇥◉⇤ ABOUT THE AUTHOR ⇥◉⇤

Maureen McQuerry is an award-winning poet, novelist, and teacher. Her YA novel, *The Peculiars*, was an ALA Best Book for YA 2013 and a Bank Street and Home Book recommended book. Her middle grade fantasy duo, *Beyond the Door* and *The Telling Stone*, were both a Booklist Top Ten Fantasy/SciFi for Youth and a finalist for the Washington State Book awards. Her poetry appears in many journals and anthologies. She lives in Washington State.

CONNECT WITH
MAUREEN DOYLE MCQUERRY!

www.maureenmcquerry.com

@maureenmcquerry

Maureen.McQuerry

@maureenmcquerry

/maureenmcquerry

www.goodreads.com/author/show/581549.Maureen_Doyle_McQuerry

BLINK®